PRAISE FOR ELLE GRAWL

"What an insidious, creepy page A
completely assured debut that wi nd
keep you looking over your should

—J. T. Ellison or

"*One of Those Faces* delivers an unreliable narrator whose paranoia is shaped by past trauma, a killer targeting women who look like her, and plenty of twists that tighten as the atmosphere closes in. This taut, chilling, page-turning psychological thriller is sure to put debut author Elle Grawl on the map."

—Loreth Anne White, *Washington Post*, Amazon Charts, and Bild bestselling author of *The Patient's Secret*

"Taut with suspense, *One of Those Faces* is a slow-burn thriller that will make you dead bolt your door during the day. Grawl's debut hypnotized me from start to finish."

—Elle Marr, Amazon Charts bestselling author of *Strangers We Know*

"Make sure to clear your schedules, because *One of Those Faces* is such a wild and compelling ride you're not going to be able to look away until the very last sentence. Grawl, with beautifully cinematic style, knocks you off balance until you feel like you're slowly drowning in nightmares right alongside Harper, not knowing which way is up or what is true. Every time you catch your breath, another revelation pulls you under. This binge-worthy, trippy thriller should be at the top of everyone's must-read list!"

—Brianna Labuskes, bestselling author of *What Can't Be Seen*

"Perfectly paced and packed with doppelgänger women and suspicious men, this creepy thriller kept me guessing all the way through! I was never sure who to trust, and I read it in a day!"

—Allie Reynolds, author of *Shiver* and *The Swell*

"Elle Grawl delivers on her irresistible premise with a story so full of mysteries and suspicious characters that your mind will spin trying to figure it all out. *One of Those Faces* is an eerie, page-turning thriller that leaves you increasingly unsettled with each new chapter."

—Megan Collins, author of *The Family Plot*

"*One of Those Faces* kept me flipping pages in pursuit of answers well past my bedtime. An utterly satisfying rabbit hole."

—Kathleen Willett, author of *Mother of All Secrets*

WHAT STILL BURNS

ALSO BY ELLE GRAWL

One of Those Faces

WHAT STILL BURNS

ELLE GRAWL

This is a work of fiction. Names, characters, organizations, places, events, and incidents are either products of the author's imagination or are used fictitiously. Otherwise, any resemblance to actual persons, living or dead, is purely coincidental.

Published by Thomas & Mercer, Seattle

www.apub.com

Amazon, the Amazon logo, and Thomas & Mercer are trademarks of Amazon.com, Inc., or its affiliates.

ISBN-13: 9781662511400 (paperback)
ISBN-13: 9781662511394 (digital)

Front cover design by Olga Grlic
Back cover design by Jarrod Taylor
Cover images: © Diane Miller, © Claude Roué / EyeEm / Getty Images; © Devil23 / Shutterstock

Printed in the United States of America

For D.K.

CHAPTER ONE

Every memory of my family is singed with fire.

Since that night when I was ten, I lose a bit more of them each year. The flames lick and burn the face of my dad until his features are gone. What color were his eyes? What about Mom? I can't even remember if her hair was long or short at the time.

The remembrances of my siblings faded the quickest. Donnie vanished one morning after a particularly bad dream a few months after I began living with Aunt Beth. I thought that I'd dreamed of Donnie when I realized I couldn't even picture what he looked like anymore. The faces of Amy and Natalie were the next to disappear, but their laughter remained. I wonder what they would've looked like as adults. I wonder what they would've become. Sometimes I still hear them giggling when I'm on the street walking by a park or on the train.

After all this time, the only thing that remains so clearly in my mind is the image of the fire itself. Waking to the glow, so sharp and blinding against the dark, empty pastures stretching behind the house, was my first memory of that night. I can still see the wooden eaves collapsing from the touch of the flames.

It's only fitting that my story ends the same way it began.

My lungs spasm.

I should've never come back. That idea replays through my mind on a loop as I drag myself along the ground, my nails cracking from the dirt piling underneath.

I cough, the dirt and ashes swirling in front of me. I collapse to the ground, stabbing pain splitting my sides.

I burrow into the earth again, gasping, inhaling the toxins.

My eyes fill with smoke, and it's hard to tell if I'm moving forward, closer to fresh air, or digging my own grave.

CHAPTER TWO

Three Weeks Earlier

It didn't take long for Aunt Beth's secrets to reveal themselves after her death.

First, it was the bills. Within days of the funeral, the kitchen table was covered in paper with scary bold font and red squares around even more frightening figures. Beth's insurance barely covered a single ibuprofen tablet in the end, but I had no idea how much the hospitals were asking for. Beth had told me she was making payments for the treatment. Looking at this enormous amount overdue, I'm not sure that could be true.

But the unpleasant surprise of the bills was just the start. What I found in a forgotten desk drawer was much worse.

I had been so reluctant to go back into her room, worried it might trigger another episode. I couldn't remember finding her body. It was one of those rare blank spaces in my memory. One second, I was opening her bedroom door; the next I was sitting on the curb as paramedics closed the ambulance door.

Grief hits me differently after I lost my family the night of the fire when I was a kid, in that it doesn't ever completely hit me anymore. And that makes it worse. I just feel numb. There's definitely sadness buried within me, waiting to bubble up, but I'm not sure it'll ever fully surface. The desire to unleash what's lying underneath is what causes me to do bad things sometimes.

Thankfully, I didn't black out upon entering Beth's room today. Instead, I just discovered the letter.

I stare down at the letterhead. Stanley, Carson, and Ridley Law LLP? That was my father's old law firm before we moved out from San Francisco to the farm. I played with Ridley's kids at the firm's annual picnic at Rodeo Beach. The flower arrangement they'd sent to the funeral for my family back then was the largest. I still can't look at lilies without feeling nauseous.

Re: Sola Property

My stomach twists. Sola? Aunt Beth and I tried to avoid the topic of that town and the farm for the past few years. Given the way we left after my mental breakdown, she always seemed worried it would trigger another.

I scan the rest of the letter.

> *It has come to our attention that the property taxes on the property at 141 County Road are delinquent. It is our understanding that the beneficiary of the trust, ALEXIS LEIGH BLAKE, will take possession of the property along with the other trust assets at the age of thirty (30). Until then, in our capacity as Trustee, we are obliged to pay the property taxes. In the future, please directly forward all property tax notices to our office so we can ensure prompt payment.*
>
> *Thank you.*
>
> *Sincerely, Jim Ridley, esq.*

A trust?

Oh, Beth.

I dial the number included in the letterhead.

"Office of Stanley, Carson, and Ridley, how can I help you?" The chipper voice reminds me of our receptionist at the magazine.

"I'm not sure . . . I found a document about a trust—for me, apparently. Ridley signed it, but—"

"Alexis Blake?" Her tone has shifted, dropping the high pitch and airiness.

"Yes?"

"We've been sending notices since a few months back."

My birthday was only a few months ago. Does Beth have those other letters filed out of sight somewhere? "I'm sorry. I didn't get any of them."

"I'll transfer you to Mr. Ridley right now. Please hold."

"Ms. Blake?" His voice comes through after one ring. Even after all this time, it sounds vaguely familiar. I remember his voice carrying through the speakerphone when my dad had to take calls at home.

"Yes. I was—"

"I'm glad to hear from you. I've been trying to get in touch with you and your aunt for some time now."

"Yes, I'm just now finding out about that." I fold over one corner of the letter in my hand. Why would Beth not tell me about this? "My aunt passed away, and I came across a letter in her paperwork. I didn't even realize we still had the Sola property." I'd always assumed Beth would've sold it at some point. It's not like we were ever going to return. Did she secretly harbor some desire to move back one day and reclaim the family farm? Maybe she hoped one day when the pain wasn't quite as fresh for both of us, she could pick up where my parents left off and restore my grandfather's farm to its former glory. I'm not sure why, but that thought makes my entire body clench.

He sighs. "Yes, it was held in trust for you since Beth didn't show an interest in selling it. I addressed that with her initially, after the, um, fire, but she was very hard to reach. But now that you're thirty—"

"How much is in the trust?"

"Unfortunately all the cash in the trust has been depleted. The only asset now is the farm itself."

Shit. "Oh." I'm still torn between sadness and anger, but anger is taking a strong lead now. I can't believe Beth would let this happen. If we'd had money at our fingertips, there's so much we could've done to make her life a little easier.

Aunt Beth died after barely living. She had abandoned any hopes she had of building her own family when I was left orphaned. And I didn't make it easy on her. Immediately after the fire, I was difficult to control, always testing her resolve. Of course, I only grew into a shittier teenager, intent on destroying myself in other ways before the grief could.

But it caught up with me. When I was sixteen and all felt lost, when I was ready to die, Beth was always there to bring me back from the edge. And later, when she became sick, it was my turn to look after her in the best way I could, considering how cash poor we were. If I'd had this money, I could've paid for her treatment outright. I could've taken her on a trip or something—anything to pay her back.

I sigh. "So, I don't understand. What *is* this trust?"

"Your father and mother set it up after your grandfather died. That's why the farm your mother inherited is in the name of the trust. And clearly, you are the sole beneficiary."

Yes, clearly. I try to recall whether my parents ever mentioned doing something like this. They must've made a special trip back to the city at some point after Grandpa died.

"I'm very sorry to hear about Beth, by the way. Sorry if I didn't say that first."

"Thank you." What a mess she's left behind for me.

"I know you must be dealing with a lot right now . . . but there is a larger issue regarding the farm."

Of course there is.

"The county is trying to recoup unpaid property taxes, so there's a bit of a time crunch . . . have you thought about whether you plan to sell?"

I haven't *thought* about the farm at all in years. Mentally compartmentalizing, when I'm able to, has been my saving grace. My brain learned long ago anything related to the night of the fire was dangerous territory. "Sell?"

"Yes, the farm. So we have limited options at this point, assuming you don't have the funds on hand to pay the taxes."

Highly unlikely. "How much is owed now?"

"$82,953."

My stomach begins to ache. "Yeah, I *definitely* can't pay that."

"I understand," he says. "Then, I'm afraid the only real choice you have is to sell the property and pay the taxes back from the proceeds."

I stare at the stack of bills beside me. I'm not sure about what selling entails exactly, but, no matter what, I need money out of this. "Okay."

"Okay? Great. If you're able to find a buyer, I'd be happy to help you with the closing. As a favor, of course. I felt just terrible all these years letting it sit there. I know this situation isn't ideal, but at least you'll get something out of it."

Isn't it ideal, though? I mean, yes, it would be better to have the trust money *and* the property free and clear. But at least I don't have to wonder if I'm making a mistake by selling it. There's no other option. "I guess."

"And, I suggest we get started on this as soon as possible."

Sola. I rest my head on my hands.

I remember the relief I felt when I saw the town shrink in our rearview mirror all those years ago.

I never wanted to return, but I guess I have no choice.

CHAPTER THREE

"Hey! Where have you been?"

I drop my empty coffee cup into the garbage bin before looking up at my boss as he approaches. "Coffee break." I cross my arms over my chest to block the new gust of wind blowing in from the bay.

Sanders's eyebrows wobble, dancing between an expression of anger and mere annoyance. He's not going to like it when I break the news to him. "I'm running a pitifully underfunded magazine here. Drink your coffee at your desk like the rest of us." He nods for me to follow him.

"How come the smokers get breaks outside?" My feet eventually move and stumble in line behind him toward the aged stone building. I hate this building. When the lease ended at our previous location a few years ago, our magazine moved into what smells like the oldest building in San Francisco.

He glances over his shoulder at me, the smirk on his lips barely visible. "So we don't all suffocate from the smoke inside."

My chest tightens for a moment. After twenty years of trying to block out the few details I remember from the night of the fire, it's all I can think about after that letter. That smell of smoke, the pressure in my lungs when I woke up outside the blaze, disoriented and shaking. I've started to wonder if I can truly live with all the unanswered questions about that night. With Beth around, it hadn't seemed to matter quite as much, but now that I'm alone, the heavy silence in the empty house reminds me of all I lost back then.

Sanders peers down at his watch and holds the door open for me. "Come on, it's 5:15. He's been waiting for you."

I let him take the lead again as we round the corner, and he opens the door to the bullpen. Most of the writers are still buzzing from their second round of afternoon coffee, and we expertly weave through them to the small conference room on the other side.

I keep my focus straight ahead as we pass Evan's open door. I've successfully avoided him all day, and there's no reason to break my streak now, especially when I won't need to be in the same room as him while I'm out of town.

"I'm sorry for the delay, Mr. Vargas," Sanders says when we burst through the door.

The old man's eyes drift past my boss's tailored blazer to me in my faded Ramones T-shirt and wrinkled, three-day-old cardigan. He's probably wondering which of us is the reporter.

"This is Alexis Blake," Sanders says, stepping aside so Mr. Vargas can also see my faded jeans that now have a coffee stain.

The man grimaces but covers it quickly enough with a polite nod. "Nice to meet you."

Sanders nods and looks down at his watch again. "Unfortunately, as I explained before, Evan, the previous lead on this, has changed positions, and he's unable to pursue it right now, but Alexis has agreed to meet with you."

The promotion to assignment editor really went to Evan's head. Apparently he can't even be bothered to finish what he's started.

Mr. Vargas's weathered gaze returns to me.

"I really have to go," Sanders says in a low voice to me as he steps past me to the door. "You're in good hands, sir."

I dive into the sagging pockets of my cardigan, stretched out from years of piling stuff into them, and pull out my phone and a small pad of paper and pen. "Sorry I kept you waiting," I say as I sink into the flimsy plastic chair across from the man. "So, let's start with the basics . . ." I unlock my phone and open the recording app. "I'm Lex. I handle a lot of our business features for the *Weekly*. I'm going to record our discussion. Is that okay with you?"

Mr. Vargas looks at my phone. "Yes, okay."

I unscrew the gnawed-on cap from my pen and tap it against the notepad. "Can you state your full name, please?"

He leans toward the phone. "Carlos Vargas," he says, almost shouting.

I force a smile. "You can speak normally. It's super sensitive."

His cheeks redden. "Oh, okay."

"So, go ahead and tell me about your restaurant." I swallow a yawn as he begins to tell me about his bayside bistro. In true Evan fashion, he'd fired himself up with a brilliant idea to feature struggling local businesses, for "human interest." He'd lined up the interviews for months before abandoning them once he got his promotion. After that, he softened me up one night with a homemade meal and an impassioned speech about all the "little guys" he'd be letting down by canceling the interviews, so I'd agreed to take over. That was, of course, before the breakup.

"And now my son is head of the kitchen." Mr. Vargas continues. "I'm really hoping it helps us turn things around. He was the head of a French restaurant in LA. His food is amazing." Apparently, I'm doing a pretty good job of feigning interest, because he smiles at me. "Do you like Spanish food?"

"I'm not sure I've ever had it." I have a feeling it's different from the usual Cal-Mex I find myself eating at least three times a week.

His eyes widen. "That's a shame. I always thought *my* cooking was pretty good, but my son? Amazing! Incredible!"

"How long has your family been in the area?"

His expression darkens. "Well, I guess it's been over twenty years now."

What is that look in his eyes? "Where were you before that?"

He shifts in his seat. "River Gap. I used to work with a farmer up there."

River Gap is a town even smaller than where my family lived north of the city. There is basically nothing but farms that way. "Yeah, it's all country living north of Sonoma, isn't it?" Hell, most people here consider Sonoma "the countryside." But past that is just nothing except wild land and terrible people. "What made you decide to come to the city?"

He stares at my phone. "Um, I really don't . . . it has nothing to do with the restaurant."

"I can turn this off." I smell dirt. I hit the button on the screen to stop recording, leaving the phone on the table so he can see it's off.

He sighs. "Please don't put this in the paper. It's so painful for our family."

I nod. "Of course."

"When my son was little, my wife died in a fire . . . back in River Gap."

"A wildfire?"

He shakes his head. "No. It started at a house near the farm we worked at and then caught over to our little house on the other corner of the property. I wasn't at home, and the firefighters only managed to save my boy."

My heart sinks. "How did it happen?"

He meets my gaze. "It was just an accident."

As was ours, allegedly. A devastating, tragic accident. Beth had always told me so. But in the rare moments I allowed my thoughts to dwell on the topic, I found myself prodding at the sparse memories I had of the day leading up to the fire. It always felt like I was searching for something, a clue, that was there before but had been wiped clean. And that's exactly why I don't like to think about it.

It's often said that the simplest explanation is usually the truest, and fires in California aren't anything new. Although I hadn't personally heard of a similar fatal fire in the area around Sola, it made perfect, painful sense how it happened. Out there, tucked away in the countryside, neighbors might not immediately notice the plumes of flames rising up from a mile away. And when they did, the volunteer fire departments sometimes had to travel a far distance to reach the flames. That last part didn't apply in our case. Our farm was just ten miles from Main Street. Beth always told me that since it happened in the middle of the night, our neighbors, the McPherons, only noticed the flames when they reached beyond the rooftop.

That strange, fuzzy sensation begins spreading through my limbs as I think about the fire. It's that dreamlike feeling that makes me almost forget that all of that really happened. It takes me a moment to pull myself back into the present. "When was this?" I ask.

Mr. Vargas glances down at his hands on the table between us. "2004."

My stomach turns. The fire that killed my family was in '03.

He shakes his head. "It just—well, it was impossible to stay there after that. Coming here seemed like a fresh start."

Fresh starts are overrated. It worked for me and Aunt Beth for the most part, I guess. But we didn't leave Sola behind until I was sixteen. The damage of living in that town for years after my family died was already done by that point. It had taken Beth too long to see what staying there was doing to me.

Mr. Vargas looks at his watch. "Well, I should be getting back to help with the dinner crowd." He laughs. "It's not much of a crowd these days, but still."

We both stand, and I reach out to shake his hand. "Thank you for meeting with me today."

He smiles. "You should come by Amor al Mar. You have to try my son's cooking. *And* he's single."

Perfect match, two childhood-fire survivors finding love. Not that Mr. Vargas knows about that. "I appreciate the offer," I say. "But I'm not really looking right now." Or anytime in the near future, for that matter.

"Oh . . . well, still I'd love for you to try our food. Anytime, come by, and your meal is on us."

I walk him to the exit of the building, and he turns to wave before getting into his beaten silver Subaru.

"How'd it go?" Evan asks, emerging from the break room before I can pass.

The scent of his sandalwood cologne makes my stomach churn. I used to find it so comforting. "It was fine." I continue walking past him to my desk.

He's hot on my heels. "Can we talk?"

"No." I grab my bag from under my chair and sling it over my shoulder.

"Look, I know you're angry, but let's be mature about this." His voice grows louder as we step outside into the parking lot.

"I'm not angry." After I caught him and the intern, I waited for anger to boil over, but it never came. I didn't even have the energy to yell at him. It felt like getting hurt by him was always an inevitability, in one way or another. It's probably rooted, like most of my issues, in my childhood trauma, but my love life is the one area that's remained untouched in therapy so far. Not for my counselor's lack of trying.

"Lex," he says as I pull out my car keys. "What happened with her—it was a mistake. I shouldn't have been here so late. I've just been so stressed with this new position and everything."

Oh yes, I'm sure the difficulty of making more money and working fewer hours is a much greater stress than burying my aunt. And on top of that, now the added stress of being summoned back to the place where my entire world fell apart as a child. "Hey, it's . . . it is what it is."

His gaze shifts. "You're always like this, you know. Can't you just feel something for once? Get angry, hit me, scream at me. God knows I deserve it."

"I'm not going to hit you." I glance back at the windows of the office. I wonder if any of them are watching. This whole thing is just embarrassing. Embarrassing that I fell for Evan in the first place. And even more mortifying for it to end in the worst possible way.

When I don't say anything more, he moans, "Come on, Lex. This is exactly what the problem always is with you. You're *always* so disconnected from everything, even me."

Deep within my gut, there is a gnawing desire to hit him. It would feel so good.

"Maybe that's why I allowed myself to fall into something with Christine. She's not like that. She lets me in."

"I'm sure she does." I walk toward the old Corolla that Beth and I shared in its little corner spot. I'd rather stab myself in the eye than continue this conversation.

"Hey! We're not done talking." I'll give it to him. His expression looks truly pained. That little wrinkle between his forehead has me almost convinced that he actually feels bad about what he did.

"Talking about what?" I ask. "About how I'm a frigid bitch with no emotion? I think I get the point."

He shrinks a little. "I didn't say that! I just think you . . . hold things in sometimes. I know you still must be a wreck after Beth . . . let me give you a ride home."

"You can relax, Evan. I'm not angry with you, and let's just reset, okay?" This experiment between Evan and me was doomed from the beginning, not only because we work together but because I'd been playing a part with him the whole time. Caring about and working on a relationship didn't come naturally to me.

"*Reset?* We've been dating for almost a year. I'm not a robot. You can't just expect me to forget about our relationship."

"Give it a try. It wasn't that difficult for you to forget a few days ago."

He averts his eyes, and I take the chance to make my escape into my car. Evan mumbles something I can't quite make out and turns toward the building.

I glance down at the envelope from Ridley's letter in my passenger's seat. Maybe in addition to getting some money, going back to Sola will give Evan a chance to cool down. Although it seems impossible that any good can come out of this.

2003

When my parents first told us we were moving to be closer to Grandpa, I was excited. But after seeing his house for the first time, I wasn't so sure. I could finally understand why Grandpa always came to visit us in San Francisco rather than the other way around.

"We're really going to live here?" I glanced over my shoulder at the house.

"Come on, Lex. It's got great bones," Dad said, wiping his forehead with the back of his hand.

Bones. I thought that was an odd way to phrase it, but it was accurate. The aging wood farmhouse clung to the frame well enough, but there were gaps in the roof apparent even to me at the age of ten. The paint was peeling off of nearly every surface. But the shape, the huge, glorious shape of the house was still good, a shadow of what had once been a rancher's mansion.

Dad handed me another box in what seemed like an endless loop. I tilted forward on my tiptoes to see into the U-Haul at the others still stacked up to the ceiling. I couldn't believe all of that had fit in our cramped city apartment.

"This is taking *forever*." I sagged under the weight of the box and leaned against Dad's side.

He laughed, nudging me gently with his elbow. "Okay, you're off box duty, kiddo. Go bring me the Tall One and you help your mom inside."

I grinned. Good, this was Donnie's problem now. I bounced back into the house, tossing the box just over the threshold, realizing too late the letters that read *fragile: cups*. Thankfully no one was nearby, so I jogged away from the scene of the crime. Donnie was on a ladder in the living room, using a screwdriver to tighten the ceiling fan. Donnie had been taller than my parents for a while, but in the months leading up to the big move, he'd shot up several inches, becoming even lankier than usual. I was surprised he needed the ladder.

"'Sup, Mini?" He grinned at me before climbing down.

Usually I'd snap at the nickname, but in that moment I was eager to issue his new assignment. "Dad said he needs you to move boxes." Although we'd all helped unload the initial few boxes, everyone had quickly scattered to do other tasks, leaving me and Dad at the van.

Donnie rolled his eyes. "Tell Dad to—"

"'Tell Dad' what?" Dad appeared in the living room behind us, setting a huge box by the covered sofa. He raised his eyebrows at Donnie.

"Uh," Donnie sputtered. "Tell Dad I'll be right over?"

Dad smiled and exchanged a look with me. "I had a feeling that was going in a different direction. Where are the girls?"

I shrugged. From the distant sound of their giggling, they were probably already decorating their rooms at the other end of the house.

Dad sighed. "Donnie, you're coming with me. Lexi, go gather the girls and help your mom, okay? She's probably trapped under a thousand paint cans somewhere around here." He eyed the half-peeled wallpaper before leaving the room.

I walked to the back of the house, turning down the corridor with framed black-and-white pictures full of people I didn't recognize, following a dull banging sound. As I passed the back door, a flash of gray and blue appeared at the corner of my eye. I paused, watching Grandpa standing on the porch, leaning against a rocking chair. He was so still. What was he looking at?

Grandpa had always been goofy. All funny faces and farmer's jokes the entire time I'd known him. Until last Christmas when he came to our place in the city. He seemed so sad and serious, his eyes barely focusing on any of us even when we were right in front of him.

He turned to look at me as I opened the door and stepped out beside him. He stared before a gentle smile parted his lips.

"What are you doing, Grandpa?" I walked up beside him.

"Emma? What are you doing here? You should be at school." He sounded frustrated but wound an arm around my shoulders.

"I'm not Emma, Grandpa. That's Mom. I'm—"

"You shouldn't be here when he comes back."

I peered up at him. "Who, Grandpa?"

He gripped my hand so hard I yelped. "Stay away from him."

"Grandpa!" I struggled in his grip.

The porch door swung open. "Pa?" My mom ran to us and put her hand on Grandpa's shoulder. "What's wrong?"

He looked over at her, and his eyes narrowed. "Emma?"

She nodded, glancing at me and slowly uncoiling his grip. "Yeah, Pa. It's me. Did you need something?"

He shook his head. "That boy, Emma. That boy shouldn't be here. You shouldn't let him come here at night."

That boy? Was he talking about Donnie? It didn't make sense, but I couldn't wrap my mind around any other possibility.

"Okay. You're right. I'll tell him, Pa." Mom led him back to the rocking chair.

He glared at me as he settled into his seat.

"Why don't you sit down for a little bit, okay? We'll go get you some water. It's hot out here."

He turned toward the barn, relaxing against the chair.

Mom took my hand and brought me inside. "Are you hurt, Lexi?"

I sniffled as I peered at Grandpa through the window. "Why is he mad at me?"

She stooped down to meet my eyeline. She had speckles of pale-yellow paint on her face and large splatters over the front of her denim overalls. "He was just a little confused."

"What boy was he talking about?"

She sighed. "I don't know. Will you go get him a glass of water?" She looked down at my wrist, my skin still red from where Grandpa grabbed me. "Are you okay, baby?"

I pulled away from her and wiped my nose with my arm. "Yeah."

"Good girl. Let's get the water together." She straightened and placed her hand on my back, guiding me down the hallway to the kitchen.

I glanced over my shoulder. Grandpa was still sitting and staring at the barn.

CHAPTER FOUR

When Aunt Beth and I left Sola, we left everything there. We packed what we could from Beth's small house near the church and sold it. I imagined the remnants of my family's scorched house sitting abandoned often over the years. The splintered wood and tumbled bricks, frozen in place as the grass grew around it, haunted me when I stopped to think about it. At some point, I remember Beth talking about leasing the acreage to ranchers for grazing, but eventually she stopped mentioning it altogether. Who would build on land where an entire family had been wiped from existence?

I roll down my window, and my ears pop as the elevation dips behind the mountains and the tree line begins to break. The clean air rushes in as it whips my hair across my face and neck. It's strange seeing all this empty land again. It doesn't even feel familiar anymore, just like it's all from an old dream.

By the time I arrive in town, it's pitch black. My headlights flash on the Railroad Crossing sign and I take a right.

I wonder what happened to everyone I knew from school who never left. I'd been curious enough to check up on a couple of the girls I knew in high school on Facebook before, only because the person I actually cared about didn't have an account. Drugs and pasture parties by thirteen, pregnant by sixteen. Thankfully, I missed the latter.

I glance at the dark pastures, and I can spot a light on at the main McPheron house as I pass. I shift in my seat as I think about him. Surely Kael's not here anymore, although I can't easily picture him existing anywhere else.

I won't be able to see anything at the farm this late. But maybe I can unknot this tangle in my mind if I see just the shadows of the wreckage. Maybe it'll lessen the blow.

I'm not sure where to enter the farm until I see the old, leaning mailbox by the road. I pull over and kill the engine before the headlights can reveal the area where the house used to be.

I open the door and step out onto the driveway, dirt crunching under my shoes as I approach a looming, dark mass. A small flash of light appears above the broken frame of the crumbling house.

I halt midstep, wondering for a moment how stupid it is to keep going before I continue toward the ruins. Chatter drifts to me in the cool air as it whips my face.

"Show us a sign," one of the voices—a girl's—pleads. "Who did this to you? To your family?"

"Don't ask that!" A male voice scoffs. They both sound so young. "It was an accident."

I slow my pace, careful to stay on the grass instead of the loose gravel below. Under the moonlight, I can barely make out the outlines of five heads huddled in what used to be our living room, the walls and roof peeled down around the group.

"No, it wasn't," a third voice intervenes. "It was arson. Someone did it, they just never found out who . . ."

"It was the dad, that's what my mom told me. He went crazy and killed them all and then set the house on fire—"

"You shouldn't be here," I call out over the rubble.

One of the girls screams, and all five heads shoot up in the dark before a flurry of phone lights shine into my eyes, blinding me.

"Who are you?" a guy shouts. He sounds more aggressive than I'd bargained for. I wonder if I've made a mistake in instigating this confrontation.

I step over one of the crumbling walls, blinking against the light shining into my eyes. "This is my property. You really shouldn't be here."

The kids start whispering. It makes me angrier. It's bad enough that they treat my family's tragedy like a local ghost story, but now they're probably going to portray me as a Boo Radley type when they tell kids at school about tonight. But maybe that's fine. People left Boo Radley alone for the most part.

"You're . . . um . . . the Blake girl?" a girl manages to ask after a second.

My eyes have adjusted now, and I can see her terrified gaze, pale and ghostly from the light of her phone. "What are you guys doing here?" I ask, sidestepping her question.

The girl who spoke grabs a bag from the ground. "Nothing. I'm so sorry. We didn't know anyone lived here."

I don't correct her. Maybe if they think I have a house hidden somewhere around here on the back lot, they won't return.

The boy who spoke first is taller than me, I realize at this distance, and he bounds toward me and stops a few feet away. "No one's lived on this property since—"

"Look, kid," I say, kicking at a rotten plank on the ground. "Call the sheriff if that would make you happy."

The other kids retreat to the opposite side of the house, climbing over the ruins in the dark. The guy in front of me is the only one who remains after a minute. He stares at me and then glances over his shoulder before following his friends, the lights from their phones bobbing as they sprint across the field. They must live close by or have a car parked near the railroad.

I turn on my own phone light, flashing it over the house to make sure no one's stayed behind, huddled in a dark corner somewhere.

No stragglers. But the light catches on some clutter that was in the middle of the circle the kids formed. I stoop to get a closer look. There are three small candles in mason jars staggered around the outer edge of a crumpled piece of paper. One candle is black, another white, and then red.

I grab the note, unfolding it and holding my light closer to the surface. On the right, the word *NO* is scrawled in pencil and on the left, *YES*. At the bottom of the page is a shakily scribbled pentagram.

How original. I guess these kids were too cheap to spring for an actual Ouija board.

I jump as leaves crunch behind me. Maybe that huge kid came back.

My eyes dart around the remnants of the house, straining to see into the darkness surrounding me. The flashlight on my phone doesn't reach quite as far as I'd like. "Hello?"

Nothing.

I take a few steps toward the caved-in door to leave, pausing to listen again. Still quiet, only the buzz of crickets.

I direct my light toward the barn. The words **Evil Was Here** are unevenly spray-painted along the tin door. Great. Just one more thing to take care of.

As I continue to the road, I feel like someone is watching me. My pulse doesn't return to normal until I jump into my car and lock the door.

I always forget how absolute the darkness is out here. No streetlamps. No storefronts. Just black. Not a single traffic light until Penman. The fact that my headlights illuminate only a few feet ahead on the highway unsettles me, as if anything could appear on the road in front of me. That happened quite a lot when I was younger. People at the feed store would exchange stories of their latest near misses with deer or coyotes all the time.

I relax my grip on the steering wheel as a flickering red sign appears. The motel is more run down than the pictures on Google Maps led me to believe, but I expected as much. The sign above is missing a glowing red *T*, and the outside could use a new coat of white paint all around. My car is one of only two in the parking lot.

I brace myself for the worst as I grab my duffel bag and lock my car. When I walk into the entrance, no one is sitting at the desk. "Great," I mutter. I survey the area, noting the yellowed wall calendar from two years ago and the rolling chair with huge puffs of stuffing poking through the synthetic leather. Footsteps approach before the front door swings open. The man winces when he sees me at first. Then in a second, he smiles. It's not a pleasant smile but one that makes me clutch my bag a little tighter.

"Hi there," he says, walking behind the desk. He doesn't sit but remains on his feet, looming above me. His eyes narrow and drift to the neckline of my shirt and then to my bag. "Need a room?"

God, there better be dead bolts on these doors. "Um, yeah."

He nods and scribbles something illegible on a blank piece of paper in front of him. "How long?"

"I don't know."

He sucks his teeth. "Card."

"What?"

"I need a card for the file."

Nice try. "I'm going to pay each night in advance in cash." Thankfully I had the good sense to withdraw what was left in my bank account before coming out. The nearest ATM is at least an hour away.

His smirk disappears.

"How much is it?" I ask.

"Seventy-five."

"Per night?"

He sighs. "Per week."

"What makes you think I'll be here for a week?"

He narrows his eyes. "You're here to sell that farm, right? You'll be lucky to make it out of here in less than a month."

I stare at him, stunned for a moment. Do I know him? I take in his dirty, sun-bleached plaid shirt, the shade of reddish-pink matching the sunburn on his face. "How do you know I'm here to sell—"

"Everyone knows."

Right. I forgot how impossibly quick word of anything out of the ordinary spreads here. And that was even before everyone had cell phones.

I turn my back to him and open my wallet, grabbing a fifty and two twenties before shoving my wallet into my bag. "I need change," I say as I hand over the cash.

He grabs a copper key from the wall behind him and slides it toward me. So old school. "You'll be in room twelve." He fishes a few wadded-up bills from the pocket of his jeans and tosses them onto the counter.

I take both the key and the money. "Which side is that on?"

He stares at me and nods behind him. "This side. Up the stairs."

That's the side of the building where the parking lot lights are out. Great. I rush out the door without a second glance at the man and squint at the side of the building where he gestured. Judging by how empty the lot is, it's impossible that more than one other person is staying here, yet he still booked me in the room in the farthest, darkest corner.

I shuffle up the rickety staircase and scramble to unlock the first door. The smell of musty, wet carpet hits me before I can take a step inside. I twist the dead bolt and appraise the room. There's a TV, but one of those super old ones with a dial rather than a remote and a set of rabbit ears on top. The comforter on the bed clearly had a vivid red floral pattern but has faded to an odd dull brown that kind of resembles dried blood.

I set my bag on the drawer next to the TV, triggering a wisp of dust.

I don't want to see the bathroom, but I desperately need a shower. The restroom isn't too bad. Clearly the tiles have been cleaned and the mirror wiped. A small paper-wrapped soap sits by the faucet beside a tiny new bottle of lotion. I wish I'd had the foresight to bring my own towels, but the two folded on the counter are spotless, at least the portions that are visible. There's one lingering long hair in the base of the tub that I can't pretend I haven't seen.

I run the water, watching as the hair floats down the drain before I disrobe. It's a quick shower rather than the luxurious one I'm craving, but the hot water makes me feel sleepy. And that's really the point.

Thankfully I'm exhausted enough from the long drive to lie down on the bed, my wet hair sinking into the pillow. The white sheets still have a faint scent of bleach, so that's a good sign, right?

I open my voice mail and click the last one from Beth from a few days ago.

"Hey Lexi, I was hopin' to catch you before you get home. Please pick up something for dinner for us. We got some of the leftover turkey chili you made and I just can't eat it again. Ha ha! Love ya, girl, but you and me shouldn't cook for a while maybe. See you in a bit."

I smile and scroll through the other messages left by Beth. It was a quiet habit that I formed when I first got a cell phone. Back then, everyone left voice mails, and I couldn't bear deleting a single one. When my cell phones inevitably ran out of space or when I needed to replace them, I would download the messages to my laptop before deleting them. After losing my family when I was little, it seemed so special to have a recording of someone's voice, portable and permanent. I wish I'd had that back when I was little. It could've really helped during my darkest times as a teenager when the weight of losing my parents and siblings was heaviest.

I let my phone fall to the mattress and stare up at the water stains on the ceiling, tracing the edges until my eyes finally close.

I hear the frantic knocking before I'm completely awake.

I scratch my fingers along the rough fabric of the sheets to make sure I'm not still dreaming. After a pause, another sharp knock sounds on the door.

I sit up, rubbing my eyes and pulling back the covers. As I approach the door, I lean forward, pressing my eye as close to the peephole as possible without touching it. Nobody is visible on the other side, only the silent, dark highway beyond the parking lot.

I step back. Maybe it wasn't a knock on my door but one of my neighbors'. Oh, because this place is so full? So far I haven't seen any of the other guests. I certainly haven't heard any moving around in the neighboring rooms.

My feet leave the floor as the motel phone on the nightstand rings. I close the distance with only a few steps and pick it up on the second ring. "Hello?"

Static erupts on the other end. I curse, holding the receiver away from my ear.

"H-hel . . ." The faint voice disappears into more garbled audio. "Help!" The moan is louder now. The quality is bad, but it's definitely a woman pleading from the other end.

"Who is this?"

There's quiet now, interrupted only by muffled breathing.

"Hello?" I swallow, my heart hammering against my chest.

The breathing grows louder, and then a bloodcurdling scream rings out. I jump back, dropping the phone, the receiver crashing onto the fraying carpet. Before I can even think about what a bad idea it is, I unlock the door and run out onto the walkway, the concrete ripping up my bare feet.

The wind blows the door open wider. Panting, I spin around, leaning against the railing to see down below in the parking lot. Silence. Not a soul nearby. And this time of night, the highway is quiet too. I turn back to my room, staring at the motel phone still dangling off the hook. I step inside and lock the door, my hands sweating as I pick up the receiver. There's no dial tone. There's no sound at all. Whoever called is still on the line.

"Who is this?"

No answer.

"What do you want?"

No answer.

"I'm going to call the police."

The sound of licking lips. "Oh, is that so?" The voice sends a chill down my spine. It's distant and airy, like someone is intentionally not opening their mouth all the way. It sounds otherworldly.

I slam the phone down, my heart racing.

2003

Sola at night had a sort of quietness that made my thoughts echo in my mind as I tried to fall asleep. The silence made every creak of the settling farmhouse deafening. I twisted under my blankets for the fifteenth time, squeezing my eyes shut.

Back in our old San Francisco apartment, the nights had been so loud, like a chaotic lullaby I'd become accustomed to. The sirens, the revving of engines as they climbed the street near our place.

I opened my eyes and rolled onto my back, staring up at the glow-in-the-dark plastic stars Donnie and Dad had formed into the Little Dipper and Big Dipper for me.

A deep voice drifted through the air, just beyond my closed door. Back in San Francisco, I always slept with my door open. But in this house, the idea of waking up and staring out into a dark open doorway made my stomach drop.

"What are you doing?" the voice whispered. "You shouldn't be here." It sounded like Grandpa grumbling.

I sprang out of bed. I turned the doorknob and padded out into the hallway, my bare feet cool against the floor.

"What do you want? I'm calling the police!"

My heart pounded as I followed Grandpa's voice toward the kitchen. There was a loud shuffle and a clatter of a chair hitting the floor. I picked up my pace and whipped around the corner.

Grandpa was crouched on the ground, clinging with one hand to the edge of the table.

I rushed to him.

He peered at me in the dark briefly before directing his gaze to the open window on the other side of the table.

My arms nearly collapsed under his weight as I tried to help him to his feet. "Grandpa?"

He panted as he steadied himself. "That boy, Emma. He did this."

I didn't think to correct my name after the strong reaction that had provoked earlier.

His eyes were still fixed on the window. "Lock that window."

I let go of his arm and obeyed, the cold night air rustling my pajama dress as I tugged the window closed and latched it. Beyond the glass was darkness like I hadn't seen before. Pure, solid dark. If I hadn't seen the pasture and the side of the barn from this same window earlier in the day, I might've thought nothing existed except this house.

When I turned around, he had already sunk into a chair at the table. "Grandpa?"

"Go back to bed," he said gruffly. "I'll keep an eye on things."

I walked over to him and pulled out another chair. I couldn't imagine going back to bed. I trained my eyes at the window. I didn't know what Grandpa was waiting for, but it made my pulse quicken.

CHAPTER FIVE

I barely slept the rest of the night, that scream playing through my mind every time I closed my eyes.

As the sun peeps through the blinds, I finally give up on sleep and roll out of bed, when I hear whistling.

I stuff my feet into my sneakers and tug my hair up into a ponytail before slipping on running shorts and a T-shirt so faded I can barely make out the band's name.

I walk out the door and lock it behind me. The guy from the front desk is standing outside the lobby, a cigarette between his fingers and an old pair of headphones over his ears. He continues whistling until he sees me out of the corner of his eyes.

I pick up my pace to get out of his line of sight. I don't love the idea of running along the highway, even though it's likely to be pretty slow this early on a Sunday—surely everyone's in church by now. I continue around the back of the motel to the dirt road.

I begin jogging, the grit of the dirt kicking up behind me with each step and rubbing in between my socks and skin.

My thoughts refocus in time with my breath.

Kael.

Beth, the house.

The house. What house? It's just ruins now.

My heels sink heavier into the dirt at the thought. But that's why I'm here, after all. To sell that godforsaken property.

The call. The scream.

I can still hear the garbled woman's voice through the receiver. It had sounded so familiar.

I turn my head toward the empty fields as I bound farther down the road, spotting a man on a tractor in the distance, cows moving sluggishly away from him as if they're trudging through mud. Here, everything seems to move so much slower.

Except for me. I push ahead, entering a part of the road where the fence line meets a row of tall trees. The dirt road curves into a large loop back to the motel.

Once the trees stop and give way to barbed wire fences, I spot the plume of dust rising along the upcoming crossroad before I hear the sound of tires grating along the gravel. As I grow closer to the motel, a black Lincoln SUV approaches the parking lot. The dust begins to settle, and a man with pure-white hair steps out.

I slow my steps. The well-manicured beard I remember is gone. But that smile is the same. It's an expression that is supposed to be disarming to his sheep at the church, but it fills me with tension.

He's clearly dressed for Sunday service in what's probably the only tailored suit in the county. "Lexi?" His voice floods me with the memories of all those sermons—passionate words slinging toward a nodding crowd.

I wipe away the sweat from my forehead and dig in my pocket for my key. "Reverend Butcher?"

His eyes drift to my running clothes. "Will you be joining us at church?"

"No," I say without hesitating. "Speaking of which, what are you doing here?"

He glances toward the motel. "Just checking on things."

I'm not even sure how to respond. Why would he possibly need to check on—

"I took over the motel a while back."

Cool. Just one more reason to hate this place. I nod, eyeing the door to my room.

"I heard you were in town . . ."

I back away in the direction of the staircase. "Join the club." I climb the stairs to my room and unlock it, the door wheezing on its hinges.

"Lexi!" he calls.

I turn around.

"I—" The smile is gone, replaced by pursed lips and a furrowed brow.

"What?"

He stares at me. "You should really come to the service."

A deeper, older resentment starts to claw at my stomach. As if attending a sermon put on by him, the very gift of God, will solve everything. I watch him for another moment before closing the door.

My heart races as I drive over the cattle guard and pass the old cars and trucks abandoned in front of the white wood-frame house. I have no idea what I'll say when Mrs. McPheron inevitably comes out to see why a strange car is here. Will she even recognize me? I just want to know what happened to him. Where is he now?

I park in front of the barbed wire fence that runs down the pasture beside the main house and the small house, a white mare staring at me as I close the car door. Oh, the horses. An ache settles in my stomach when I look more closely at the horse. I don't recognize her, but this smell and her deep and almost-human gaze as I approach the fence, that's familiar.

I walk past her into the open barn, my shoes crunching on the pebbles and loose hay. The horses at the wooden gate shift toward me, but the previous focus of their attention—a man at the other end hunched over an overturned wheelbarrow—remains with his back turned. Those shoulders, broad and taut under a thin gray T-shirt, clinging to his back with sweat. That faded army-green baseball cap. God, is that the same one from back then? How old is that?

I stop in the middle of the barn, unable to bring myself closer. What does he look like now after all this time? Although I'd hoped, I never really expected to see him here. I'd been prepared to see his parents, but what if *he* doesn't recognize me?

"Hello?" I say stupidly, as if I've wandered in here by accident or something.

He straightens, and I realize he must've grown another four or five inches since I last saw him. He turns around, his cheeks and nose flushed under his sun-kissed skin.

A dimple appears as his lips tug into a grin. "Sexy Lexi? Is that you?" He closes the gap between us, taking off his canvas gloves. "Wow."

I can't help but smile at the high school nickname. As much as I'd resented it then, I'm flooded with nostalgia. "Yep, it's me. Although I'm considerably less sexy than I used to be."

Kael surveys me, his green eyes drifting from my plain T-shirt to my distressed jeans. I suddenly feel like I should've made more of an effort to dress up. "Clearly you haven't seen what's happened to everyone else after high school." He laughs. "But seriously, you look great. Lexi two point oh." He wipes the back of his hand across his forehead, leaving a streak through the wall of sweat that's gathered along his tan skin. The smile fades from his face after a moment. "I just heard about Beth . . . I'm sorry, Lex."

I extend my palm to the gelding behind the fence, letting him nuzzle at it before I stroke his snout. "Thanks." I continue petting the horse. I forgot how good this texture—grit and fur—feels. It's healing. "She got sick a while ago. But I thought she had a little more time. We both did." I step away from the horse and am almost immediately gently pulled into Kael's grasp. I love that he hugs without asking, unlike Evan. I mean, it's my own fault that Evan asked. He knew I generally hate hugs. But I don't hate this. Kael smells like sawdust and hay and sweat. In the best way.

He pulls back quickly. "Shit, I'm disgusting right now," he says, lifting his hands in surrender as if I've flashed a gun at him. "Sorry."

"It's okay. It was a nice reminder of what you used to do back then."

On the days when he was grossest, after hours of cleaning out stalls, mending fences, and training horses, he'd chase me around and hug me just to get all the ick of the day on me too. I was usually a big mess those hot summer days myself, but I'd play along, acting as if I didn't want to touch him. In truth, I lived for those hugs, for those all-encompassing arms around me.

He frowns. "It's hard to imagine Beth is gone. She was such a force." He stares at me. "But what brings you back to Sola?"

The seriousness of his tone takes me aback. "What? Are you not happy to see me?"

He shakes his head. "You must've been doing better in the city. Why would you want to come back? Nothing good has ever happened to you in this place."

Not *nothing*. Kael and I happened here. He was my first, and possibly my only, love. "If you must know, I'm only here to finally sell the farm."

"Really? Oh."

His tone conveys all of my worries in an instant. Seeing those kids at the ruins of my family's old house last night confirmed everything I feared. This town hasn't forgotten about the fire either. "Yeah, I think my chances of finding a buyer near here are pretty slim. Why are bumpkins so superstitious?"

He sighs. "Hey, I'm a bumpkin, but I'm not superstitious. And I'd take it off your hands if I could, you know that."

I gesture around the barn. "Sell a few of those stallions I saw in the front pasture and maybe you can."

It's meant as a joke, but his face falls.

"Why? What's wrong?"

"Nothing."

"Come on, what's going on?"

"I'm losing money on this place. A lot. Even if I sold every horse here, I wouldn't be able to pay shit." He walks to the bench by the barn entrance and grabs a canteen, unscrewing the lid before taking a sip.

Desperate to change the subject, I nod over to the wheelbarrow. "What was going on over there?"

He follows my gaze and laughs. "Oh. Whisper got pissed this morning and kicked the damn thing across the barn when I brought him out to change his shoes. I thought it was worth a shot to see if it was salvageable."

I glance around. "Whisper? You kept him?"

"Of course! He's your horse."

Warmth fills my limbs. Whisper *was* mine at one time. He was the one horse my family had owned among our dairy cows. Beth had comforted me when we gave him to Kael's family before moving away. It had helped that I trusted Kael and his dad to look after Whisper, my best friend. I'd come to terms a long time ago that they'd probably sold him at some point over the years.

"Can I see him?"

He waves for me to follow him. "Grab some peppermints and let's go see your boy."

As we pass through the barn opening, I pause by the beaten stereo on a shelf and dip into the glass jar of soft peppermint candies, grabbing a couple before catching up with Kael.

He opens the gate for me, and I deftly sidestep the horse shit gathered in front of me. "I put him out in the pasture after he destroyed the wheelbarrow, but he always hangs around by that pond."

"He's still a firebrand, I guess." Whisper had always been spirited to say the least. Arabians often are. My parents and brother had never known what to do with him, but he and I had clicked. Even when he spooked, I never reacted with fear for some reason, even though he towered over my young frame. But he calmed quicker with me than he did around others.

As soon as we leave the corrals, I spot him. Whisper's beautiful roan coat has faded with age, but it still shines brilliantly in the light from the setting sun.

Kael nickers as we approach, and Whisper turns, his eyes immediately locking onto me before he trots toward us. Kael instinctively steps between us, probably thinking Whisper is about to charge me. It's easy to forget how big horses are until they're bounding toward you like a thousand-pound dog. But Whisper slows a few paces away and dips his head in my direction.

I raise my palm up to his snout, and his whiskers tickle my skin. "Hey, buddy," I say, edging closer and rubbing his neck. I pause to unwrap one of the peppermints, and he flicks his ear, nuzzling me as I place the candy into the center of my flat hand and he vacuums it up. "I wasn't sure he'd recognize me," I say over my shoulder to Kael.

He steps beside me, patting Whisper's neck as I feed him one more peppermint. "I would've been shocked if he didn't run up to you like he did. Sometimes I get the feeling he's still looking for you when I bring him into the barn."

That thought jabs at my heart. There really isn't anything purer than the love of an animal. And I'd walked out on him.

To be honest, I'm a little shocked Kael's parents decided to keep him, especially with how headstrong he'd been. His dad I think always harbored a special affection for difficult animals (and me), but Mrs. McPheron wasn't one to tolerate nonsense. I glance toward the empty driveway in the distance by the main house. I suppose Kael's living in his grandfather's smaller house just a few yards away from the barn. "Where's your mom? I didn't see her car."

Kael scratches the other side of Whisper's neck. "She's at church. She goes early to help the nursery."

"And you don't? Go to church, I mean."

"Nope." He steps beside me as I unwrap another peppermint. "So how long do you reckon you're going to be in town for?"

"Until I sell the goddamn property."

He smiles.

"What?"

"No, it's good," he says. "You're going to be here for a while then."

I decide against elaborating on my dilemma. No need to sour the mood with talk of squandered trust money and property taxes. "Don't take this the wrong way, but why are you still here?"

"What do you mean?" I can see from the sudden flicker in his gaze that he knows exactly what I mean.

"I mean, are you just visiting your parents or . . ." *Did you never leave?*

He shifts his weight. "Well, I got into USC, so I lived in LA for a couple of years."

Relief washes over me. "Really? That's great! What was your major?"

"Engineering. Started with industrial and then switched to mechanical."

In a school district that valued sports over academia, Kael had always put grades first. While other football players skated by with Cs that really should've been Fs, Kael studied before every practice and after every game to earn his As. "Wow. I always knew you were more than a pretty face."

His lips remain in a hard line. "But . . . Dad died before my junior year."

I look away from Whisper and meet Kael's eyes. "Oh. Kael, I—"

He shakes his head. "It's fine. Well, I just mean, it's been so long now. Anyway, after his accident, I dropped out to come help Mom. Fast-forward a decade and I'm still here."

I want to ask what happened to his dad, but I hesitate. This must've been why he mentioned he was struggling to keep the ranch afloat. "I'm sorry. I really had no idea."

"Yeah, I know. But that's how it always is, right? You think you're free and clear of this place and it drags you back in somehow." He chuckles.

Is that what's happening to me? Have I fallen into the Sola trap by coming back here? What if I never escape again? My chest tightens.

"So," Kael says after a moment. "You know how the last decade has chewed me up and spit me out. What about you? Surely if you've been in the city this whole time, things must be going well."

"It honestly hasn't been too bad. I've been writing for a local magazine. It's really only in the past week that shit's hit the fan."

He raises his eyebrows.

"Well, Beth passed away and then I found out my boyfriend, um . . . it doesn't matter . . . we broke up."

"All that in one week?"

"Yep."

"Sounds like you could use a drink." He's looking at me as if I'm still the bad influence his parents reluctantly hired at Beth's urging. When we were fourteen, I gave him his first beer after he caught me drinking at the bridge down the road from Beth's house. That was the moment I realized he was actually good company rather than just the golden boy at church.

I laugh. "I wish, but I already have a headache without the alcohol. I'll let you buy me a drink later."

"Any time." He grins. "Maybe we can toast to the worst years being behind us?"

"God, I fucking hope so." Sometimes I think I have a hard time taking recent bad things seriously because when the worst scenario imaginable already happened, all the other pain can feel a little muted.

"So where are you staying while you're here?"

I nod vaguely across the fields. "A motel down the road."

He furrows his brow. "We don't have a motel 'down the road.'"

"Yeah, it's in Penman."

"Isn't that a little out of the way?"

"Just a hop, skip, and a jump. Is that what people say?"

He rolls his eyes and smiles. "Don't try to be cute and folksy. You're a San Franciscan. It sounds so wrong coming from you."

"Okay, fine. It's only twenty minutes away. See? That doesn't sound quite as whimsical." I shake my head. "It's actually a relief to have somewhere outside the border of this town to rest."

He stares at me. "You know, it's really not that bad here."

"So far, I haven't really seen anything that backs up that statement." I laugh. "I mean, except for you. But you don't count. You're too good for this place." Whisper inches forward and nuzzles my unclenched hand, huffing in disappointment when no food is found.

"Do you know how long my family's lived here?"

"Probably as long as the Rawlings." I can vaguely hear Grandpa's voice in my ear. *"My father's father built the old barn on our farm."* That's why they never tore it down. Grandpa and Beth repaired and repaired it until it was a patchwork of different-colored tin.

"Nope, longer. We've helped build this place. So, maybe it's kind of a shithole . . . but, it's *our* shithole."

"That's exactly why we have different perspectives of this place," I say. "It never mattered to anyone here that my mom was raised here, or that Grandpa was a third-generation farmer. *I* was an outsider." Sure, my siblings and I weren't born here, but we still had ties to this land. But the people here couldn't bear to be cordial even out of respect to Grandpa.

"That's not true—"

"It is. I'm a Blake, not a Rawlings, to these people." And that's fine. I never wanted to be treated by these people as one of them. I just wanted to feel accepted on *any* small level. I wanted my voice heard and not discarded because I wasn't "part of the community" even though I had nowhere else to go.

He frowns.

"And that's unforgivable." To be an outsider—a judgmental, questioning outsider. And that's exactly what Dad did best—ask questions. "They hated my dad."

"Come on, everyone loved your mom. They worshipped her, Lex."

"I'm sure they did at some point." How could they not? She had been so easy to love. Fierce, whip smart, gorgeous. Although I'm sure most people only cared about the latter. The first two didn't have much value in a woman here, at least not a young one. Beth was one of the only exceptions. "But she was a disgrace when she returned with my 'city slicker' dad, right? I'm sure even your parents had some colorful opinions about that."

He shakes his head. "Never. I mean, they heard stuff, of course."

"From the church, right?"

"Where else? But, to be fair, it's not like your parents really approved of this town, either, right?" Kael glances down.

Maybe that is fair. But I'm not willing to admit it out loud.

"So, what can I do to help you? With the land, I mean. I imagine it's not in great shape."

"It was hard to get a great look at it last night, but that's pretty accurate."

"Hmm." He looks at me.

"What?"

"I'm just worried maybe you've bitten off more than you can chew. Maybe you're not ready to do this right now."

He thinks I'm too emotionally fragile about the property? "It's not like I came here for fun. To be honest, Beth left me in a really bad spot. I *have* to sell the property . . ." I stop short of explaining why, hoping he can interpret the desperation in my eyes.

He holds my gaze. "Okay, then let's make it happen."

CHAPTER SIX

Being in this town is draining, as if with every breath I take here, I become more hollow and the town stronger. Whatever energy I gained from seeing Kael again after all these years is already gone. I couldn't bring myself to stop by the farm. Maybe Kael was right. Maybe I'm not ready to deal with this right now.

I pull over at the Ringer Bros. convenience store at the corner where Sola becomes Penman.

If it's like what I remember, there won't be much to choose from for lunch, but there will be microwaved grocery store pizzas on display under a Fresh sign and an endless sea of Funyuns bags gathering dust.

I push through the door, the familiar stench of mildew and burnt grease filling my nostrils. No one's in sight. I shouldn't be surprised.

I stare at the pizza under the glass display by the counter, watching as a single fly dances along the oily cheese. Okay, so no pizza.

I turn my attention to the coolers full of drinks at the very back instead. The lights buzz louder and flicker as I open the fridge door and pull out a carton of coconut water. As the door slams back into place, I spot a shelf at the very corner of the room, elaborate candles and crystals dramatically at odds with the display of Hostess desserts on one side and the mounted deer head on the other.

I walk toward the shelves, one in particular catching my eye. I pick up the emerald pillar candle, my fingers swiping through the dust that's gathered over the parchment label. Some small words have been scrawled in intricate calligraphy, but they're difficult to make out in the dim light.

"Hi, can I help you?"

I spin around, my eyes landing on the pale-faced woman behind me. It takes my brain only a second to remember where I've seen those ice-blue eyes and smile that perpetually looks like a scowl. She used to have orchid highlights in her hair, but they've been replaced with electric blue.

"Janna? Is that you?" After the words leave my mouth, anxiety and excitement tumble together in my gut.

The girl turns around, tugging on the mess of black-and-blue hair that's fallen from her ponytail. "Oh my God! Lex?" A smile flickers across her lips but then disappears. "I heard you were around. I was sorry to hear about Beth. I loved her." She frowns.

While Beth wasn't a huge fan of Janna Butcher, despite the fact that she was the preacher's daughter, Janna had always been partial to Beth. I assumed it was because Beth had the grit Janna's mom lacked. Or maybe it was just that compared to her home, even my broken family was more stable than hers. Everything in Janna's world had been so strange.

She wipes her hands on her apron and glances at the candle I'm holding. "Resurrection candles? Do you know how to use those?"

I gently place it on the shelf. "Oh, no." Janna believing in this garbage to rebel against her reverend father was one of the reasons I'd distanced myself from her. I'd wanted to believe, too, at first, but I had long accepted that nothing exists past our physical world. All this mystical bullshit made just as much sense to me as the natural world did to Janna. I'd always been a little jealous of her in a way. I *wish* I could believe. Who wouldn't? "I actually found some kids on the property last night, and they had a candle like this. Do you know anything about that?" I can't quite hide the annoyance in my voice. My tolerance for supernatural paraphernalia has only deteriorated over the years.

"I'm so sorry. I had no idea. A lot of kids will come in here and ask about these things. When they buy them, I always explain that they're to be used in cases where there's a *personal* connection to the conjurer. But you know, the kids here. There's nothing better to do, is there?"

Nothing better to do than play Bloody Mary with my dead family? Yeah, I guess she has a point. I swallow the comment that settles on the tip of my tongue. "I get it. To be honest, I'm a little surprised you're allowed to even sell this"—Shit? Garbage?—"*stuff* here."

"Oh . . . well, actually, this is my place now," she says, smiling and clasping her hands together, in the way we used to talk as teens about exciting things we'd get to do as adults.

"Wow! That's amazing, congrats." In that case, I guess I'm more surprised that she's selling *only* candles and crystals. "How did you manage that?" At some point the last Ringer brother must've died. I can't imagine them parting with this place otherwise.

She glances down. "I studied to get my Realtor license a little while back and really started looking for a place to invest in while I build my real estate work. I mean, my dad paid for the store, but I found it and brokered the deal and everything."

Of course. She had always been able to somehow manage to overlook her father's misdeeds when money was concerned. An entire store seems like an extravagant gift, especially for a reverend. "That's great."

"Yeah, well, it's a work in progress. I kept the pizza and the food how it was because people expect that now. But soon, I'm hoping to turn this place around." Her eyes brighten. "And, speaking of . . . if you need help to get that property sold, I'd be thrilled to do it."

My gaze immediately drifts to the blue hair peeking out from her thick black waves. Her family's well connected here. Maybe people in town aren't quite as conservative as I remembered and won't have reservations about dealing with an eccentric Realtor. Who am I kidding? Any potential buyer probably won't be a local. "Um, yeah, okay. That'd be great." It's not like I really had a better plan other than googling to find a Realtor in this area.

Her grin becomes genuine, the edges of her plum lipstick folding into the creases around her mouth. "Amazing! What's your number? Maybe we can meet this week to look at the property. And if you still have a good vibe about this, I'll bring the contract and we can get started!"

"Yeah, sure." I raise my coconut water. "Well, I'm just going to grab a couple of other things and head out."

Janna takes the green candle from the shelf and holds it out toward me. "Are you interested in trying it out?" I must make a face because she shakes her head. "I'm sorry. I know you think all of this is stupid, but . . . I don't know. We all get a little curious sometimes, don't we?"

I really regret committing to seeing her again. "Mm-hmm."

She sighs. "I shouldn't have said anything. It's just . . . once you sell the land, you're going to be losing the connection."

I don't want to find out exactly what she means by that, so I accept the candle. "How much is it?"

She waves her hand. "Oh, no. It's free." She smiles. "I'll be at the counter whenever you're ready to check out."

I watch her walk down the aisle and disappear around the corner, the wax from the candle softening under my searing skin.

CHAPTER SEVEN

I stare through my windshield at the rusted iron archway of Lakewood Cemetery, downing half the bag of Bugles and the coconut water I bought from Janna.

I grab the candle from the seat beside me and toss it into the back. It's stupid, but after last night and talking with Janna, I wanted to stop by. Not for a "connection." Just to see what's left of them. To see the reminders that they were actually here once.

My feet are heavy as I walk into the graveyard. I remember the last time I was here. The day of the funeral was so sunny it seemed wrong somehow.

I sink onto the leaves, brushing away the dirt from the gravestone with Mom's and Dad's names.

I'd always wondered why they were buried here of all places, but I now realize this must've been part of the paperwork my parents handled with the lawyers. My grandparents on Dad's side could barely look at me during the service, even though they sat directly beside me. Beth held my hand the entire time.

I move on to Donnie's stone beside Natalie's and Amy's. They aren't nearly as unkept as I'd expected them to be. I'm honestly surprised they haven't been vandalized. Maybe my grandparents visit regularly, if they are even still around. Although I can't imagine them driving all the way to the middle of nowhere to visit a bunch of rocks if they never showed an interest in seeing me. The cards with checks in them had stopped around the time I turned eighteen, and it's been a while since I got the last sporadic Christmas card.

My phone buzzes in my pocket. It's a text from Sanders. I click on the notification.

Good work, he wrote simply and attached a link. I click it, and a high-resolution photo appears of Carlos Vargas standing beside a young man with his same eyes. They're both smiling in front of a small restaurant by a pier, their arms crossed over their chests, the neon sign between their shoulders. Below the photo is our series title, Small Biz San Fran, and my byline.

I almost forgot that I even wrote this up last night when I couldn't sleep. I'm glad they were able to edit it into something usable. Sanders must've rushed it for the digital edition that went live today. I scroll up to the photo again. In another world, I would've definitely taken Mr. Vargas up on his offer to meet his son.

I'm drawn out of my own thoughts at a faint rustling sound behind me. I look over my shoulder, my heart jumping at the sight of a man in the distance. The mist from the nearby lake still weighs heavily in the air, and I can barely make out the shape. His broad shoulders and arms blend into a mass of fog.

I immediately squeeze my eyes shut like I used to when I'd hear that voice at night in the farmhouse. Those sounds and shadows that were shrugged off as an old house settling. Maybe, just like I've come to understand of the ghost back then, the man isn't really here.

My spine tingles as if someone's whispered along my neck. I steel my nerves and open my eyes. I'm alone among the gravestones.

My feet begin walking in the direction I saw the man before I can completely register the action. If what I saw was real, following a mysterious man into the fog can't possibly end well. The grave markers end, giving way to a thicket, the distance between the trees narrowing as I go deeper.

After a moment, I stop, panting and listening. The mist is low in the trees, thinning around the trunks. I scan the thicket and see nothing. Nothing but green and brown.

I walk back to the cemetery, my pulse still echoing in my ears as I break through the clearing.

"There you are," a deep voice calls out. I look toward my car and see Sheriff Larson approaching from the dirt parking lot.

He looks nearly the same as before, but his cowboy hat is a little worse for wear and his gait a bit wearier than I remember. He twitches his mouth into something that could almost be mistaken for a smile, his mustache wiggling. The facial hair is different. I bet he grew it after one too many comments about his baby face. He was still new to this area when we'd moved in and was considered a pushover by the old-timers here. Maybe the mustache helps.

"Hi, Sheriff." I was a mouthy sixteen-year-old the last time I saw him, but of course he still remembers me best from the night of the fire. He was my first memory of that night as well. His kind brown eyes moist at the edges from the smoke as he tried to coax me away from the burning house. He never stopped looking at me with that same pitying expression for as long as I lived in Sola. "What are you doing here?" I ask, still trying to catch my breath as we meet.

He stares at the trees and then back at me. "I was following up on a call near the old schoolhouse. I spotted your car from the road as I was heading back to the office. I heard rumblings you were back in town. I was hoping you'd have the good sense to stay clear of this place. If *you're* back, that means something bad must've happened."

"Well, I'm not back by choice."

"Yes, I heard about Beth." He frowns. This must cement the idea of a family curse in his mind. Beth was barely older than him. Much too young to die, but so was the rest of my family. "It's a real shame. She was one of the good ones."

"Thank you." She was *the* good one. That's why I'm grateful she at least got out of Sola before she died.

The lines around his mouth deepen. "So I imagine you're out here trying to deal with the farm?"

I nod. "Happen to know anyone in the market for a haunted hundred-acre farm?"

"That's not funny." He's not as good humored as I remember. That's what being stuck here for too long can do, I guess. "I wanted to make sure you hadn't run into trouble out here."

"Trouble? What kind of trouble?" I can't help but glance into the trees again. Who was that man? If he was visiting a grave, why wouldn't he have gone back to the gate rather than disappear into the thicket?

Larson furrows his brow. "You've got a lot of eyes on you right now, Lexi. Ever since you came to town."

"Oh, I know." I roll my eyes.

"Look, let me give you our office's number in case you need to call directly," he says. "We're on the 911 route now, but if you have a different area code . . . well, there's no telling where they may direct your call." His tone is so solemn.

"What exactly are you expecting is going to happen to me? Why would I need to call 911?"

He shakes his head. "Oh, I don't mean anything by it. In case someone gives you trouble on the farm. I don't like the idea of you meeting buyers out there on your own."

He's right. I was lucky those kids last night didn't call my bluff. I probably wouldn't have been able to even get in touch with Larson. "Oh, okay." I can still read something, unspoken, behind his eyes. "Well, you don't have to worry about that. I have a Realtor now." I pull out my phone, changing screens from the article to my address book before handing it to him. "You can type in the number. That's probably easier."

As he types, I glance in the direction where I saw the man earlier. The mist has completely dissipated. Should I tell Larson about the man? What's he going to do? Whoever that was has just as much right to be here as I do.

"How long are you planning to stay here?" He returns my phone and gestures to my family.

"Oh, I'm leaving now." I walk beside him as he leads the way to our cars.

"Is anyone giving you a hard time?" he asks softly. His lips curve into a sad smile as he stops by his cruiser and looks at me.

"Don't look at me like that. I've barely been in town a day, so nothing too bad yet. It's just beginning."

He continues to stare at me. "Don't take that nonsense from any of them. You don't deserve to be treated that way, here or anywhere."

"Don't worry about me. I'll be fine. Fuck them all."

He chuckles. "Atta girl." He opens his car door, his hand leaving a print in the dust gathered outside.

I unlock my phone to pull up directions to the motel when I remember the article. Mr. Vargas's son. Something had bothered me since he mentioned the date of that farmhouse fire. It was probably a coincidence, but River Gap isn't far from here. "Sheriff?"

He was about to duck into his seat but pauses to look at me, resting his hands on the roof of the car.

"Do you know about a fire a while back in River Gap?"

He narrows his eyes. "What year?"

I recall what Mr. Vargas said during the interview. "2004?"

"Nothing comes to mind. Why?"

"No reason."

He studies me for a moment, perhaps trying to decide whether to press me further or leave it for now.

"I actually need to ask you about something else." I swallow. I had tried not to think about these details for so long, but now that I'm back here, the constant questions gnaw at the edge of my mind. "I want to get a copy of the report from the night of the fire."

He stares at me, his expression impossible to read. "No."

"Wow. Okay. I expect this kind of shit from everyone else here, but not you."

He stiffens his chin. "Your father and your mother would tell you not to go diving into this stuff. Not now. What good would it do? Hell, I know Beth would say the same."

Beth is exactly the reason I haven't been able to close all these doors from the past. She always said it was an accident but never explained how it had started. And, although I hadn't admitted it myself, those stupid séance kids' accusation had rattled me.

"It was the dad."

Was there possibly even a little truth to it?

"Look, you did your part. You somehow managed to keep all the sordid details out of the hands of the gossiping masses around here, and I appreciate it. But *I* deserve to know what really happened that night."

His posture changes, and he squares up as if he's bracing for a hit to the gut. "It was an accident, Lexi. A tragic accident. You should let it lie."

"Are you going to make me put in a FOIA request?" Freedom of Information Act. It's been a while since I've had to use that beautiful tool. There aren't many reasons to use it at the *Weekly*. "There's probably an even easier way to request it since I'm a direct relative."

"You can do what you need to. The reason the busybodies here never got the details is because there are exemptions to FOIA, and this was an ongoing investigation."

"*Was*. But it's been twenty years, so how can you still consider it ongoing? Also, if it was an accident, what is there to investigate?"

His shoulders slump. "Do you really want all the details, Lexi? That was a terrible night . . ."

I glance toward the thicket at where I just chased a shadow. I need to know what's real and what was a product of my childish rationalization of the tragedy. Were my memories some kind of respun version of a truth I hadn't wanted to accept? "Yes," I say.

He shifts his weight. "Give me a few days to pull everything together. What exactly are you looking for?"

"Everything."

CHAPTER EIGHT

My hands are raw from scrubbing.

I lean back on my heels, surveying my handiwork so far. The spray-painted letters on the barn are definitely beginning to fade. The combination of the unsettling prank call and Janna's enthusiasm for getting this place sold gave me a burst of renewed energy to clean this place and get the hell out of here. Larson can email me the answers I'm looking for.

Before dawn, I drove to the Ringer Bros. store and bought the biggest bottle of isopropyl alcohol I could find in the first aid section along with two rolls of paper towels and sponges.

Hours later, I'm finally starting to see some progress. I've been so focused, almost in a trance from the rhythm of spray, wipe, wipe, that I haven't noticed the sound of songbirds until now.

I hoist myself up, balancing against the door as a wave of dizziness washes over me. The heat of the sun sends a new bead of sweat down my forehead.

Part of the reason I had come so early was so I could avoid the first look at the entire farm in daylight. But now I can't put it off any longer. My eyes drift over to the giant oak tree where the ancient, sun-bleached tire swing still dangles. The rope that Dad had replaced at Amy's insistence is wrapped so tightly around the branch, like it's holding on for dear life.

I walk past what's left of the house, eyeing the discolored tin of the barn against the blue sky and distant hills. I grab the key to the padlock that the law office gave me and pop it open, the tin door screeching as I slide it. It's so dark inside, the only light coming in through gaps in the roof. As my eyes adjust, they land on the old, leaning workbench in the corner. Once Grandpa's table for repairing odds and ends, it became Dad's desk when we moved in. When he wasn't toiling out on the farm, he would come in here and stay for hours. All the times I'd wander in to check on him, he'd be hunched over and scribbling into a notebook or reading the *San Francisco Chronicle* he drove over an hour each way to get on Sunday mornings.

I run my hand over the top before I can think better of it, my fingers gritty from the dust and grime that's gathered. I wipe my hand across my jeans, turning around to survey the other side. The loft is completely empty, not even a stray piece or two of hay left at the bottom. The men Beth hired to cut and bale the hay must not have used this barn for storage. I wonder if that's due to convenience or superstition.

Other items I'm sure were still here the last time I saw the barn are gone. Only a few of the rusted antique farm implements that used to hang by the entrance are still up. And all our bikes are missing. Those were perhaps the only things of value ever housed here and probably stolen within weeks after my family's demise. I could even guess which family across the railroad from us had done it. They stole from the living easily enough.

The corroded barrels used to house grain, dog kibble, and deer feed are on the dirt floor. I half expect something to scurry out like the raccoon used to occasionally, but these, too, have been empty for a while.

As my eyes adjust, I walk deeper through the swinging door to the milking parlor. Even though a cow hasn't been in here for a long time, the whole place reeks of cattle.

I don't have the first clue what to do with any of this stuff. Part of me feels like I should keep the remaining antique farming implements, but I can't imagine waking up every day to see those in the house.

I stand up and walk deeper into the barn, gazing up at the rafters. At least the structure is intact. It's just a matter of decluttering. I kick one of the old feed barrels toward the door. It barely moves, and a sharp pain shoots through my toe. I bend over, placing both hands on the barrel, and shove it. It still doesn't budge. It must be lodged on something. I push once more, harder. The barrel rolls this time, and so do I, slipping and falling onto the dirt.

I lay there for a moment as the dust settles, something dull digging into my stomach. I sit up and feel in the dirt, my fingers closing around plastic. I lift the object closer to my eyes. It's a cassette tape, covered in layers of grime, some of the reel slack and protruding from the bottom.

I haven't seen a cassette in . . . well, a very long time. Whose tape is it? Is it an artifact from my family?

How can I play the tape? Will it even work if the reel is a mess like this? I vaguely recall fixing tangled film on an old videotape forever ago when the VHS tore it up. I think the video played well enough after that.

I get to my feet and dust off my jeans before stepping out of the barn. In the stronger lighting, the tape looks a little worse than I originally thought. What are the chances Kael still has a cassette player?

I hold it between both hands as if it's going to fly away. I walk past my car and down the road toward Kael's place. I pause as I turn onto his driveway. His truck isn't parked in front of the small house. Still, it's worth a try.

I continue up to the door and knock. I wait for a rustle of movement, but nothing comes. I hear a horse nicker in the barn, but other than that, quiet. I knock again.

"Kael's not in right now."

I jump and spin around to see Mrs. McPheron standing behind the porch steps. Her arms are crossed over her chest, in contrast with that open, sweet smile she's wearing. "Oh, okay. Sorry, I was working on the property and I had a question, so I figured—"

"He ran into town for the day. He should be back this afternoon." She's wearing a pale-yellow shirt without a single wrinkle, but her jeans have small spots of dirt. She must've been out in the pasture and saw me approaching. "Is it something *I* can help you with?"

I smile and shake my head. "No, but I appreciate it. I'll just give Kael a call later." I walk down from the porch.

"How's it going over there?" She nods down the road toward the farm. "Kael told me you're trying to sell it."

"It's slow going. Do you know of anyone looking to buy?"

She dusts her hands on the sides of her jeans. "No, but I'll keep an ear out. I'm sure you already know this, but just holler if you need any help over there. Kael and I are always more than happy to help a neighbor out." She turns toward the house. "I'll tell him you stopped by," she calls over her shoulder. I glance down at the cassette in my hand as I walk back to the farm.

I can't explain why the possible contents of the tape weigh so heavily on my mind. Maybe it's the same reason I can't quite let go of Mr. Vargas's mention of their fire. Maybe it's because repressed curiosity can't stay buried forever, and maybe only now I'm ready to ask questions again, even if they lead nowhere.

The hair on the back of my neck rises as I notice the large pickup truck in the farm driveway. Whoever it is must've arrived while I was speaking with Mrs. McPheron.

As I approach the truck, it becomes apparent no one is inside the cab. I gather the unspooled tape and tuck it carefully into my jeans pocket. "Hello?" I call toward the ruins of the house. Hopefully it's a potential buyer, although I feel like an idiot for even thinking it's possible.

"Hi there!" The voice doesn't come from where I expect, and I jump. A man emerges from the dark barn. He clearly must've attended church this morning and is still decked out in his Dockers and loafers. "Oh, I hope I didn't give you a scare." As he comes closer, I realize just how tall he is.

I dig my keys out and hold them tight. It's a habit I've developed after taking three different self-defense classes over the years. Officer McCraw always endorsed eye gouging when necessary. "I wasn't expecting anyone."

"Yeah, sorry," he says, casting a glance over his shoulder toward the barn. "I heard this place was open again." He turns back to me. "You should really keep the barn locked when you're out."

My muscles tense as I realize just how many steps it would take me to run past this guy to my car.

He smiles as he looks closer at me. "You're the Blake girl, aren't you? Alexis, right?"

"That's right. But I go by Lex."

He nods. "Wow, you've grown up so much. You definitely favor your mother."

Chills break out along my arms. "You knew her?" It shouldn't surprise me so much. Judging by his face and worn hands, he's around the age she'd be if she were still alive.

"Oh yeah. Emma and I were in school together." His lips twitch. "She was an amazing woman. I know this is over a decade too late, but I was so sorry to hear what happened to her—to your family."

I loosen my grip on my keys. I believe he really means it. "Thank you."

"I hope this doesn't sound weird, but the least I could do is buy you a meal or a drink sometime. You don't even necessarily have to eat it with me," he adds. "I just always felt terrible that I couldn't do anything more for you. Your mom really meant a lot to me."

This last part makes my stomach sink. What's that supposed to mean?

"Not right now, of course." He lets out a nervous laugh. "I'm sure you have your hands full at the moment."

"Yeah, okay. Sure, why not?"

He pulls out an old Android phone from his jeans pocket. "What's your cell phone number?"

Shit. Given the creepy phone call the other night, I don't love the idea of giving out my cell phone number. But what can I do? "Uh, 415-678-6554."

He beams at me. "Okay. I'll give you a call." He turns and walks toward his truck.

I hesitate, thumbing the keys in my hand. "Wait. I'm sorry, what was your name?"

He looks over his shoulder at me, one hand on his open door. "Tom Miller."

CHAPTER NINE

When I arrive at the motel, my search for cassette repair takes a back seat to googling Tom Miller. Other than the property listed in his last name with the tax appraisal district and a private Facebook page, I don't find much. His address doesn't seem familiar to me. It's a two-acre lot with a simple house closer to Beth's old house than the farm.

I click back to the Facebook tab. I don't like the idea of adding him as a friend, but how else can I skulk through his photos? What if there are some throwback pictures with Mom?

The sudden knock on my room door makes me freeze.

"It's me, Lex! Open up!" Evan's voice shouts from the other side.

Realizing it's only Evan and not the mysterious caller from last night doesn't provide nearly as much relief as it should. I lower my feet over the side of the bed and walk to the door. It bursts open the second I unlock it.

Evan's eyes immediately dart around the room as if he's expecting a man to walk out from the bathroom wearing only a towel. "So, this is where you're staying?"

I close the door behind him. "What are you doing here?" Sanders. He was the only person I told where I was staying in case of an emergency. And I highly doubt this is an emergency.

"You really thought you could just sneak off and I wouldn't know?"

"I didn't 'sneak off.' I told Sanders that I had to take some time off to deal with a personal matter."

He narrows his eyes. "Well, I wish you would have talked to *me* about it. I am your direct supervisor, after all."

I sigh. Of course Evan would barge in here and make everything about him when he wasn't even an afterthought to me. "I didn't want to talk with you because I knew you would make it weird. And that's exactly what you're doing right now—you're making this weird, Evan. Besides, I told the only person who actually matters where I was going. If you had questions as my *supervisor*, this could've been an email."

He puts his hands on his hips. "I didn't know what else to do."

Tell him what he wants to hear so he'll get the hell out of here. It's the logical choice, but I can't. "You're not my problem anymore. It's entirely inappropriate that you're here right now."

"You can't ignore me, Lex. We work together." He steps toward me, trying to look intimidating, I guess. But I'm close enough to his height that he'll need to try harder.

"I know. So leave me alone and go do your job."

"You can't talk to me like that," he spits. "If you want to make things difficult, I can make them difficult."

Wow. He really is unhinged more than I realized if he thinks he can talk to me like this. "What exactly is your plan? You want to *bully* me into getting back together? Or do you just want to put me into my place as your underling? How do you see that working out?"

He takes a step back. "I'm not trying to push you . . . but things can't go back the way they were."

Yeah, of course. When we got together, he and I were at the same level. "None of this matters because after I'm done here, I'm out of the *Weekly*."

His eyes narrow. "What?"

I'm probably more surprised by this pronouncement than he is. After paying off debts and our house in the city, there won't be much left, but it'll be enough to buy me time to figure out what's next. In this moment it's become clear that going back to the *Weekly* isn't an option. Not while Evan is there. "From this conversation, it seems like you're planning to make my life miserable at the office. And since I have a lawyer now, I don't see why I need to put up with that."

The stubborn line of his lips falters for a moment. "What lawyer?"

"The one who's been managing my trust all these years." God, could I sound any more like a trust-baby asshole? But it's worth the expression on Evan's face. "I think he'd be very interested to hear about this whole situation." Obviously, Jim Ridley isn't that kind of lawyer, but I just want to scare him. A modicum of fear and shame is the least of what he owes me for this little outburst.

Evan lunges for the bed, slamming my laptop shut and scooping it into his arms.

"What are you doing?" I can't help the hint of panic that rises in my voice.

"Finally some kind of reaction." He steps toward the door, clutching the laptop tighter. "Clearly if you're not going to be with the *Weekly* anymore, I have to confiscate your work laptop."

"I don't have a work laptop, you idiot. None of us do." I'm reminded annually that the budget doesn't allow for one.

He opens the door. "Regardless, you have the company's intellectual property on here. We'll need to scrub it first if you're no longer an employee."

I can't recall the last time I had the urge to hit someone, but the desire is strong at the moment. "How old are you? You're really going to steal my laptop?" I follow him out onto the landing.

"I'm not stealing it. This is protocol!" He retreats down the stairs toward his car parked in the front.

I grab his arm before he can open the car. "Evan, give me the laptop. You're not leaving with it."

He violently jerks his arm back, breaking my grasp. "You can have it back in San Francisco."

I wrap my hand around his wrist, his metal watch pinching my skin. "Evan—"

"Let go." He cradles the laptop in one arm and raises his other hand, using it to grip my forearm. The pressure of his fingers increases as he digs his nails into my flesh.

A car door slams nearby, and he releases me.

Kael appears, walking around his truck. "Do we have a problem here?" He stands beside me, surveying Evan.

"Who are you?"

"I'm Kael. Who are you?"

Evan wrinkles his nose. "Kale? Like the leafy green?"

Kael's expression remains neutral. "I wouldn't know. We mostly grow up on raw beef out here."

I would laugh at this encounter if my entire body didn't feel like it's on fire right now. I'd assumed I knew the real Evan after working beside him and dating him, but I guess the incident with the intern should've tipped me off that he wasn't the man I thought he was. More than that, though, I don't relish the idea of explaining to Kael that I'd ever been romantically linked to Evan.

Kael eyes the laptop and looks back at me. "Is that yours?"

Evan frowns, extending it toward me before I can respond. "I guess we can scrub it for data when you get back."

I take it from his hands, fighting the urge to shove him. "Don't come back here, Evan."

He looks between Kael and me one more time, fumbling for his keys before unlocking his Prius and jumping in.

I stand beside Kael and glare at Evan until he disappears down the road. "Raw beef?"

Kael looks down at me. "Yep. Why do you think our football team is the best around here?"

My muscles relax. "Well, thanks for your help."

"No problem. I was just trying to minimize the damage. You looked like you were winding up to hit him, and with a personality like that, he can't afford to take a face shot."

The laugh I've been holding back finally surfaces. "Then, *he* should be thanking you, I guess."

"All jokes aside, what did I walk in on?"

I scan the parking lot, noticing that the blinds in the front office are raised. I bet that creeper probably watched this whole thing go down. Hell, he might be on the phone right now, recounting a play-by-play to Butcher or Mr. Handley or something. "Let's talk in my room." I lead him up the rusty staircase and hurriedly close the door behind us. "Already put up enough of a show for everyone."

Kael looks around the dark room, illuminated only by the small lamp on the nightstand. To be honest, I'm scared of turning on the ceiling fan light. It appears cleaner this way. "Seems like things didn't get too out of hand in here with that guy."

"That was Evan. My editor . . . and more recently, my ex-boyfriend." I gently toss my laptop to the bed. "He's harmless."

His eyes widen. "He didn't seem harmless when I pulled up. He looked like he was getting ready to hurt you."

I shake my head. "He would never." I glance down at the red skin on my arm where he gripped me. "I told him I'm planning to quit when I get back to the city, but to be honest, I think he's having a hard time with our breakup." Maybe part of the reason is that he actually wanted to hurt me or at least a bigger reaction out of me after his betrayal. Maybe he can't stand how easy it was for me to separate myself from him.

"You're not quitting because of him, are you?"

"It doesn't matter." I sink onto the bed. "I've been in that same job for too long anyway. It's time to move on." Although I don't really relish the idea of starting from scratch somewhere else.

"But—"

"Drop it, Kael. Please."

He sighs. "Okay."

"So, what are you doing here anyway? I thought you went to town today."

He shrugs, leaning against the wall. "Yeah, I had a farrier job over there this morning. Mom told me you stopped by."

"Oh." Right. The cassette. I open the nightstand drawer and pull out the tape. "I found this in the barn this morning. I was going to see if you still had a player."

He takes the tape into his hands. "I think I do, but I obviously can't run it through like this. It'll shred to pieces." He sits on the bed next to me. "What's on it?" He gingerly inspects the tangled reel.

"I don't know. Probably nothing, but I need to know. It's so weird that it would still be in the barn, right?" My detour after the encounter with the stranger had slightly derailed me. "Hey, do you know a Tom Miller?"

Kael nods, still staring down at the tape. "Yeah, he's one of the deacons, and he volunteers at the fire department."

Of course.

"He still works at the bank too. He's been a teller there forever. I mean, at least as long as I can remember."

That's right, there is a bank in town, around the corner from Main Street. I'd only been in there a handful of times, once with Dad when we first moved here and once with Beth right before we moved. I try to think if I recognized Tom as one of those tellers who gave me a free lollipop when I waited for Dad to open an account. "He came up to me today outside the barn. He kind of gave me an odd vibe."

Kael meets my gaze. "Hmm. He's a nice guy. What did he say?"

"I guess he knew my mom. He kept talking about how he didn't get to do enough for me in the past. He wants to buy me a drink."

His eyebrows furrow. "What's weird about that?"

"I don't know. Sometimes it throws me off how people here seem to know about me, but I know nothing about them." I shrug. "Speaking of that . . . something kind of weird happened the other day."

"Okay, like what?"

I lean back on the bed, my hands behind me. "I actually don't know how to even explain it without you thinking I'm losing it."

He laughs. "That's promising."

"The other day, I got some kind of prank call in the middle of the night on the room phone."

His smile fades. "What kind of prank call?"

"I don't even . . . well, it was, like, a woman screaming?" It sounds even crazier out loud. "And then some guy came on the line and started breathing."

Kael makes a face.

"I asked who it was a few times, and when he didn't answer, I said I was going to call the police."

"And?"

The memory of the strange, breathy response over the motel phone makes me shudder. "He said 'Oh, is that so?' And before the call, someone started banging on my room door. I went out and no one was there. No car or anything."

Kael frowns. "What? Why would you go out if someone was banging on your door? That wasn't safe."

I run a hand through my hair. "Yeah, it was just an automatic reaction. I was really freaked out."

"Where was Evan that night?"

I look at him. "Evan? You think he did that?"

He shrugs. "It crossed my mind. He obviously has it out for you. And he knows where you're staying."

"No. He probably just drove out today. I didn't see his car or anything when it happened."

"Maybe he parked around the corner."

I shake my head. "No. I really don't think he would do that."

He furrows his brow and looks down at the tape. "So, about this tape . . . do you want me to bring it back with me and try to respool it?"

I stare at it. "If you're free, why don't I bring it by tomorrow? I'll hold on to it."

"Yeah, sure." He sets it by the bed. "By the way, I saw your little project when I was driving home. The barn is already looking a lot better."

"Oh. The graffiti?" This day feels so long that I almost forgot how I spent the entire morning.

He glances toward the window. "Are you really okay staying here?"

I stand up from the mattress. "I'm fine. Really. And if I'm not, you're just a phone call away, right?"

He meets my eyes. "Always."

CHAPTER TEN

I hadn't really been prepared for the weight of returning to Sola. But in just a couple of days, it's become clear to me how badly I need to leave this place.

Despite a restless night of eyeing the motel phone in the dark, waiting for a ring that never came, I returned to the farm at first light.

"You really don't have to do this," I say as I hand Kael a bottle of frozen water.

He grins at me and bends down from the seat to take it. "Thanks. I can't picture you mowing."

He's right. And I'd been banking on that reaction when I started the next morning by asking to borrow his large tractor. He nearly laughed me out of the driveway. I had ridden on one with Dad before, but I had no clue how to even start one, especially not the fancy one in Kael's barn. "I could have figured it out."

He shakes his head and tucks the bottle in the seat beside him. "A simple 'thank you' wouldn't hurt."

"Thank you. Really, I mean it. I don't want this place to look like a total disaster when Janna comes out here to assess the situation."

He stares down at me. "Janna?" His smile fades.

"Yes. She's a Realtor now."

He blinks. "Well, that's news to me. I think the last time I saw her was when I had to stop by the store on the way to the auction last month. She was creeping around the back holding a bunch of crystals."

Janna wasn't above fibbing, so I'd even checked for her license registration with the state. "Yeah, well she's doing that too. Reverend Butcher bought out the shop and gave it to her, so now she's hawking séance candles to kids in town." I can't help the bitterness in my tone.

Kael notices. "They're just dumb kids, Lex. There's nothing else to do around here. Try not to take it personally."

I turn to him. "How many times have you come across people loitering on our land?"

He looks away. "Just a couple." He doesn't want to upset me. "Do you want me to bale any of this? I can help you sell it."

"Keep some for the horses and sell the rest. The money's all yours." I could really use some cash, but it's the least I can do since he refused to let me pay him for mowing.

He pulls on his baseball cap. "We'll argue about that later. I'll go ahead and get started." With the buzz of the tractor in the background, I return to my work in the barn. I thought cleaning the graffiti from the outside would be the most difficult, but it's clear now that the inside is in just as much need of TLC. The most daunting part of the work is going to be cleaning off all this dairy shit before Janna comes over.

I slip my wireless headphones over my ears and hit play on my phone before tucking it into the pocket of my jeans. I stare down from the platform at the empty milking stalls. Even above the music, I can almost hear the sounds of the cows rustling and mooing and almost see Dad walking around the now-rusted machines, checking everything as Donnie scurries after him, asking questions. Dad had picked up everything so quickly. I think on some level, no matter how he felt about the people in town, he was proud to be working on the farm. He and Mom had truly begun rebuilding what was rapidly falling into disrepair after Grandpa's decline.

I hate that I'm filled with this drive to prove to Janna that this farm is worth her time. Why do I care what she thinks anyway? She's just a hobbyist Realtor. It's not like her word is gospel.

I shake the thought from my head and grab the hose from the ground. I turn the spigot and step down to the first stall, flicking on the nozzle. It gives me a strange satisfaction, watching the cobwebs and caked-on dirt dissolve under the stream and flow toward the drain by my feet.

I reach the last stall on the east side of the barn when something just beyond the metal divider catches my eye. I shut off the water and walk around to the other side of the stall. A small bundle lies curled up against the back wall. The light from the open door doesn't quite reach this long space. I duck under the rafter that tapers beyond the stalls and get on my knees.

I pull out my phone and shine the flashlight over to the corner as I crawl toward it. It looks like fabric. All the other stalls had been covered in dirt, but this section of the concrete floor is relatively clean. I grab the bundle, and it unfolds to be a jacket, several crushed beer cans underneath it along with a single AA battery. The navy jacket is certainly worn, but doesn't appear to have been in this one place very long. As if the owner might be back any moment.

I sit back on my heels. This space between the stalls and the outer wall is certainly big and long enough for someone to sleep. Maybe there was a squatter not long ago. Whoever it was didn't leave anything valuable behind, so they probably cleared out when they realized I'd be coming back here on a daily basis. I try not to think about the idea of someone watching me without me knowing. Something about being in the middle of nowhere has always made me fearful of an unknown pair of eyes observing my every move.

I turn around to crawl out, and my heart skips when I see a man standing a few feet away. When I see him, he smiles and gestures to his ears. Damn it! What was I thinking wearing headphones? I pull them off and grip my phone.

"So sorry!" the man says, taking a few steps back. "I hope I didn't scare you."

My heart racing, I make my way out of the crawl space. There are two other young men standing nearby. "What do you want?" I snap. God, I hope Kael's not too far away.

The first man extends his hand to me, but I don't shake it. "I'm Gavin. Are you Alexis Blake?"

I look between the guys. Judging by their all-black wardrobes alone, I'm willing to bet they're not locals. "Who wants to know?"

Gavin laughs. "Us. We have a business offer. It's about the property."

Business offer? To take this entire place off my hands? Out of the blue? This has to be some type of scam. But my brain can't wrap around what benefit there would be for them. "Okay. What is it?"

The two men behind him break off suddenly, wandering closer to the remnants of the house. "We run a small business, and we're interested in renting the farm for a day," Gavin says.

Damn. I knew it was too good to be true. "What kind of small business?"

His face turns red. "We wanted to explore the property a little."

"Uh-huh." I eye his friends as they walk out of the barn and toward the house. I notice one of the guys brings his phone out and starts recording as he sweeps it around the ruins. I catch a glimpse of what looks like a dried gray bouquet of twigs in the other one's hands. Good God, is that sage? I remember the one time I let Janna burn that shit in my room at Beth's house, and I never heard the end of it about the smell. "This wouldn't happen to be a ghost-hunting thing, would it?" I wonder if I can burn a hole into him with just my glare.

"We do everything respectfully." His head shakes as if his body's betraying him. "Our mission is to investigate the locations where horrible tragedies have occurred and to—"

"Get off my property." I push past him.

"We're willing to pay!"

I slightly slow my pace. "The entire $500,000 I'm selling it for?"

"Um, well, no. We don't have enough money to *buy* it, but—"

"Then the answer is no." The one with the phone flinches as I approach. "Get out!"

They look at me and exchange a glance but continue filming.

I grab my phone from my pocket. "I'm calling the sheriff if all of you don't leave right now."

Gavin runs up beside me, waving his hands. "Please, we only want to do right by your family. It's horrible what happened to them." He's standing too close.

"You know people normally have guns on them at all times out here, right?"

His eyes dart to my waist as if I'm pointing one at him right now. "I know you think all of this stuff is kind of woo-woo, but—"

"How do *you* know I think that?"

He squirmed. "Um, well—"

"Did someone tell you to come here?"

Footfalls sound behind me in the grass. "Lex? Everything all right?" Kael walks up from behind me, his hat in his hand. He and Gavin stand at the same height.

Gavin takes a step back. "Yes, we were just talking business."

"I asked her, not you." Kael looks at me.

"They're ghost hunters." I cross my arms over my chest. "And we're done talking. Thank you for your interest. Please leave and go fuck yourselves."

"Okay, okay," Gavin stammers as Kael takes a step toward him. "Can I at least give you my number in case you change your mind?"

"No. Leave."

The men in the house head toward the old van at the end of the driveway. Gavin turns and joins them. Kael follows them to the edge of the property and watches as they drive away. Once the dust on the road begins to settle, he turns back.

"People are vultures," I say once Kael reaches me. "They wouldn't take no for an answer."

He shakes his head. "This is why I said you shouldn't be out here alone. They snuck up on you, didn't they?"

I shrug. "Those idiots . . . the weird thing is, that guy Gavin said he knows I don't like this kind of bullshit. How could he know that?"

Kael looks away from me.

"What?"

He sighs. "I wasn't going to say anything, but I've seen them before."

"How? Where?"

"At Ringer Bros. They run around with Janna sometimes."

Anger takes the place of confusion. "Of course."

"I'm sure she didn't tell them to come by or anything. She probably just mentioned it and—"

"That little rat," I say. "I can't believe she would do that to me. Although, I should have figured."

Kael watches me.

"Sorry. I'm just sick of this stuff. I'm sick of the worst day of my life being reduced to a curse or ghost story." I massage my temple. "My family deserves better than that."

"I know." He shifts weight onto the other leg.

"What? You think I'm overreacting?"

He shakes his head. "No, definitely not. But . . . never mind."

"What, Kael?" I try to even out my voice again.

"I just . . . those guys are creeps, but I wouldn't completely write off all that stuff as BS." He glances down at his feet. "You're going to think less of me, but after my dad died, I kind of started believing there might be something after all this."

"Yeah, I get that," I say. "There's nothing wrong with that. Of course, I don't think less of you for that. I really wish I could believe it too."

He looks up at me and forces a slight grin. "Anyway, I'll get back to mowing. Are you going to be okay alone in the barn?"

I nod. "Yes. Thanks for checking on me, but I think I've had enough rescuing for the time being. I'll take on the next guy that harasses me."

He grins and gestures to the headphones around my neck. "Maybe play the music on your phone's speaker instead, okay?"

I slide them off and watch as he walks back to the tractor.

By the time Kael finishes the mowing, his skin has browned a little more than before. And I can feel how tender my own skin has become from the sun as I ride in the seat beside him.

The sun is beginning to set as he pulls into the driveway. "I'm starving," I shout over the rumble of the engine.

He smirks. "I told you not to get a salad."

When I ordered our lunch from the café, I couldn't remember the last time I ate a fresh vegetable since coming to Sola, and so I opted for the "deluxe" salad. In reality, it was one sliced cherry tomato over a bed of iceberg lettuce doused in ranch dressing.

He parks between the main house and the barn and shuts off the engine. "Don't worry. I'll make you something." He extends his hand up to me after he jumps to the ground.

I take it, savoring the heat of his skin. "You can't cook," I say, hopefully disguising my disappointment when he releases my hand once I'm beside him.

He walks ahead onto the porch of the small house and opens the front door for me. I haven't been inside since his grandfather lived here. "You've been gone for a while, Lex. There's a lot I can do that might surprise you."

It sounds like a promise.

"And speaking of surprising skills, before we eat, I'm going to fix that tape of yours. Did you bring it?"

"Oh. Yeah." My hand flies to my bag. I adjust the strap on my shoulder to dig in for the tape. I had folded it into a piece of copy paper to keep the reel from getting torn. "Wait, you really know how to fix it?" I had resolved myself to trying to track down a back-alley cassette dealer in Tenderloin when I got back to the city.

"I actually spent last night watching tutorials on YouTube," Kael says as I set the tape in the palm of his hand. "It's pretty straightforward. It looked like the tape popped off the hub and then got tangled, and that's an easy fix."

"I have no idea what any of that means, but sounds great."

He smiles. "It'll probably take a little while, though. Let me go grab my tools." He walks down the hall. I hear a bit of rummaging, and then he returns with a plastic bag and a small box. He lays out the contents of the bag on the kitchen table, including a roll of really thin transparent tape and a new shell shrink-wrapped in plastic. "I grabbed a couple of things just for this."

"Kael." It's nice. Too nice. "Why would you do that? I could've taken it into town and found a knockoff RadioShack or something."

He laughs. "It's really no big deal. It looks fun, actually." He sits in one of the wooden chairs. "Give me twenty minutes . . . uh, or closer to thirty maybe."

I glance out the kitchen window at the barn. "Why don't I feed the horses, then? It's around time, isn't it?" The horses have all moved to the front pastures, their tails thrashing impatiently.

"Really? Do you remember how to?"

I shrug. "Yeah. One can of pellets per horse and then a fourth can of the alfalfa pellets, right?"

"Yep, that's about it," he says. "You'll probably have to lead Whisper to the corral. He eats alone there."

I nod and walk outside. I guess Whisper's still starting fights over food. He's waiting for me at the fence near the barn. I enter the corral and open the gate for him to join me. He immediately trots to me and whinnies. I latch the gate behind him and leave him by the trough.

The old Folgers coffee can we used to measure food is still in the feed barrels by the old radio and peppermint bowl. I divvy out Whisper's food and then load two open feed bags into a wheelbarrow and cart it to the front pasture, where over a dozen horses have gathered. They all begin whinnying when they see me. They all huddle and start devouring the food as soon as I pour it into the bowls at the fence line. I make sure the two fillies get enough in their smaller corner of the pasture before I stalk back to the barn.

Whisper watches me, gnawing on some leftover hay in the trough from this morning as I crumple up the empty feed bags and toss them by the door. I approach him and lay a hand on his snout. "You like it here, right?" In the years since leaving, I often daydreamed about what it would be like if I had the money to stable Whisper in the city. Instead of going home after school (and later, work), I would picture taking Beth's old car out to the stables and riding him around by the ocean. The stable would need to be by the coast. Whisper would love to listen to the waves breaking.

Whisper nods his head at me.

"Soon I'll take you out for a ride. How about that?"

"Hey." Kael appears at the entrance. For a second I expect him to tease me about talking to a horse, but his face is pale. "I fixed it. I think you need to hear this."

My heart sinks. "Okay." I walk to him, and he leads the way to the house.

"Sorry," he says, opening the door for me. "I started playing it because I wanted to make sure it actually still worked. I didn't want to get your hopes up."

"It's fine." The recorder is on the kitchen table. I sink into the seat beside it.

"I'm a little scared it won't survive a rewind, but here we go." Kael sits across from me and hits the rewind button.

I tap my fingers against the table as the recorder clicks at the beginning of the tape.

Kael looks up at me and presses play.

A faint buzzing sound emits before a familiar voice.

"What do you think, Lexi? What should we name her?"

The shock sends chills along my skin. Dad? The audio is crackly and distant, but there is no doubt.

A young, chirpy Lex answers, *"Peaches!"*

Peaches was one of the puppies I raised. Her fur had these little light-tan patches that reminded me of a peach. I look up at Kael as the audio continues.

"You got it!" my dad says. *"Peaches it is. What about this little guy? Oreo?"*

A pressure begins to build in my chest.

"No, what about Rocky?" my child voice counters.

Dad laughs. He had such a great laugh. The distorted audio doesn't do it justice.

I stop the tape. "What is this?"

Kael seems wary, his eyes studying me for a read of my reaction.

"Who recorded this?"

He raises his eyebrows. "I just assumed it was your dad."

I lean back in my seat. "Why would he do that?" I try to imagine my dad toting around a tape recorder. I'm not sure I ever even saw him with a cassette before. He had plenty of CDs in his car, but never a cassette. Not that I can remember. I shake my head. "I just . . . I wasn't expecting that." Although I'm not sure what I *did* expect. The tape was on our property. It made perfect sense that it would've belonged to one of us.

"How are you doing?" Kael asks after a moment.

I shrug. "Yeah. I'm a little creeped out, but it's fine, I guess."

"Do you want to keep playing it?"

"No." I feel like if I hear more, I might throw up. I'm not sure why, but a wave of nausea begins to form in my stomach. "I just need to . . . wrap my head around this. I wasn't expecting to hear him."

"I get it." He stares at me. "Lex . . . no, never mind."

"What?"

He shakes his head. "Forget it. It's definitely not what you want to hear right now."

I'd like to hear anything to get my mind off this weird tape. "Let me be the judge of that."

He sighs. "Earlier, I mentioned how things changed a little for me when Dad died. But I didn't explain why."

I lean forward in my seat. "Oh, okay."

"He died in the barn." He looks away from me, rubbing the back of his neck. "He had a heart attack and fell from the loft while trying to get help. His ankle snapped and . . . he couldn't . . . well, anyway. It took him a long time to die. And it was probably really painful."

My stomach sinks. "Kael, I'm—"

He waves his hand. "It's fine. There's a point to this, I promise." He stares straight down at the table. "After that, I dropped out of school and moved back here to take care of things and help Mom. And, I'm not really sure how to explain it, but as soon as I stepped into the barn, I just had this *feeling*." He glances at me. "Like someone was standing behind me. All the time. Like, if you were to go into the other room and I was following right behind you and watching you."

I'm not sure what to say. I've felt that before too. But the brain is powerful and weak at the same time. As my undergrad psychology classes taught me, our minds can conjure sensations without the ability to filter them as false.

"It was weird. I would turn around sometimes in the barn, expecting to see Mom standing behind me, but no one was there. I tried not to think about it too much. I figured I was just being jumpy since I'd been away from home for a while. But then . . ." He shakes his head. "Something really strange happened."

It's hard to imagine something bad enough to shake Kael.

"I couldn't sleep one night," he continues. "I thought I heard Whisper rustling around in the barn, so I decided to go check on him. When I got out there, he was frozen and snorting. I could see the whites of his eyes. He was spooked. I tried to calm him down, and then, all of a sudden, something moved out of the corner of my eye. I turned to look, and I got pushed over. My head hit the edge of the stall. I didn't black out right away, but as I started to pass out, this shadow appeared—standing over me."

My heart begins to pound. I imagine the shadow. The night I saw the ghost in Grandpa's room, standing over his body, before I blacked out. The solid black mass illuminated only slightly by the moonlight creeping in through the window. It was only a shape, a shadow, but I could *feel* it watching me. It was some kind of deep, animal instinct. Like a rabbit sensing a nearby coyote.

I feel that same sensation in my throat when I saw the figure as a child—like a ball of cotton is wedged there and I can't swallow it down.

A layer of goose bumps spreads along my skin. For a moment I feel as though I might see the shadow in the corner of my eye, and that knot settles into my stomach. Maybe that knot never entirely disappeared.

I recall the figure at the cemetery.

"It was this dark mass. I couldn't really make out any features before everything went dark," Kael says. "While I was unconscious, I started to hear a voice." He pauses.

"What was it?" I ask after a moment.

"I don't know. It was this deep, low whisper—a man's voice. It was saying 'Get up' over and over again. When I finally woke up, I'd been dragged out of the barn and my mom was standing above me. She said a voice had called out to her for help. She thought it was me and came running out, and there I was, my head bleeding out onto the ground. I had a concussion." He shifts in his seat. "I know this sounds silly, but I really feel like that shadow—the voice—it was my dad. It doesn't make a lot of sense, but I think he's the one who dragged me out of the barn."

I bite my tongue.

He looks up at me sheepishly. "Come on, let's hear it. You think I'm crazy."

"No. Not at all." I meet his eyes. "I guess I'm a little jealous that you've experienced something like that." I have long discounted any instances of perceived spirits from childhood. Or so I thought. Children's brains are steeped in a kind of surrealism. They don't see the big picture of how the natural world works. As we grow, the less mysterious the world becomes.

He raises his eyebrows.

"I mean, not that I'm sure it wasn't terrifying. I just . . . you seem so sure it was him. I wish I had that."

"I'm *not* sure. But it was enough to make me question things."

I tap the recorder with my finger. "This isn't paranormal."

"I know." He rests against the back of his chair.

"You think I should let Janna's friends conduct their little ghost hunt?"

He furrows his brow. "God, no. But you're back here, and it seems to me like you're looking for answers. Maybe just keep an open mind about what the past might be trying to tell you."

2003

My eyes opened in the dark before I realized what disturbed my sleep.

A low, deep mumble carried across the room. I froze in bed, winding my fists around my blanket.

Maybe it was a dream.

The sound persisted as I strained my ears. Was it coming from outside? It could've been a coyote maybe.

It suddenly stopped. I peered around my room, focusing my eyes on the closet doors, barely ajar. My heart began to race. Did I close them completely? The cat might've opened them again on his own.

"Get out!" The roar sent me to my feet.

I opened the door to the hallway and ran to Natalie's room, then dove into her covers.

"What? Oh my gosh!" She sat up and glared at me, tugging the blankets away.

"There's someone in my room!" I whispered. I glanced toward the door and edged closer to Nat.

She stared out into the hallway. "What? No there isn't."

"I swear!" My voice trembled. "He just yelled at me." My body shook as she touched my shoulder.

"It was probably just a dream. Let's go check it out."

"No!"

She sighed. "Okay, then let's go get Dad. Is that better?"

I remembered how he snapped at me earlier at dinner. His flashlight had gone missing from the barn, and he was convinced I'd moved it. "Please! Can I just sleep with you tonight?"

She shimmied under the covers. "Whatever. But you're out if you start kicking me in your sleep again."

I pulled the blankets over my head, listening to the sound of my breathing fill the space. The voice I'd heard was familiar.

Maybe Nat was right. Maybe it was from a dream.

CHAPTER ELEVEN

The second I enter my motel room, I toss Kael's borrowed recorder onto the bed and sink into the rumpled duvet. I stare down at the recorder. Part of me couldn't wait to leave Kael's house to listen to the rest of the tape. But now that I'm alone, I want to toss it against the wall. Curiosity wins out, and I press play.

Several minutes of the tape run in silence, my heart racing in anticipation. Finally a voice breaks through.

"Why did you bring them to church?" My father's voice is cold.

There's a long pause before my mom answers. *"I thought it'd be good for us to get back into the community here."*

"It's just . . . you've never shown an interest in religion before, but our first week in town and you suddenly need to go to church?"

Mom sighs. *"I really just wanted the kids to meet everyone before the school year starts."*

"Okay. Well, next time, take the girls and Donnie if he wants to go, but leave Lexi here with me," Dad says.

"Fine. If that makes you feel better."

"Feel better?" Dad snaps. *"God, Emma, the least you can do is keep her away from all that. I've been more than understanding, and I was willing to move because of your dad. I thought we had an understanding of how things would go once we were here."*

A loud clatter sounds through the recording.

"Paul," Mom whispers, her voice quivering. *"Stop. I won't bring her again. I'm sorry."*

There's a long pause. *"Did you hear that?"* Dad asks.

A slight click sounds, and the recording goes quiet. I wait for a few more minutes, but nothing else comes up.

I stare at the recorder as the tape continues to roll in silence. I'd already had a hard time accepting the idea that Dad would've recorded this, but especially now.

I rewind the tape.

The venom in Dad's voice raises goose bumps along my arms. Why would he ever talk to Mom like that?

I can't imagine either of them would record an interaction like this. Unless . . .

I lean my head back against the wall, a sinking feeling growing in my stomach. Unless Mom recorded the argument because she was scared. I close my eyes, thinking back to those occasional weekend mornings when I was little.

I try to picture what Mom looked like when they eventually came out of their room late in the day. She never had scars or bruises, at least not that I remember. But her eyes were red and puffy when they joined us. Dad was usually quiet those mornings. He'd immediately make Mom a cup of coffee and then bring me with him to grab takeout for all of us. By the time we returned home, Mom was smiling again, and the tension seemed gone from Donnie's shoulders.

Were they always fighting like this? And if so, why?

Instead of driving to the farm, I go straight to Ringer Bros. the next morning.

Janna is draped across the front counter, a large book in her hands. She doesn't look up until I'm standing right in front of her.

"Is this some kind of joke to you?" It comes out more accusatory than I expect. Probably a side effect of listening to that tape over and over again all night.

She laughs. "What? Nice to see you too."

I stare at her. "I told your ghost-hunting buddies no, but I bet they already told you that."

She raises her eyebrows. "Oh. You're upset about *that*."

"My entire family died a fiery, horrible, and probably painful death on this property that they worked so hard to keep. I can't believe you would think I'd be interested in exploiting their deaths like that."

"I know," she says softly. "That's not what I was trying to do. In fact, *I* wasn't trying to do anything."

"Seems like you told your buddy Gavin to give it a try and see if I'd let them film their *Blair Witch Project*."

She shakes her head. "They were already going to approach you, and I warned them that you would definitely say no. That's all." She closes her book and sets it by the cash register.

"Oh."

"Yeah, I knew you'd flip out when they asked you. Speaking of spooky stuff, what did you do with that candle?"

I'd almost forgotten about the candle. "Um, it's still in my room. Why?"

"It's interesting. I would've figured you'd thrown it away by now."

"I wouldn't read into that. I've just been busy."

She smirks. "Whatever you say. And I'm sorry for Gavin. I really did try to get him to leave you alone."

I wish she had tried harder. "Well, I'd appreciate it if you didn't spread it around that I'm spending time at the farm right now. It'll probably just attract more attention."

"Of course. For the record, I didn't tell Gavin anything like that."

I forgot that being around Janna was like this. As much as I considered her my best friend for some time, it's hard to ever know when to believe her. The longer I knew her, the more I realized how she would bend the truth about trivial things as a defense against the constraints of her reality. My phone begins to vibrate. "Okay, thanks." I wait until I'm out the front door and in the parking lot before I answer the call. "Hello?"

"Hey, um, I'm sorry to be bothering you right now," Sanders says.

Uh-oh. Here it comes. There's no telling what version of events Evan told Sanders by now. "It's fine. What's up?"

He exhales a heavy sigh on the other end. "Well, is Evan still with you?"

"What?"

"This is awkward, but I figured maybe you guys got back together and he ended up staying longer than expected . . . and that's fine. It's just put me in a bit of a bad spot with workload having both of you out."

My heart sinks. "What? No. We didn't get back together, and I haven't seen Evan since the day he came out. He hasn't come back to the city yet?" Could Evan be around here somewhere? Is he messing with me?

"No . . ."

I clench my fists. "Have you heard from him at all? No emails or texts?"

"Nada. Honestly, that makes me a little concerned. Do you know where he might be?"

He's not my problem anymore. I'd said it to his face, but I bite my tongue with Sanders. I know he appreciates workplace drama even less than I do, and there's no reason to tell him I'm quitting right now. "I'm in the middle of something. I'll let you know if I hear from him." I end the call and glance toward the street. If Evan is skulking around somewhere, surely I would've seen him by now.

The store door swings open beside me. "Hey," Janna says. She seems completely unfazed by my outburst. "Speaking of the farm, why don't I stop by to check it out tomorrow?"

I blink, still thinking about Evan. "Um . . . yeah. Okay."

CHAPTER TWELVE

The last thing I want is to be alone right now. Between the tape, the ghost hunters, Evan, and the fact that Janna's coming to the farm tomorrow, I need a distraction. I need to hear someone else talk so I don't spiral.

Originally, after spending the rest of the day working on the barn, I planned on picking up dinner and going back to my room, maybe going for a jog, and then binging Netflix on my laptop with Evan's stolen password. I figure he deserves it after the shit he pulled.

I park in front of the café. It's busier than I expected. For some reason, the thought of going in alone, all eyes on me, makes my stomach sink. I pull out my phone.

"Hi," Kael says when he picks up after the second ring.

"Hey. Um, I was wondering if you wanted to grab some dinner with me?"

"Oh." His voice drops. "Actually—"

"You find me repulsive, don't you?" I tease.

He laughs. "Definitely not."

"Then it's because of the whole 'town pariah' thing, isn't it?" I lean back against the headrest.

"You are *not* a pariah," he says. "But I, uh, have a thing."

"Wow. You really are trying to avoid me? And very badly, I might add."

He hesitates. "Uh . . . I actually have to spend the night at the fire station."

I turn and look down the street at the large tin building near the church.

"I'm a volunteer firefighter."

I freeze for a moment. How can I respond to that? "You're kidding." The thought of the flames makes my chest tighten. Not just flames, but *Kael* in flames.

"I'm not actually," he says. "I'm sorry. I wasn't really sure how to bring it up before."

I kick at the concrete step outside the café. "You have to spend the night there?"

"Yeah. We all spend a night—sometimes two if we're short a person—at the station. That's how the night calls get handled."

"Oh, okay."

"Sorry."

I sigh. "No, it's fine." I guess it's another meal sitting on the motel bed tonight.

"Do you want to come hang out *here*?" he asks.

"Is that allowed?" Even if it is, I'm not sure how I feel about being around all that fire equipment. Imagining Kael in uniform is a new fear I didn't realize existed.

"I mean, as long as you don't distract me, I don't think it'll be a problem."

The prospect of being around Kael outweighs the dread of being in the station. "Distract? No, not me. I'll come over in a few then."

"Lex?" Kael grins at me as he cracks open the side door of the station.

I hold up the bag of Styrofoam boxes. "I brought dinner to you."

"You're a saint." He opens the heavy metal door for me and takes the bag as I hand it to him. "Patty melts?"

"Of course." As far as I'm concerned, there's nothing else worth eating at the café. Except for the french fries and, on the right day, the fried catfish.

He gestures for me to follow him.

I stare at the looming fire truck as we pass it, and he leads me into the kitchen off the main room.

"Thanks for coming. I felt bad for leaving you alone for dinner," he says, grabbing a couple of plastic glasses from above the sink. "Coke or lemonade?"

"Lemonade, please." I've missed that shitty powdered lemonade everyone here seems to keep a pitcher of in their fridges. It reminds me of hot summer days and coming into the house to hear the clink of a spoon stirring.

"And thanks for the food." He opens the refrigerator and pours the murky yellow beverage into our glasses. "You saved me. I was about to make us a couple of very sad tacos." He sits down across from me and hands me one of the glasses.

"What makes a taco sad?" I take one of the boxes and slide it over to him.

"Well, we're almost out of groceries here, so I was just going to grill some Vienna sausages and toss them in a tortilla."

I almost spit out my drink. "That's not sad, that's diabolical."

He laughs. "If you think *that's* bad, don't even get me started on my 'leftover soup' recipe."

"Stop, I don't want to lose my appetite." I bite into my melt. The taste of the toasted cheap white bread and the local ground beef is unmatched.

"Good call."

I fish a few ketchup packets out of the bottom of the plastic bag and hand them to Kael.

"What about you? You don't want any?"

I grab a mustard packet and wave it.

He makes a face. "That's right. I forgot about that. To be honest, I'm not really sure you have a right to judge my taco-making skills if you're still eating your fries with mustard."

I rip open the packet and squirt the contents into the corner of my box. "It's delicious." I dip a fry in and then extend it to him. "You've just never had the guts to try it before."

He meets my eyes and takes the fry. He examines it between his two fingers for a moment before biting it. He continues to chew silently and then holds up a finger. "No. There's something wrong with you. This is awful."

I snicker. "Okay, we both have no taste, I guess." That would explain a lot of Beth's criticisms of my cooking in the past.

My gaze drifts to the flash of the fire engine through the small window in the kitchen door. Joking with Kael takes out some of the sting of being here. The sight of the truck feels a little less intimidating than how large it seemed to me when I was ten, with its big lights and noise on the worst night of my life. Maybe that's what made me turn away from all of this as much as possible before. "I'm interested in how this whole situation works." I point to the bunk room behind us. It's hard to see the equipment without thinking of Kael's father lifting his face shield and leading me away from the burning house that night. "You have to spend the night here, and you *don't* get paid for it?"

His lips curve into a crooked grin. "That's correct."

"Who routes the daytime calls?"

"So, *all* the calls are routed through the county's 911 center, but we always have someone available at the station. A couple of part-timers trade off as needed during the day."

It's a good system, I guess. Especially in a rural area like this. But at night, even if the station is attended at all times, the witnesses who can report a fire are limited. That was the problem with our fire. It probably took the McPherons too long to catch the scent of smoke while they were sleeping. "Part-timers?"

He swallows a mouthful of french fry. "Yeah, Millie is here most days, and then Reverend Butcher spends a lot of time here, too, during the weekdays."

An involuntary shiver runs through me at the mention of Butcher. "Do you really think a fire will get called in tonight?"

His eyes drift to the handheld radio at the edge of the table. "You never know. But we also don't *just* respond to fires. Most of the time, it's car accidents out here. It's rare for a night to pass without at least one of those."

I nod. "So, who's the brains of this whole operation anyway?" For as long as I can remember, Mr. McPheron was the chief.

"Of the department? Well, it's a team effort, obviously, but Reverend Butcher is the chief now."

My stomach drops. "Really?"

He glances down at his sandwich. "Yeah, he got elected a few years before Dad died."

I guess I shouldn't be surprised, but I am. "Why? Your dad was doing it for so long."

"I don't know . . . everyone liked Dad well enough, but Butcher has always had more sway, hasn't he?" He leans back in his seat. "And before the election it came out that someone had been stealing funds from the department."

"Stealing? There's no way anyone thought your dad had anything to do with it!"

"No." He shakes his head. "I don't think anyone thought that. And maybe stealing is the wrong word. Some of the money had gone *missing*. Everyone figured Butcher might be better at managing the funds since he has experience doing that for the church."

"And?"

Kael grips his glass of lemonade. "So far, so good."

I find that hard to believe. Although, what do I know? He's managed to somehow keep the church running all this time. "Do *you* think someone stole the money?"

"I have no idea, Lex." His eyes betray something more.

"Think you'll ever want to run for chief?"

He shakes his head. "Never. I'm barely keeping my head above water between this and the ranch as it is." He shifts in his seat. "I've been thinking about that tape from the other day . . . did you listen to the rest of it?"

As much as I'd like to forget, I've been thinking about it too. "I did. And it was interesting." I stare down at my empty box. "After the part we listened to together, it turned into an argument between my parents. My dad seemed really upset."

He furrows his brow. "What were they fighting about?"

"Church."

He looks confused. But he can't possibly be more confused than I am.

"I'm trying not to dwell on it, but between that and the phone calls . . . well, it's pretty unsettling."

"Have you received any more calls since last time?"

I shake my head. "And hopefully it stays that way," I say. "Actually, something kind of weird happened. You remember Evan came to the motel the other day?"

"Yeah, of course."

"Well, I got a call from our boss at the magazine, and apparently he hasn't been back to the office yet. It's strange, but I really don't think he's still around. Maybe he's at his mom's place or something, but if he is still here and hiding out, I'm worried about him. It's not like him at all to behave this way."

Kael sighs. "Either way, you should report it to the sheriff. You can think you know someone and still not really understand what they're capable of until it's too late."

Too late? I can read between the lines what that may mean. "What you saw of him last time wasn't normal. He can be a little overbearing maybe, but he was just upset." His baseline has always been a little chaotic, but he's not forceful. And he's definitely not the type to lie in wait and stalk someone. "Anyway, I'm not supposed to be distracting you. Are there duties you're neglecting while you listen to me?"

Kael grins and stands up from his chair. "Want to see what I was working on before you got here?"

I follow him into the bunk room. Hats, shields, and boots are lined up. A stiff brush is cast down beside one pair.

"It's my turn to clean the PPE." Kael leans against the doorframe.

"Sounds like a fun night." I pretend to glance at my watch. "I better head out."

He rolls his eyes. "Oh, come on, you're going to leave just before the good part?"

I slowly walk toward the door. "Hey, *you're* the volunteer, not me."

"Touché." He unlatches the back door. "Are you headed back to the motel?"

"I guess."

He purses his lips. "Lex . . . please keep an eye out, okay? Be careful."

I'd be lying if I said I don't enjoy it a little when he worries about me. "I will. I'll even text you when I get back to my room if that makes you feel better."

He smiles. "It does. Thanks." He stands with the door remaining open until I get in my car and turn the key in the ignition. He raises his hand in a small wave as I start to roll out of the driveway.

Despite what I told Kael, the idea of going back to my room alone right now fills me with a deep dread. Once I reach the edge of town, instead of turning toward the motel, I continue until I see a sign for the one bar in the county.

Everything is going much slower here than expected. Instead of settling in early for another restless night of sleep, maybe I can at least check some work emails.

I park between the two other cars in front of the bar and grab my laptop bag from the back seat. When I step inside, the bartender nods to me as I walk to the far corner opposite of the flat-screen

TV. Some football game is playing, but the sound isn't too loud over here.

I sink into the booth just as the bartender appears.

"What can I get you?" From his bloodshot eyes, it looks like he's either been working all day or just downed a shot from the tequila bottle that's sitting on the bar counter behind him.

"Whiskey on the rocks, please."

He leans against the other side of the booth. "What kind?"

"The cheapest one you have."

He snickers. "All right. I'll be right back."

I wait until he's back behind the counter before I pull out my laptop. I stare at the home screen for Outlook until my drink arrives and I finally remember my password.

"Try not to let it touch your tongue," the bartender says and then walks away.

I stare at the tumbler and give it a little shake. I take a quick gulp. Jesus, that definitely burns.

My phone vibrates on the table.

Kael: Are you back yet?

I hold up my phone and snap a picture of my drink, the bar and TV in the background.

I took a detour, I type back and send it with the picture.

"Lex? I thought that was you."

I look up as Tom approaches my booth, hands in the front pockets of his jeans. "Oh. Hi."

He smiles and glances at my laptop. "Can I join you?" He already sits down before I can respond. "Why don't I buy you that dinner I owe you?"

"I actually already ate."

He nods and drums his fingers along the table. "Do you mind keeping me company while I eat then?"

Yes, I do mind. Please leave. However . . . I glance at the 589 unread email notifications that have appeared on my screen. "Sure." I close my laptop and slide it into my bag.

"Perfect." He turns in his seat and waves at the bartender.

The bartender makes a face but hurries our way.

Tom pushes a menu across the table toward me. "Order anything you like. It's on me. I'll get you another drink too." He points to my glass. "Whiskey?"

"Scotch." If it's free, I might as well upgrade. I down the remaining slush that's already forming at the bottom of the glass. I eye the menu. If I have to sit here and listen to this weirdo reminisce about the good ol' days, I might as well get some free food. "And I'll get a cheeseburger too."

When the bartender arrives, Tom turns to him. "Two whiskeys and two cheeseburgers please. No pickles on one."

I set the menu down. "And extra pickles on the other."

Tom faces me again once we're alone. "What a coincidence, right? Running into you here. It's a little out of the way from Sola, isn't it?"

After the second run-in with Tom over the course of a couple of days, I'm not sure I'd call it a coincidence. "It's the only nearby bar, from what I hear."

He nods. "Yep, that's right. It's pretty funny, isn't it? About an hour to the west of here, there's nearly nothing but weed farms, but in Sola you can't even get a decent drink unless you can drive to the edge of the county." He shakes his head. "How are you liking being back in town?"

"Uh . . ." Surely I can think of one nice thing to say.

"I heard you've been running around with the McPheron boy again." Again? He watches me for my reaction.

"He and I are old friends." I cross my arms over my chest. Jesus, is everyone here tracking my every movement?

He grips his glass. "He's a good kid. A lot like his dad. And he's probably the best one we have on the team."

"The team?"

"Yeah, we're both with the VFD," he says. "And let me tell you, he's dedicated. He came up with this really interesting system for—"

"How long have you been with the department?"

The gaze in his eyes shifts. "I know what you're thinking, but I wasn't on it when . . . well, you know. I actually joined up about a year later. Things weren't going so great at home with my old lady, and I was looking for any excuse to—"

"Did you hear anything about how the fire was started?" If I have to listen to this guy, I might as well get something out of it.

He sighs and leans back in his seat. "Lexi, you're barking up the wrong tree. As far as I know, it was a freak accident. You know how windy it can get up here."

The biggest casualty fire this Podunk town has ever seen, and that's all he's heard about it within the fire department?

"What did you expect me to say? Sola's not a town where crazy things happen, you know that. It was just a tragedy."

I hold his gaze. "I don't know. It's hard to put a lot of faith in a corrupt fire department."

His eyes narrow. "What?"

Good, I struck a nerve. He's pissed. "I heard there was a bit of a money problem a while back."

"Who told you that? Was it Kael?"

Shit. I didn't think this through. I don't want to put a target on his back. "No."

"Larson?"

"No. I, uh . . ." I shake my head and look down. "So, how did you know my mom again?"

His posture relaxes a little. "She and I were in school together. We'd known each other since kindergarten, actually. Not that we were . . . well, everyone loved her. She was a little too popular for her own good."

What the hell is that supposed to mean?

He laughs nervously. "I just mean that's why we weren't really that close. She was too high in demand. And then, in high school, you know, there was a little inner circle."

"Inner circle?" Sounds like a strange way to say my mom probably thought this guy was a weirdo too.

"Yeah, it was mostly footballers and cheerleaders, not dorks like me." He smiles, but it doesn't reach his eyes. "But you know how that is. I hear you were pretty popular in high school too."

I study him. How does he know what I was like in high school?

"But Emma was always too good for this place," Tom continues. "She never planned to stick around."

The food arrives, and Tom takes a fork and knife and begins cutting into his burger. "What did you get up to in San Francisco?" he asks between bites.

"What?"

He waves his fork toward me. "What were you doing out there? What became of you?"

"Oh . . . um, I work for a magazine."

He nods. "A writer?"

"Yeah."

He grins. "Your mom loved to write. College?"

"Excuse me?"

He pauses with another piece of burger outside his mouth. "Did you go to college?"

"Oh. Yeah." Not a good one, though. I'm sure if Beth had bothered to sell the farm earlier, I could have afforded a degree worth a shit. I swallow the hint of resentment creeping up my throat. I've tried not to judge Beth over the past few days. After all, I can't fault her for avoiding the unpleasant task I'm currently suffering through.

"Good, good," Tom says. His gaze shifts. "She would have been proud of you."

Instead of being comforting like he probably intends, the comment is unsettling. "I thought you said you weren't that close with my mom."

He snorts. "True. But of all the kids at school, she was the only one who was nice to me. It was nothing to her, but to me . . . well, it meant a lot." He settles deeper into his seat. "I'm really sorry." His face has become pale.

"For what?"

"Your family. That never should have happened."

I shift in my seat. I need an exit strategy. Something about Tom makes my skin crawl.

"Emma was there for me and a lot of people. I feel like we really let her down by not taking better care of you. You're one of us, after all."

One of them? "That's not true. I was born in the city. And I'm a Blake. Not a Rawlings."

He holds my gaze. "Your blood is here. Like it or not." He swirls his glass of scotch. "This place is like a black hole. You only think you can escape it, but it just keeps drawing you back in. Your mom said something like that to me when she came back the first time."

The first time? "You mean when we moved back?"

His eyes shift. "No. It was just Emma for a time. She came by herself to visit with family for a bit."

I scan through the memories filed in my mind. Mom never came here on her own. In fact, she never brought us to Sola at all until we moved here. "When?"

Tom begins to gnaw his lower lip. "I don't remember the year exactly."

The way he's avoiding my gaze makes me nervous. Why is he suddenly clamming up like this? "It must've been when I was very little. I don't remember her leaving and going on a trip alone."

"Oh . . . well, I think it was when Amy was little. She'd just turned two."

When Amy was two? That would've been before I was born. "How long was she here for?"

He finishes the remnants of liquor from his glass. "A few months, I think. Maybe six? But it was so long ago."

"Six months? Alone?" With three little kids at home?

He stares down at the table. "Well, your parents probably didn't see a point in bringing it up to you. They seemed a lot better when they all came here."

The argument from the tape plays through my mind. "Do you mean something was going on between them when my mom came here alone? Were they separated?" Did Mom leave my dad?

He squirms in his seat. "I only know tidbits about all that. I shouldn't have said anything. Look, I know it's probably not easy to hear about your parents having a hard time, but lots of married couples go through rough patches. To their credit, at least they stuck it out. Our divorce was really hard on my son. People don't realize how that messes with a kid."

Anger begins to stir in the pit of my stomach. It's as if Tom spitting this out has tampered with the pristine image I have of my parents. I obviously never thought they were perfect, but this definitely doesn't comport with how my perception of them has remained over the years, frozen in time. Now I can't even picture the people he's describing. "Thanks for the drink, but I need to head out."

He follows me toward the door. "Lexi, I—"

I spin on my heel. "What?"

He shrinks back. "I'm sorry. I didn't mean to upset you."

I push through the door and walk as fast as I can until I reach the safety of my car. My heart is racing. I wring the steering wheel between my clenched hands and stare at the sign above the bar. Thankfully, Tom doesn't follow me out.

My phone buzzes in my pocket, and I pull it out. It's Kael calling. "Hey," I answer flatly.

"So instead of choosing to clean with me, you decided to drink? Your loss." He laughs. "How's the whiskey?"

"Kael . . . did you ever hear anything about my parents?"

He hesitates. "Like what?"

"Tom came up to me at the bar, and he had some interesting things to say about them. Did you ever hear anything about marriage problems?"

"No, not that I can remember at least," he says. "What did he say?"

"Apparently my parents were separated before I was born. Mom left Dad and my brother and sisters and stayed alone in Sola for six months." I shake my head. "Maybe it had something to do with why they were arguing on that tape." Why is there a tape at all? I still haven't figured that out.

"I had no idea. Why would he even bring that up?"

I release the remaining hold I have on the wheel and lean back in the seat. "I don't know. He started acting really cagey after he brought it up. I had to get away from him before he blurted out any more trivia facts about my parents . . . they seemed happy, didn't they?"

"Yeah. I thought so. Stressed maybe, but they definitely were happy together. And they were always nice to everyone . . . well, almost everyone."

"What's that supposed to mean?"

"It's no secret your dad wasn't a big fan of the church. I remember one time we were at the feed store, and he made some biting remark to Mr. Handley about him being a deacon or something. Mom was there, and she definitely noticed it. I mean, I was a little kid back then, but it stuck out to me because it was so out of character. Just little stuff like that. People around here have long memories about that kind of thing."

"That says more about the type of people who serve as deacons here than it does about my dad," I snap.

"Hey, you're not wrong. I'm with you on that. The church here certainly seems to attract a lot of *interesting* characters. I should know . . . I work with them."

"Work with them?" I set my phone on speakerphone and place it on the dashboard before I shift gear into drive.

"They're all firefighters too."

I turn the steering wheel and roll forward onto the main road. "The deacons? They're all firefighters?"

"Yeah, it's kind of an inside joke. They even have their own Bible study group called the Flamebearers. They tried to get me to go when I got back, and that's actually when I stopped going to service. It was all just a bit much."

He's right. When I reflect back on it, all my deacons growing up were also the same ones who served up dishes at the annual fire department barbecue fundraiser. Maybe I just didn't notice too much because the deacons weren't the *only* firefighters. I turn up the strength of my headlights as I drive farther away from bar lights. "Well then, it's no mystery that Butcher was elected chief, is it?" The real mystery is that it took so long. I guess that's a testament to how much people respected Kael's father that they would allow a nondeacon to hold a position of power in town for so long.

Kael exhales on the other end of the phone. "It certainly isn't."

"So, you're the only one not in their little cult Bible study?"

"Yep."

"Aren't you a rebel?"

He laughs. "It gives me a bad feeling. I mean, the 'Flamebearers'? Come on. Besides, I just don't really know how I feel about all the church stuff anymore these days."

"I get it." It took Beth years away from Sola and some very patient people at her new church in the city to help deconstruct so many harmful beliefs formed at Sola Evangelical. And that was fine by me. I stopped attending church as soon as I turned eighteen, but I didn't begrudge Beth her devoutness. As long as no one is getting hurt, people can believe whatever they want.

"Are you okay? After hearing all of that about your parents?"

I turn into the motel parking lot, my eyes scanning for Evan's car on the off chance I'm wrong about him. "Yeah. I'll be fine. Well, I'm at the motel now. I'll talk to you later."

"Okay," he says softly. "I'll be up cleaning and polishing old boots if you need someone to talk to."

"You don't get to actually sleep there?"

"Most people catnap here and there on night shifts, but I can't ever seem to get comfortable."

I get out of the car and shut the door. "I probably won't be able to sleep much tonight, either, if that makes you feel any better."

"It doesn't. If I was at home, I'd play you some music." I hadn't been working at the ranch very long when we found Mr. McPheron's old Emerson record player and rock albums. We found them tucked at the back of the loft after Kael crawled up there to find me reading a magazine instead of sweeping.

The crate peeked out from behind the stack of folded saddle blankets I was propped up against. The records clearly hadn't been played in forever, so we were shocked that the player still worked. After looking through the collection, Kael was quick to realize his dad must've hid them in the barn, as they probably weren't conservative enough for his mom. I think that day really changed how Kael saw his father. Mr. McPheron was a quiet rebel. A man with secrets.

"That's sweet, but I can play music on my phone." I finish climbing the stairs to my room and pull out my key from the back pocket of my jeans.

He clicks his tongue. "It's not the same. Insomnia can only be cured with the beautifully imperfect sound of vinyl. Everyone knows that."

I smile as I step in through the door. "God, you're such a music snob."

"I know. I'm the worst."

I toss my bag onto the floor by the bed, but a spot of color on the nightstand catches my eye. A red light flashes on the motel phone. Someone has called and left a voice mail.

"Lex? Am I really that bad?"

I stare down at the flashing button. "What? No. Sorry, I got distracted."

"Well, *try* to get some sleep, okay? Good night."

Who would leave a message? If it *is* Evan doing all of this, listening to the voice mail is exactly what he wants. Maybe he really is trying to scare me. "Good night, Kael." I reach toward the motel phone and punch the delete button.

CHAPTER THIRTEEN

I've been dreading this. I can't exactly pinpoint why. Maybe it's because this means it's really happening. I really am losing this place forever.

Janna's bottom lip is almost raw from how hard she's gnawing on it. Her black eyebrows knit together as she kicks a stray brick, scribbling onto the screen of her iPad with a stylus. She's definitely playing the part of Realtor today, trading in her distressed skinny jeans for a pair of black straight-legged slacks and an eggplant button-up tunic that could be mistaken for a formal shirt from afar. She's even pulled together a neat bun, highlighting only a single strand of blue hair to bind it.

"So?" I prod. I made a point to take her to the barn, making sure she took note of the intact cubicles. I spotted some wood rot on the trim of the walls, but that will be easy to replace.

Janna finally meets my gaze with a sigh, tucking the iPad under her arm. "Yikes, right?"

"Yeah, I guess. But it could be a lot worse, honestly."

She nods. "I think we have to level it."

"The remains of the house? I guess I was thinking—"

"No, the whole lot. The barn has to go."

"Janna . . . the barn is the only thing of value. There's still a full system in there for dairy ranchers and—"

"Does the equipment even run?" She raises her eyebrows.

"I'm not sure yet." To be honest, I've never used it before, so I wouldn't even know where to begin checking it. "I can ask Kael to help me figure that out."

A smile breaks out along her icy expression. "Oh, Kael? Interesting. I bet he was pretty excited to find out you're back in town."

I can feel my cheeks redden. "No. I mean, no more excited than he should be."

"Sure. He was the first person you went to see, wasn't he?"

Damn it. "He has my horse."

She rolls her eyes, and for a moment, it's like we're sitting at the cafeteria table in high school again. "Give me a break. You used to tell me everything. *Everything*, Lex."

I had. Back then, who else was there to tell? Beth would've had a fit and moved me out of town earlier if she'd found out what Kael and I got up to in the stables. Janna perfectly fit the role as a stand-in for what I would've confessed to my sisters if they'd had the chance to become teenagers. And she did so happily, as an only child.

"Okay, okay," she says in response to my silence. "I'm just saying, I'm glad you guys are back in touch . . . no pun intended." She turns to the barn. "But I'm sorry. I really don't see someone in the area buying this place with any existing structures on it. Leveling the house is a start, but the barn has to go too."

I survey the faint remains of the spray paint on a patch of the tin exterior. *Evil was here*. "A fresh coat of paint can do wonders."

She glances at me out of the corner of her eye. "That's not the problem."

"I know," I say quietly. This place is cursed. That's why no one will touch it. The barn is the only reminder that a family lived here and they were happy once. But that's the same reason I can't let go of it. Not yet.

She looks down at her Apple Watch. "Well, I need to head out, but we'll talk soon, all right? Come by the store and we can figure this out."

As Janna climbs into her Mercedes, my phone begins to buzz in my pocket. I wait until she's out of the driveway before I answer. "Hello?"

"Yes, Alexis? It's Jim Ridley." The lawyer sounds relieved that I answered. "I was just following up. Have you been able to check out the property yet?"

I sigh, glancing into the barn. "Yeah. I actually had a Realtor come out and look at it with me."

"Oh, a Realtor? That's a good start."

Good. At least I've done something right.

"Look, I really want to help you out with this, so once you have an offer, let me know and I can drive out there. If someone's interested, I want to make sure you don't let go of that property for too little." His optimism makes me feel more hopeful than I've allowed myself so far. "I expect you'll take some kind of hit given the time constraints, but I want to make sure you get a fair number. At least enough to give you a good amount after the taxes are paid."

"I don't want to put you out."

"You're not," he says. "Your parents would want it this way. Anyway, save my number. Give me a call if anything changes or if you have any questions, okay?"

"Okay. Thank you." I'll take any help I can get.

CHAPTER FOURTEEN

Kael raises the brim of his hat and stares at me. "You know I'm not a dairy guy, right?" His face is covered with a thin layer of dirt. I caught him at his forge at the back of the stable. From behind I thought for a minute it was his father. He was the only one I'd ever seen back there, shaping and cooling horseshoes.

He sets his hammer on top of the forge, wiping a streak of sweat from his forehead and redistributing the soot along his brow.

"Yes," I say, leaning against the stable door. "But you're, um, handy, right? I figured you might at least be able to tell if the equipment is worth saving."

He grins. "Okay. Want to check it out now? I'm already dirty, so why not?" He wipes his hands on his black apron and casts it to the side. "Did you walk here?"

"Yeah." I needed the time to think after what Janna said.

"Then I'll spare you the misery of being trapped in a car with me right now." He laughs, walking beside me away from the barn and toward the path I cleared, cutting through the grass between our land. He doesn't smell bad, though. He clearly put something on this morning, either aftershave or deodorant, that has a scent of pine. Mingled with the smell of his sweat, it reminds me of a forest after a heavy rain. And fire. He has a stench of smoke radiating from him. "So, why are you suddenly looking into the dairy stuff?"

"Well, Janna came over to appraise the place . . ."

He raises his eyebrows. "Uh-huh."

"And I believe her first impression was 'yikes.'"

He shakes his head. "Typical Janna. This place isn't that bad. The land is solid enough attraction." As we step into the barn, he says nothing and wanders over to what my Google searches have informed me is a homogenizer. I hadn't known what it was years ago when Dad bought a new one after Grandpa died, but I do remember it cost $20,000. It had only been used for a couple of months before the fire.

He stoops down and tilts the stainless steel machine forward.

I take a deep breath. His silence is killing me. I sit on the edge of a concrete platform that oversees the milking cubicles, watching as he jiggles and taps various components.

Finally, he walks over and sits beside me.

"Well?"

He sighs. "Dairy farming is highly regulated, right?"

"I guess . . ." I don't like where this is going.

"So, I don't see a state audit going particularly well if a farm is using equipment that has been sitting here unused for over a decade. Most of this stuff is refrigeration based, and the cooling systems probably aren't as reliable as they should be."

Shit.

"However . . ." He stands up and knocks on the nearest metal cubicle door, swinging it open and picking at the rust that's formed by the hinge. "This barn has great bones. It might not be the prettiest to look at from the road, but the structure is solid. Even if the new owner wanted to cow-calf or raise horses, the way it's built up inside is perfect."

Bones. I guess that's better than nothing. "Janna wants to tear down the barn."

Kael frowns. "Why?"

"She thinks no one will buy it as is. She wants to clear out the rubble from the fire, and I get that. But the barn? It's not *that* bad."

He nods. "No offense . . . I know Janna's your friend, but I wouldn't necessarily depend on her. Has she actually even sold anything yet?"

"Probably not. But, it won't hurt to give it a try with her, right? And we're not friends, not anymore."

He shrugs.

"Speaking of Janna, her dad owns the motel now? Is that true?"

"Yep. He owns half the town now."

I kick at a pebble by my feet. "That's disconcerting."

He tilts his head to the side. "Why? If not him, someone else would've done it."

"He's a horrible person . . . in my opinion."

He raises his eyebrows. "Oh? Self-righteous Reverend Butcher has skeletons in his closet?"

"Maybe it's not earth shattering enough to everyone else here, but the way he treated his family is fucked up to say the least."

"In what way?"

"Never mind. Just, I'm not thrilled to hear how he's thriving as a pastor *and* monopolizing the entire town. That's not weird to anyone else?"

"No, of course not. He can do no wrong. 'God has blessed him in business.'" He points a finger to the sky.

My stomach twists. Of course there's a lot that goes unseen in this town. Why wouldn't they choose to turn a blind eye to the faults of their preacher?

"What has he done to his family, though?"

I shake my head. "Forget I said anything. It's not really my thing to share." As far as I'm concerned, my promise to Janna didn't expire. I should've said something all those years ago, but since I didn't, revealing it now is just gossip.

"Okay." He glances down at his boots. "Well, I'm glad you came over today. I thought you were avoiding me."

"Why would I avoid you?"

His eyes flicker to me again, soft but worried. "About the fire stuff . . . it was probably weird for you at the station. And then when you came with dinner there—on top of all the stuff with your parents, it just must be a lot."

"Forget about it. I'm fine. Really. But, I have to admit, I was a little surprised that you're into all of that now and volunteering. Isn't it dangerous?"

He sighs. "After Dad died and I came back here, I needed something more than just the ranch. And the department was struggling. I figured it's no more dangerous than working the ranch every day." He laughs. "The odds that I'll get kicked in the head by your horse are much higher."

I remember the other night at the fire station. Even just thinking about what all that equipment is meant to protect him from makes my fist clench.

He gazes across the open field toward the ranch. "Enough small talk, want to skip to the good part?"

I stare at him, reading a little too much into that mischievous smile. "The good part?"

He gestures to the stables. "I'm pretty sure he's been waiting for you all day."

Right. Whisper.

—

"Are you ready to ride?" Kael walks behind me, grabbing the saddle draped over the railing.

I had been so excited at the idea, but now I wonder if I even remember how to. Whisper's not easy. He likes me, sure, but one wrong move and he won't hesitate to buck me off.

"Come on, you'll be fine," Kael says, as if he's reading my mind. "He's really mellowed out with age." He opens the gate and enters the corral, seamlessly distracting Whisper with a peppermint before sliding a pad and saddle on his back.

Whisper sniffs my palm for candy. “Please don’t kill me,” I say to him softly. He stares at me, and I’m sure he understands what I’m telling him. Whether he’ll grant my request, however . . .

“Okay, the old girl’s ready.” Penny lopes beside Kael, barely glancing at me before nuzzling Whisper’s side. “Let’s go. Do you need help getting on?”

“No, I’m good.” I tug on the horn and the back of the saddle to make sure it won’t flip under my weight and do my best impression of a confident horsewoman, swinging one leg over the side of the saddle, praying silently that Whisper won’t shoot off into the horizon. My hands relax around the reins as I sink against the seat. So far, so good.

Kael’s already somehow on Penny, smiling at me. Whisper begins following after Kael and Penny without prompting. Kael glances over his shoulder to me as we ride farther away from the barn and into the wild grass. “To the lake and back?”

I nod and take a moment to pat the base of Whisper’s neck as we move forward. It’s been a while since I felt so light and free. That’s what riding Whisper used to be for me—a way to escape and let go of all that weighed me down back then. The load is a bit heavier now.

“You doing okay?” Kael waits for me and Whisper to catch up.

“Yep.” I point to the lines of trees on our right as we pass. “That’s new.”

“Oh. Yeah, Dad got an orchard started a while back. Right after I left for college, I think.” His eyes latch onto the trees for a moment longer before he turns straight ahead again.

“You must miss him.” There isn’t much to define Mr. McPheron in my mind other than he was quiet and slow to anger, and he would *always* remove his hat when he entered a building.

He shrugs. “I had some great years with him.”

“That doesn’t make it any easier.” When people know what happened to my family, they seem to feel like they can’t express grief to me.

Like I'm going to undermine their loss because nothing can possibly amount to mine.

He glances at me. "It does, though." He looks like he wants to say more but stops himself.

I imagine he wants to add that he's better off with more memories. But, in my opinion, that makes it worse, not easier. Each year, my limited memories of my family fade a little, and losing them becomes a tad less painful. Kael had his dad around for more than half his life. That's hard to erase. "What kind of trees are they?"

"Peach, walnut, apple. I'm sure you can guess which one is most popular around here."

We're nearly to the ravine ahead, but if I squint at the orchard, I can see a spot of red. That must be an apple the horses have missed. I turn my head to the front just as the first glimmer of water appears up ahead.

The ground begins to decline, the full lake coming into view. Kael dismounts Penny in one swift movement and grips the horn of my saddle, extending his free hand to me. I grip it and dig my heel into the stirrup while swinging the other leg over. I manage not to kick Kael in the face and lower down beside him.

Whisper leads the way to the water's edge, admiring the view of the mountains on the other side before bowing his head and lapping at the lake.

There are so many great views in the city, but nothing beats this. The stillness and quiet. It almost hurts my ears. The water is a translucent green that gradually becomes a deep emerald blue away from the shore. That's where that steep drop-off is. The one that Kael used to warn me not to swim past, but I did it anyway. I look at him. He's staring ahead at the water as well.

"Don't even think about it," he says.

Can he read my mind? "What?"

He shakes his head. "You're definitely not a strong enough swimmer to get away with that again." He winds Penny's reins around her saddle.

I slide off my sneakers, gripping his forearm to steady myself as I pull off my socks.

"Lex—"

"Relax, I just want to wade in." I release my grip and set my shoes beside Whisper, then walk into the shallows. The water's so cool on my skin, but not cold like the Pacific, the heat from the sun absorbed by the large stones lining the shore.

After a moment, Kael splashes in next to me, his boots abandoned by Penny. He's standing so close it's hard to resist the urge to reach for his hand. "Is it weird? Being back?"

"A little. It brings up a lot of . . ." Anger. Sadness. "Feelings." I kick up some water as I finish, clear droplets raining down on the green ripples. "It's like I'm sixteen again. But not in a good way. Everyone's treating me like I'm still an angsty teen with a chip on my shoulder."

He laughs. "Welcome to my hell. Everyone still asks me about that goal I kicked in 2010. Over ten years ago and I hear about that game at least once a week."

"Yeah, well, it *was* a pretty great kick." I missed it because I was too busy hiding under the bleachers from the head cheerleader, but video of the kick made it to the highlight reel at the next pep rally.

"I know you're not sure how long you'll be around, but you're welcome to come however much you want. To see Whisper." He's looking at me, and even though I'm still staring down at the water below, I can feel the heat of his gaze.

"Thank you." But I'm desperately hoping I'm gone by the end of the week. "I might stop by to see this view again too." I nod to the sun beginning to set across the lake.

"Yeah, it's something, isn't it?"

"It really is." I walk a couple of steps back toward Whisper and sink onto the ground. I stretch my toes toward the water as Kael sits beside me.

"God might not have blessed us with much out here, but I never get sick of the scenery," he says.

"I thought you said you weren't a church boy anymore?"

He looks toward the sunset. "I'm not. But that doesn't mean I don't believe in God."

"Hmm" is all I can manage in response.

He gestures at our surroundings. "This is my church now, I guess. That's how it was for my dad. He never went to church except for holidays, but he'd come out here and go fishing every Sunday morning, and I honestly think he was closer to God than any of the deacons." He glances down at his hands.

My parents never really talked about God. And neither did Grandpa, for that matter. He went diligently his entire life, but I can't remember a single instance of him attributing anything in real life to a higher power. "Do you think we go anywhere after this?"

Kael shifts. "I don't know. I don't know a lot of things, and I'm okay with that."

"Same." Except I'm not okay with it. It eats me alive.

CHAPTER FIFTEEN

I forgot how sore horseback riding used to make me. My legs tremble as I walk up the motel staircase. Even though I smell like horse, I collapse onto the bed.

I wince as the room phone begins to ring.

I lie still for a moment, staring at the ceiling, listening to the sound before I shoot up. It's just the guy at the front desk, I tell myself.

I sit up, my palms sweating as I pick up the receiver. "Hello?"

"No, Donnie!" It's my own shrill voice when I was a child, playing through the receiver.

My heart stops.

"Come on, Lexi," my brother says on the other end. *"It's time to go to bed. Wash out your glass and put it in the dishwasher."*

Little Lex blows a raspberry. A clang of a glass. *"Dad said I could—"*

"He said *you could stay up until nine . . . and what does the clock say?"*

My indignant little grumble plays over the audio. A rash of sweat sprouts along my back and neck. "Who is this?"

The sound suddenly cuts out. A second passes in silence before a small crackle and more audio starts.

"You must think I'm a fucking fool, Emma!" Dad's voice yells through the receiver.

The volume makes me jump. Faint sounds of crying play on the other end. *"Paul, please . . ."* It doesn't sound like my mom, her voice so quiet and weak.

A loud crash sounds in the background. *"If you keep pushing me, I can't be held responsible for what I might do,"* Dad says.

More weeping.

"Do you understand?" The anger is gone from his voice, replaced by a frigid calm.

Mom sniffs. *"I made a mistake, Paul. How many times do we need to go over this?"*

A chair scrapes the ground. *"I'm sorry,"* Dad says. *"Every time I think I've moved past it, something like this happens, and I just . . . leave Lex out of it, or we're going to have problems here."*

Mom clears her throat. *"I'm really trying—"*

"Stop. I don't want to talk about this anymore. It is what it is."

The line goes dead.

My hands shake as I set the receiver down. I sit on the edge of the bed, my heart racing. It takes me a moment before I remember. I haven't used a landline in so long. I pick up the phone and dial *69.

"Your call cannot be completed at this time. Please hang up and dial again."

Damn it. The number must have been blocked. I set the phone down again and walk over to the window. Part of me wants to rip back the curtains, but the other part of me is terrified I may see someone standing there.

I turn around and retreat to the bed. I put my back against the wall and tuck the covers up over my bent legs and up to my chin.

This position feels familiar. It was my go-to whenever I heard the farmhouse creak at night all those years ago. And the whispers of the ghost I was sure was there. I stare at the door until my eyes hurt.

CHAPTER SIXTEEN

I must've fallen asleep somehow. In the morning, I woke up still huddled in the corner of the bed. I couldn't get out of the motel room fast enough.

"I thought I might find you here." I sink into the seat opposite Sheriff Larson. I decided to try to catch him at the café with his first cup of coffee. I'm not sure I've ever encountered him this early in the morning before. His uniform is crisp, and his graying hair is wavy without having been crushed under the weight of his hat all day.

He sets down his newspaper and blinks at me. "Lexi?" He peers at the rest of the empty café. "What can I do for you?"

"Have you processed my request yet?"

He lifts his cup and drains the last few drops. "Not yet. I'm still working on it. Believe me, I will let you know once it's ready."

"I figured."

He studies me from across the table. "Is there something else that's on your mind?"

I glance down at my hands. "You knew my parents."

He raises his eyebrows. "Yes, I did."

"And you were very close with them."

He holds my gaze.

"I remember you would come over a few times a week for dinner." The talk at dinner was benign enough, but what did he and Dad say when they slipped away afterward to have a beer in the barn?

"Yes, your parents invited me over a few times."

"Why?"

He sets his mug down. "You know why."

I shrug. "No, I don't. They were just nice?"

"Well, yes. But also, they were outsiders here like me. And, to be frank, they were some of the only normal people around here."

"Normal?"

He nods. "Yeah, I mean, I came from Seattle to this place. It was a big adjustment. And they were going through the same thing. They were extremely kind to me during that time."

I replay my conversation with Tom in my mind. "Did my dad ever mention any marriage problems they were having?"

He steels his expression. He knows something. "What do you mean?"

"I don't know. Tom Miller told me—"

"Why are you talking with Tom?"

"Why shouldn't I?" It's not like I've much choice in the matter. Tom is the one making a point to talk with me.

He shakes his head. "He's always running his mouth about a bunch of nonsense. You'd do better to keep away from him."

"Well, he mentioned that my mom and dad may have been having problems before we moved back here. Did Dad ever say anything about that to you?"

He stares down at his empty coffee cup, perhaps wishing he could busy his mouth with drinking rather than talking with me about this. "Lexi, why are you asking me this?"

"I want to know if it's true."

"Why? Would it change anything you already know about your parents?"

"It doesn't matter," I say. "I have a right to ask questions about my own family." I've gone long enough without knowing.

"You had a beautiful, *happy* family, Lexi. And that's exactly how you should remember them." His tone isn't entirely convincing, but I can tell this is the most I'll get from him. He grabs his cowboy hat from the edge of the table. "How much longer are you going to be around here?"

"Are you sick of me already?"

He stands up from his seat. "I'm not sure this place is good for you."

CHAPTER SEVENTEEN

I steer my car onto the dirt road past the railroad tracks. As I drive over the first bump, a splash of coffee escapes from the top of my to-go cup from the café.

Mrs. McPheron's car isn't parked out front, but Kael's truck is by the barn, although I can't see him.

I park and grip my coffee cup before getting out of the car. I walk into the barn. Kael is nowhere to be seen, but Whisper turns to look at me and taps one of his hooves against the soil.

"I thought I heard a car pulling up."

I spot Kael approaching. "Hi, I wasn't sure if you'd be awake." I sip my coffee.

"You're up so early these days. I don't remember you as a morning person."

That's because I wasn't. I used to grumble into the stables when Beth would drop me off in the mornings to help Kael feed the horses. But adulthood brought coffee—glorious coffee—and early-morning jogs. Suddenly mornings didn't feel quite as bad anymore. Memories of that call last night, though, jolted me awake faster than caffeine ever has.

He leans over the railing beside me. "Is everything okay?"

I pat the soft flesh of Whisper's muzzle, his whiskers tickling my palm. No. Everything is not okay, but I'm not even sure where to start.

"Yeah." I want to tell him about the latest call, but something stops me. If those stupid town kids were gossiping that my dad had something to do with the fire . . . what if Kael had heard the same thing? What if I told him about the argument I heard over the phone, and it only made my dad seem like a monster? I look into Whisper's eyes. "I think I want to go for a ride. Want to come?"

"I'm sorry. There's a dressage competition in Dunnigan Hills that I'm working. It's going to take all morning."

"Oh." I thought maybe going for a ride might give me the courage to say more to him.

He gestures to Whisper. "Do you want me to help you saddle up?"

"No, it's okay. Have fun."

He stares at me for a moment as he moves to the open stable door. "If you're still here when I get back, want to grab a bite?"

"Yeah, that'd be great." I turn my attention to Whisper as Kael exits. I grab a blanket from the top of the shelf and drag a saddle from where Kael left it on a wooden post. "You feeling up for a short trip?" I say quietly to Whisper as I step into the pen. I'm not sure he understands me, but he's uncharacteristically patient, waiting for me to adjust the straps and position of the reins and saddle.

The low morning sun glistens over the tops of the grass. It reminds me of how the sunrise looks reflecting on the water at the beach, fragmented and alive as the light rolls on the waves to shore. This might be a great time to head to the lake.

Where am I?

I blink, my eyes focusing on the trees at the thicket, the sunlight burning the back of my neck. I stagger back into the grass, lifting my hands to wipe the sweat from my forehead. That's when I see it.

Blood staining my hands, under my fingernails. Is it *my* blood?

My breath quickens as I look up. I scan the horizon, noting the broken grass that marks a path toward the woods. There's no sign that it's anyone else's blood other than my own.

I feel my waist, my arms. Everything is dull to the sensation of my own touch. Am I in shock?

How long have I been here?

The sun is already directly overhead. The last thing I remember is riding Whisper.

Oh God, what if it isn't my blood?

I spin around, my eyes focusing on Whisper. He seems okay. He stands under a tree at the edge of the thicket, beckoning and then stepping back. As I approach, he trots farther away.

I smell it before I see the red peeking through the dense trunks and leaves. The scent grows thicker in the air as I reach the trees. It's rancid. Thick.

I step over a fallen log and truly see it for the first time.

It's impossible to know for sure from the appearance, but the scraps of shirt identify the body as human. The corpse is torn, huge chunks of raw flesh missing or peeled away, exposing the meat underneath.

I try to feel the sensation through my body, to remind myself that I'm really here. I'm really staring down at a body. I'm really covered in blood. My legs begin to quake as I make my way to the clearing. Whisper is still standing close by, his hooves tentatively approaching.

I pull my phone from my jacket, my fingers leaving a bloody trail on the screen. I miss the right buttons a few times before I actually succeed in dialing. As soon as the phone stops ringing, I blurt it out, not even waiting for a greeting. "I need help."

"I called the game warden," Sheriff Larson says, eyeing me and then glancing at Kael.

I'd stood for nearly thirty minutes, absently stroking Whisper's coat and staring at the red mass nearby, before Larson arrived. "Game warden?"

Larson nods. "It's clearly a cougar attack."

I can still see the mauled body. "How can you be so sure? Who is that?"

"I'm not sure. As far as I know, no one has been reported missing or whatnot."

Kael shifts his weight, bringing his body closer to mine. "What happened?"

I focus on his face rather than the deputies moving behind him. An ambulance left with the body only a few moments ago, but they're still looking around the area. "I don't know."

Larson had looked at me the exact same way when I told him I didn't remember how I found the body. Now they both stare at me, their lips pressed into hard lines.

"How are you feeling?"

I sip my peppermint tea, focusing on the mismatched decor in Kael's kitchen to replace the images in my head. "I mean, it's hard to be at a hundred percent after seeing a mutilated corpse . . ."

Kael nods, leaning over the table toward me. "I know."

"Who would've been out there in your fields?"

He shakes his head. "I have no idea."

"Do you really think it was an animal?" I'd noticed the doubt on Larson's face even as he said it.

He frowns. "It's possible."

I set the mug down with a thud. "What kind of animal would gnaw away at someone like that and not eat any of it?"

"I don't know. But until we find out what happened, you shouldn't go out alone."

No argument there.

He runs a hand over his face. "In fact, I'm wondering if maybe you should stay here for a little while."

"I don't think so. Can you imagine what the yakety-yaks of this town would say if they found out I was staying at an unmarried man's house?"

A small smile forms on his lips. "I mean, it's definitely less of a scandal than you staying at a married man's home, right?"

"Nah, I'm pretty sure they're both equally guaranteed to get me to hell." I shift in my seat, studying the creases that have appeared along his forehead. "The motel is safer. It's farther from here."

He shakes his head. "Do you really care what people might say?"

"Me? No. But you should. You're the one who has to continue living here in harmony with the locals once I'm gone." Staying here with him would be wonderful, but also . . . complicated. More complicated than I want to take on at the moment. "Let's not panic. I'll just stay alert."

He opens his mouth and then shuts it. But he doesn't have to say anything. The intensity of his gaze says it all. He's rattled.

And so am I. But for a few different reasons. "Kael?" I squeeze the handle of my mug, nearly hard enough to break it off.

"Yes?"

I inhale, trying to form the sentence in my mind before I speak it. "I don't remember what happened today."

"You're just in shock."

"No. I blacked out before I called Larson. I don't remember getting close to the forest, and I don't know how long I was standing near the body." I lean away from him.

He furrows his brow, pausing for a while before asking the question. "Has this happened before?"

"Yes. From the night of the fire, I have these periods where I'll lose time occasionally." I honestly think it started before the fire, though. If

I had to pinpoint the first instance I'd lost time like that, it was probably the night Grandpa died.

"Why are you telling me this?"

I sigh. "I guess there's a part of me that's scared." It's the same fear that lurks at the back of my mind when I think about the fire and all that I can't remember from that night.

He meets my eyes. "Scared of what happened?"

Does he really not understand what I'm trying to say? "No. I'm scared that maybe I did something."

He shakes his head. "Come on, Lex. Whoever that is was long gone before you got there with Whisper."

"We don't know that, though, do we? At least not yet." Part of me was praying for an autopsy finding that he did die from an animal attack of some sort.

Kael takes a long drink from his cup. "How exactly could you have done *that* to him? And why? You don't even know who that was."

True.

"And there was no weapon on you."

"I had his blood on my hands."

"From checking on him," he says quickly. "You were just checking on him first. For all you knew, he could've still been alive."

"Maybe. But the simple truth is, I don't remember."

His lips twitch.

"What?"

"No . . . I just was thinking about how calm you were," he says, looking down at his hands. "If you really didn't remember anything, why weren't you more upset about finding that scene?"

There are two explanations really, aren't there? The first is, I had a hand in doing that to a human and on some level remembered it. I only vocalize the second option. "Honestly, when was the last time you cried?"

He shrugs. "I guess when my dad died. Why?"

"I haven't cried since I was ten." I shift in my seat. I can't remember the last time I have unloaded all this stuff on someone. Probably before Beth got sick when I told her what my psychiatrist said. "A few years ago, I found out I have some kind of problem that numbs me to certain things in my life. Sometimes my perception of reality is a little distorted, and I just emotionally shut down." The PTSD diagnosis was expected. According to Dr. Mattheson, the first child psychiatrist Beth brought me to, it made perfect sense that my mind would block out the specific memories of that night. It was also expected that the nightmares and flashbacks would cause me to have panic attacks at night. It wasn't until much later in my midtwenties that they began to realize I was having repeated dissociative episodes.

I search his expression for what I'd always feared seeing on Evan's face if I confessed this to him. But Kael doesn't look at me with anything other than compassion, his eyes soft as he surveys me.

His hand finds mine, and he awkwardly closes his fingers around mine. "How often does that happen?"

I let my skin soften under the touch of his coarse hands. "I don't know . . . when something big happens, I kind of just don't feel like it's really happening. I just kind of space out. Not often, but sometimes."

His grip tightens around my hand. "Now that you've mentioned it, I think I've noticed when you kind of . . . fade away sometimes."

Interesting. In nearly a year of dating Evan, he'd only prodded me, trying to bully me into crying when he felt I should be upset. Other than that, he'd never seemed to notice. "I don't know why I told all of that to you. You think I'm crazy now, right?"

He smiles. "Not at all. Apparently, I have a lot more faith in you than you have in yourself. It's ridiculous that you would even entertain the idea that you'd kill someone."

"Under the right circumstances, anyone is capable of killing."

He brushes his thumb over my knuckles. "Not you. And not like that."

I'm not so sure. But he did make a compelling point. I don't even know whose body that was. "It's getting late. I should head back."

"But—"

"I appreciate the concern, but I'm not sure what you think is going to happen exactly. That there's a murderer waiting for me in my room or something?" I slowly retract my hand, standing from the couch. "Besides, you said it was an animal, right?"

He rises beside me, rubbing the back of his neck. "I don't know. I just have a bad feeling. Weird things have been going on since you got back."

I grab my car keys from the table. "Correlation doesn't equal causation." Although right now in particular it's hard not to mistake the two.

He follows me to the door, the light in his eyes fading as I open it. He trails behind me and opens the car door for me.

"What did you mean you can tell when I 'fade'?"

He leans against the open door. "That's what you're worried about?" I can see from his slightly curled lips he means it as a joke, but his expression quickly turns neutral once the words leave his mouth.

"I'm just curious. How do you know?"

He sighs, glancing over to the fields between his house and the stables. "It's hard to describe, but it's like you don't really see me."

I nod. "For the record, I always see you, even if it doesn't seem like it."

He smiles. "Good."

I'm not sure of so much right now. But Kael, looking down at me, is completely real to me in this moment.

CHAPTER EIGHTEEN

The lingering sense of dread from the incident at the ranch hung over me all night.

I lay awake, sorting through the cloudy feelings and memories, not only about finding the body but also about my family. And about the farm.

Sometimes it feels like my mind is my greatest asset and my greatest enemy. Maybe my brain's ability to block out certain things has allowed me to survive, but at the expense of clarity and the truth.

Larson was absolutely right.

The sooner I can get out of here, the better. In a matter of days, I've somehow managed to get sucked in by rumors and completely lost track of the real reason I'm here. I need to get a handle on this whole farm thing.

I turn onto the dirt road toward Kael's place. If I can borrow his hose again, maybe I can finish cleaning up the milking stalls.

Maybe at this point I should just do what Janna says and level the place. I'm running out of time to sell. And it's not like I have many other hopes to get someone to buy this place.

As I start down the driveway toward the small house, I spot Butcher standing beside Kael. They're both standing on the porch. Kael looks like he just woke up; his hair is disheveled, and he's keeping his distance from Butcher.

Kael looks at my car and then quickly lowers his gaze to the ground. Butcher pats his shoulder before walking to his black SUV parked by the house.

I get out of my car right as he begins to pull out of the driveway, his gaze darting to me for a moment before he turns onto the road.

"What was that about?" I ask once I reach Kael.

He rubs the back of his neck. "Oh. Nothing."

It definitely isn't "nothing." "Why is Butcher out here? He's really trying to sell you on that Flamebearers bullshit?"

"Something like that. Coffee?" He opens the front door to the house and holds it for me.

The hose can wait. I need to know what Butcher could've said to make Kael look like someone just kicked him in the stomach. I step into the house.

He bounds to the coffee maker and pours into two mugs, handing one to me. He takes two huge gulps of coffee before looking at me again. He sets his mug down and runs a hand through his hair.

I narrow my eyes at him. "What was that really about with Butcher? What did he say to you?" Maybe I'm reading too much into it. Maybe Kael's just tired.

He sighs. "I'll tell you . . . but I don't want to talk about it after that."

"Okay."

"He wants to buy the ranch." His brows knit together, and he opens a cabinet by the stove, extracting a box of Pop-Tarts. It was hidden behind a container of Raisin Bran.

"What? Where does he get off—"

"Lex, please." He hands me a foil-wrapped packet and then opens one for himself.

"But—"

"I know." He bites off a corner. "It doesn't matter. Obviously, we're not selling. But it just . . ." He shakes his head and takes another bite.

"Is anyone bothering to ask how someone like a preacher in the middle of nowhere is acquiring all this land?"

Kael shakes his head. "Don't make this into something it isn't."

"I'm serious. His only job is full-time preacher, right? Where is he getting all this money from?"

"He owns businesses."

I raise my eyebrows. "The motel that has maybe two guests a month? You can't possibly believe that place is generating enough income for him to buy up this town piece by piece. If anything, it's losing money."

"What do you want me to say?"

"I want you to say it's weird . . . and that the only reasonable explanation is that he's taking advantage of the congregation."

He narrows his eyes. "That's a big accusation."

"I know. But it has to be true. There's no other way. And it's astounding to me that no one has cared to look into it before."

"People around here don't like to stir up trouble. You know that."

"If he's doing this, don't you think *he's* the one stirring up trouble?"

He sets the remaining Pop-Tart on the counter. "He used to be some bigwig at that oil-supply company over near the coast way before your family came to town. He probably just saved up a bunch of money."

"Enough money to support a failing motel and a convenience store, and buy up old ranches?"

He stares straight ahead at the wall.

"And, I hate to point this out, but you did say someone is stealing from the fire department."

He whips his head toward me. "I never said that."

"You did, but then you backtracked for some reason."

He rubs at one of his eyes. "Did you come here for something? Or you just saw Butcher's car and wanted to badger me about this?"

I know he's tired, but his tone still takes me off guard. "Maybe you should go back to bed and try waking up again on the right side."

"God, you're right. I'm sorry." He leans his head against the cabinet. "I shouldn't have snapped at you."

This whole problem is Kael's to deal with. I have my own messes to clean up. I cross my arms over my chest. I need to refocus, yet again. Less Butcher, more barn. "And for the record, I came over to steal your stable hose."

"You're planning to work on the barn today?"

"I figured I might as well do what I came here to do."

He sighs. "Maybe you should take it easy . . . after yesterday."

That's exactly why I need to keep pushing. I need to get out of here. I can still feel that wet, thick blood on my hands.

"How are you feeling about all of that?"

I shrug. "I don't know. I'm trying not to think about it at all." According to Evan, that's what I'm best at. Burying unpleasant thoughts.

CHAPTER NINETEEN

As much as I hate it, there's something therapeutic about manual labor. And hosing down empty stalls sure beats cleaning out ones filled with horse or cow shit. By the time I finish my work at the farm for the day, the sun is setting, and the only thing I can think about is that patty melt. I drive to the café right before closing and pick up two.

It's dark and raining when I arrive at his house. I grab the to-go boxes and exit the car. I can smell the faint scent of smoke in the air. Someone must be burning brush.

The porch light is on as if Kael's expecting me. I walk up the steps and knock on the door.

There's no response, not even a movement nearby to indicate he's getting ready to answer the door. I glance behind me, and I realize his truck isn't parked. Of course. He has a life completely separate from me. Why wouldn't he be out with friends? It's not like he would put his entire life on hold when I drove into town.

Ah well. No shame in eating alone.

I gaze across the pasture on the way to my car, and that's when I see it. Probably a quarter mile away at a neighbor's property, flashing lights revealing a thick screen of smoke, white against the black sky.

No.

I drop the boxes on the porch and sprint down the driveway, my hair flattening in the rain. The flames come into view once I pass the thick cluster of trees near the edge of the road. My feet pick up speed when I spot Kael's truck yards away from what used to be a barn but is now an inferno.

My steps slow as I near the fire, searching the shapes of the men spraying water from hoses toward the barn. None of them seem like Kael. I move forward but only inches before my feet freeze entirely. My body begins to tremble as I realize Kael isn't outside. I open my mouth to shout his name, but I can't move, hypnotized by the roaring flames.

I collapse to the ground, trying to focus on breathing, but I feel as though my throat is tightening. The surge of water on the fire causes it to shrink, columns of smoke and ash flying above the barn.

After a moment, another man emerges from the opposite side. Even in uniform with his mask in position, I recognize Kael's gait. He turns away from the other men and raises his mask.

"Lex!" Kael rushes over to me, tossing his helmet onto the grass beside us. His gloves are gone, and he cups my face in his bare hands. "What's wrong? Talk to me."

I shove against his shoulder, but I can't speak. I want to hurt him for making me feel this way.

He glances toward the barn and, seeing that the fire is under control, helps me to my feet. "Give me one second. Stay here." He jogs to the other men and helps one wind the enormous hose back onto the small fire engine.

By the time he returns to me, the jacket of his uniform swung over his arm and his truck keys in hand, anger has replaced the fear in my body.

"Did you walk here?" he asks, opening the passenger door for me.

I still haven't found my voice yet, but I sink onto the seat and slam the door closed.

"What happened?" he asks again as he appears in the cabin beside me and turns the keys in the ignition.

I look out the window as he reverses out of the dirt driveway. I can only manage to shake my head.

He reaches into the back seat of his truck and pulls out a sheepskin jacket, draping it over my shoulders. "Did you come here because of me? You were worried something happened?"

I shiver into his jacket. "I came to your house and you weren't there. And then I saw the smoke." I swallow.

"You must be freezing. Do you want me to take you to the motel?"

I push my drenched hair away from my forehead. "No."

"Okay." He's silent as he starts down the dark road. "I've been doing this for years," he says after several minutes.

"I know."

"And I go to training in Sacramento several times a year."

I sigh. "I know. Look, I just wanted to make sure you were okay. Is that so bad?"

"No. It's sweet," he says, glancing at me, his expression barely visible in the glow from the headlights ahead. "I just don't want you to ever feel scared like that again."

"I wasn't scared." But I was. I was scared that the fire was going to take everything away from me again. For a moment, I'd seen my future and what it would look like without Kael in it. I couldn't lose him along with everyone else.

He reaches over with one hand and grasps mine. "Good." He turns down the ranch driveway, and his little house appears past the barn. "Let me grab you something to change into," he says once we're inside. He throws his gear down by the door, a puddle of water appearing beneath it immediately. "The bathroom is down the hallway if you want to change or warm up or anything."

I accept the folded stack of T-shirt and gym shorts he hands me and close the door behind me. I squeeze my hair with the towel and then drape it over the edge of the bathtub. I tug on the borrowed clothes and emerge minutes later to see Kael wiping up the kitchen floor where his gear had been. His hair is still dripping.

"Can I throw these in the dryer?" I ask, holding up my wet and discarded jeans and sweater.

"Yeah, I'll take those for you." He takes the bundle and walks into the utility room. The machine whirs in the distance, and then he reappears. "So, do you—"

"Do you have anything to drink?" I have a feeling he was about to ask me if I wanted a ride back to the motel. And I hate that I don't want to leave just yet.

"Yeah, of course. No beer, but is whiskey okay?"

"Okay? I prefer it." I sink onto the sofa, debating whether to pull the nearby throw blanket over my shoulders when he joins me, handing me a tumbler glass of caramel-colored liquor.

He cranks the dial on the radiator across the room. "Are you warm enough?" he asks, sitting beside me.

I nod, taking a sip. "Yes, and the whiskey certainly doesn't hurt."

He drinks from his glass, his eyes drifting to look at me in his periphery.

He still smells like smoke. And damp wood. "Did anyone get hurt?" When I blink, the backs of my eyelids still burn as if I'm staring at the blaze.

"No. No people, no animals that didn't get away. And the rain really helped keep it at bay."

I nod.

"Lex," he says. "How do you feel about me?"

Right now? I'm angry with him. Angry that he would make me feel this way.

"Okay." He sets his glass on the coffee table. "I'll go first . . . I'm crazy about you."

The tension leaves my body.

His fingers lock into mine. He looks up at me, gauging my reaction. "Why did you really come back here?"

Is it possible on some level it was for him? I relax under the warmth of his touch. "You know why, and it definitely wasn't for you." I turn to him. "You're not supposed to be here anymore, Kael. I can't think of a worse place for you."

He studies me. "Really? Then where am I supposed to be?" His tone is playful, but I catch a hint of sadness in his eyes.

"I don't know. Teaching at a university somewhere. Or running some kind of tech start-up."

He shakes his head. "It was always going to be this way. Eventually, I was going to end up back here in Sola. This is my home." His hand retreats across my skin.

I forget what we're talking about. I can't lose this moment with him. I've thought about being with him again so many times after I left. "Don't stop." I cup my hand over his.

He leans forward, his lips brushing against mine before they meet. His hand leaves my stomach and strokes my hair as our kiss deepens. His other palm rests in the small of my back and guides me closer into his arms until I can feel the warmth of his chest through my shirt.

He pulls away, his face still so close to mine. "Is this—"

I kiss him again before he can finish the question. No. Maybe it's not okay. And maybe we shouldn't reignite all this, but I can't imagine letting him go. My hands search for the waistband of his pants, eagerly tugging them down along his hips. He does the same to my shorts, laying me down on my back and straddling me on the sofa before removing his pants entirely.

We don't speak again, but our eyes lock in the dim living room; his breath is falling on my neck as we move together, the leather beneath me creaking until we're both spent.

We're silent for several moments as I stroke his soft brown hair. "I've been wanting to do this since the day you came back," he says, resting his chin on my shoulder.

"You've been wanting to fuck me on your couch?"

He gazes down at me. "I'm serious. I've never stopped thinking about you, Lexi." I almost can't handle the intensity of how he's looking at me right now, the spark in his hazel eyes.

"I don't think I've ever really stopped thinking about you either."

He rolls onto his side, leaning against the back of the sofa, his feet still tangled with mine.

"But I still hate that you're still here," I say after a moment. "And I hate that you're a volunteer firefighter." I look at him to see his reaction.

He remains unmoved. "I'm sorry. But I'm in this community. I want to do my part. Besides, you know how important it is to have volunteers. We're out here on our own away from all help, and minutes matter."

"I don't care."

He dares to glance at me. "You can't possibly mean that. Especially not after—"

"No one in this town is going to let their neighbor die like that again, I assure you." The words almost burn my tongue on their way out. "Just out of curiosity, how many people have died in fires here since my family?"

He shakes his head but doesn't speak.

"Do you know the real reason Beth moved us away? It was eating me alive to stay here, everyone suddenly acting like they were there for me, when I knew they didn't give a shit. If anything, they were happy that the outsiders were gone." I take a deep breath, leaning away from his arm. "I tried to kill myself."

His head jerks up. "What?"

"A couple of times, actually. But the first time was when I was sixteen." I hate saying this last part. It probably feels like a betrayal, being with him and then hiding how much I didn't want to exist anymore. I always thought it must've seemed so sudden to him back then. We had finally gotten closer, and then I disappeared for a long weekend, and when I came back, I told him Beth was moving us out. When he asked me where I had been, I lied and said I was visiting my other grandparents in the city.

I can see immediately from the shift in his eyes that he's probably remembering all of this too. "I'm . . . I'm so sorry. I had no idea you were going through that."

Apparently neither had Beth. I never cried. I never talked about the fire. And no one else ever did, at least not while I was around. I was walking through the days numb, trapped in a world where my family seemingly never existed. And it turns out that when you're numb, somehow death doesn't seem so serious.

One day, I just wanted to feel something. Even if it ended everything.

As soon as I began to feel tired from the pills, I staggered to Beth and told her what I'd done. At the last minute, I was terrified of leaving her alone to find my cold, dead body in the morning. After I threw up by the front door, I remember nothing else from that night until I woke up in the hospital two towns away.

If I hadn't found her when I did, there likely wouldn't have been a chance. And she knew it. By the time I got released from the seventy-two-hour psychiatric hold, she had already put her little house near town up for sale. She looked at me differently after that. She began telling me little stories about my mom growing up and about how my parents met.

Leaving town helped. But then, a couple of years later, I hit rock bottom again. That's when the medication started.

Kael's hand wraps around mine. "I don't know what to say."

I realize I've been quiet for the past several moments. Neither do I. I've never told anyone before. "I don't know why I told you all of that. I guess being back here . . . all that resentment toward this town is coming up again."

"And earlier tonight probably didn't help any."

No, it didn't. I can't even articulate how strong the fear gripped me when I saw his truck pulled over in the field. I felt like I was a kid again, standing outside the inferno, my eyes burning, my body trembling. I lay my head against his shoulder. I've missed being this close to him.

CHAPTER TWENTY

The warmth of the sun on my face wakes me. When I open my eyes, Kael is lying beside me on the bed, his arm around my waist. His eyelids are shut but flutter softly underneath his tangle of brown waves. He must be dreaming. I'm glad we relocated to Kael's room, under the fleece blankets. Even with the radiator running in the other room, it's still chilly.

I stare up at the popcorn ceiling. It reminds me of my old room at Beth's house in Sola before we moved.

Rapid knocking on the other side of the small house makes me jump. Kael sits up immediately, blinking and raking a hand through his hair. He looks at me and smiles. "Good morning."

I sit up beside him, pulling the blanket up to my bare neck to keep from shivering. "Good morning, but someone's at your door."

The smile fades as another sharp whack sounds at the door. "Kael?" A light but urgent voice drifts through the house.

Kael springs from the bed. "Shit! It's my mom." He grabs his jeans and a T-shirt from the floor and tugs them on. "Stay here, I'll get rid of her." He nearly trips out of the bedroom in his hurry.

I survey the room, trying to remember where I left my clothes. Ah, they're probably sitting in the dryer still.

"Yes?" Kael's hoarse voice says after the sound of the front door squeaking open.

"Oh, there you are!" Mrs. McPheron exclaims.

"What's going on?" Kael can't hide the irritation in his tone.

"Well, I was getting ready to go to church, and I saw Lexi's car out front."

I hadn't even thought about the eyebrows that would raise at my car being parked in Kael's driveway all night. It's no one's damn business, but it'll still get town tongues wagging.

"Oh yeah, she came over for coffee," Kael says without missing a beat. It makes me wonder if he's had other girls over before and used the same excuse when his mom grills him about their cars.

"Well, she's up and about pretty early."

I carefully get off the bed, trying to avoid any creaking of the springs.

"Where is she?"

I fish around the floor for my borrowed clothes before I think better of it. Coming out of the back of the house in Kael's shirt and shorts is obviously going to give up the game. I wind a blanket over my body and go to the bedroom door. The way that the hall curves completely shields me from view of the front. I look across the hall. The only thing between me and the dryer in the utility room is a few feet.

"She's in the bathroom, Mom."

I tiptoe to the dryer, pulling my clothes on and checking to make sure everything is on in the right direction.

"Well, can I come in?" The clack of heels tells me she's already managed to forge a path past Kael in the entryway.

"Why?"

"I want to say hi and—"

"Good morning!" I manage to turn down the hallway as nonchalantly as possible.

Her eyes dart immediately to my clothes and then up to my hair. Thanks to the dryer, my clothes are unwrinkled. My hair's a little flat, but at least I managed to brush through it with my fingers. "Good morning, Lexi," she chirps, glancing at Kael next. "It's always good to see you."

Kael shifts his weight impatiently. "Have fun at church. We're going to get back to coffee."

Mrs. McPheron turns back to me and smiles. "I actually wanted to extend an invitation to you. Since you're already here, it seems like the perfect chance to accompany me to service."

Kael and I exchange a panicked glance. "We're not going," he says, leaning against the open door.

"Yeah, I'm not sure I'm up for that." Not now, not ever. It seems especially inappropriate to go after what we did last night.

Her lips falter. "I understand, but . . . I really think it would mean a lot for everyone to see you after our dear Beth passed. Everyone at church is asking about her and you."

"I'm not dressed for church." Beth would've grounded me for a week if I went to church looking like this as a teenager.

Her eyes scan me up and down. "Oh, well. We're a church, dear. Come as you are."

I force a smile to keep from rolling my eyes.

Kael opens his mouth but then closes it again, his jaw clenching.

"All right, well, I'll see you two at the chapel in a bit." Mrs. McPheron steps over the threshold onto the porch. "I'm going in early for choir practice, but service starts at nine o'clock." She raises her eyebrows at Kael. "Best get there ten minutes early just in case? Okay, bye!" She hurries away down the steps to her car.

Kael closes the door. "We're not going to church." He follows me into the kitchen, watching as I plug in his coffee maker.

"Might as well just get this over with." Mrs. McPheron has a point—Beth would probably want me to put in an appearance with her old friends and accept their condolences. And I owe her that at least.

2003

Something about the church always felt off to me, even as a child.

"I'm not going," I whispered, tugging against Aunt Beth's grip. I was the only one who was still by her side in the sanctuary other than Donnie. Natalie and Amy had eagerly scampered after the other preteens as the rest of the congregation settled into the pews.

Beth looked past me to Donnie.

He shrugged. "You didn't have to bring us here. I could've taken care of everyone." Earlier that morning, I'd woken to the sound of him arguing with Beth before she rushed into my room to get me dressed. When he'd seen my confused expression, he'd clenched his jaw and led me down the hall. He kicked away broken glass on the kitchen floor as we passed. It wasn't the first time I'd seen that type of mess. Sometimes at our old place, I'd find Donnie cleaning up the mess and frying up homemade doughnut holes for us in the morning. He never explained what happened, so eventually I stopped asking. We'd all watch cartoons until Mom and Dad came out of their room around noon.

I would've much preferred that over being loaded into Beth's van and driven here to the church.

Beth released my arm, and I inched closer to Donnie. She stared at him. "Look, this isn't exactly how I pictured my morning going, either, kid."

He sighed and took my hand. "Lexi, don't you want to meet some new friends?"

I shook my head.

The organ music from the stage halted, and a dark-haired man appeared behind the podium.

"Come on," Donnie muttered, steering me away from Beth and into the corridor behind the sanctuary. Once we made it to the fellowship hall, I dug my heels into the carpet. He stopped and looked down at me. "Lexi, *please*. Will you just go to the stupid kids' Bible study?" He crouched down and placed his hands on my shoulders.

"Where's Mom and Dad?" Everyone seemed so upset in the van on the way I hadn't dared to ask.

"They're sleeping." His gaze remained steady.

"Why do they get to sleep and we—"

"Lexi," he groaned. He turned and nodded to the group of kids lined up near a small room. "Mom and Dad just needed some time alone, and Aunt Beth wants you to make some friends here. I'm going to go to the youth group. I'll come find you as soon as church is over, okay?"

I stared at the giggling kids, a knot twisting in my stomach. Even though they had barely looked my way, it felt like they were laughing at me. "Can't I go with Nat and Amy?"

"Not yet." He straightened. "Come on, it'll be fun." He nudged me toward the kids, and I tentatively closed the distance.

Now they definitely were all looking at me. I quickly shuffled behind them into the classroom. A wrinkly lady towered over all of us and narrowed her eyes when they locked on me. "Hmm . . . the Blake girl?" She looked to a younger woman handing out small Bibles to kids as they sat cross-legged on the floor.

The young woman smiled at me. "Oh, hi, Lexi." She walked over to me and put one of the tiny Bibles in my hand. "I'm Mrs. McPheron. I know your mom. Why don't you have a seat over here?"

I edged closer to the group of kids.

"Kael, move over a little," the woman said.

The boy glanced at us and scooted across the floor, closer to the window. I sat down beside him, and he blushed.

"All right, everyone . . ." Mrs. McPheron made her way to the front of the room and stood beside the old lady, who was now perched on a rocking chair. "We're going to talk about Noah's ark today—"

I set down my book on the cold tile floor beside my folded legs. The boy next to me flipped through it absently as the woman continued speaking.

"She's that new girl." The whisper came from the two girls nearby. "My dad said her mom is . . ." The voice dropped as the girl leaned closer to her companion.

When I looked at them, they snickered.

My skin felt hot suddenly, and my hands were sticky as I pressed against the floor and got to my feet, bolting for the open door. The fellowship hall was empty, so I continued running until I reached the main corridor. I could hear the rumbling voice of the sermon in the sanctuary as I stood in the dark. Aunt Beth would be furious if I burst in there while the reverend was speaking.

As I caught my breath, a new sound came into focus. The clinking of glass. A light flickered in the kitchen, and I walked toward it.

Could it be Donnie? Maybe he didn't go to the youth group after all. I rounded the corner and froze.

In the dark, a figure stood beside the fridge. As I squinted, the face of a boy came into view. He turned to me. He surveyed me for a moment and then grinned. There was a wicked glint to it.

I stepped back.

"Hey," he called. His voice was almost as deep as Donnie's. He was nearly as tall as Donnie, too, but his hair was almost to his shoulders. "Shouldn't you be in Sunday school?"

He was much too young to be an adult, but still my heart began to race. He waved for me to come closer. It took only a moment for me to obey. "Are you hungry?" He stretches out a silver dish toward me. Even in the dark I could see all the tiny white rectangles at the bottom.

I *was* hungry. Beth and Donnie had loaded us all up without breakfast. "What is it?"

The boy grabbed one and put it in his mouth. "Just bread."

I looked up at him as I reached into the dish, and he nodded. I placed two on my tongue and frowned. It tasted just like paper. It was awful, but as my stomach grumbled, I grabbed a handful.

He smiled and opened the fridge with his free hand. From the small light, I caught a better glimpse of his face. The door closed, and he presented a new silver dish, this one with tiny clear cups all filled with a purple liquid. "Do you want juice?"

The bread had left my mouth rough and dry. I took one cup and poured it onto my tongue. It wasn't until I drank the second one that I puckered. There was an oddly bitter aftertaste. "What kind of juice is this?"

"Have one more."

I didn't like the way he was looking at me, but I was still thirsty, so I had four more.

"It's blood," the boy muttered and set both dishes on the counter in front of me.

My head felt a little fuzzy, and at his words, my stomach churned. "What?" I dropped the empty cups onto the floor and stepped back.

He shrugged. "Yeah, it's the blood of Jesus."

It suddenly felt difficult to stand straight. I slouched against the counter, my heart beating fast.

After a moment he laughed.

"Good Lord!" The gasp and the flash of the overhead light startled me awake.

I was still propped against the kitchen cabinets, empty plastic glasses scattered around me. The boy had disappeared, and Aunt Beth was standing over me.

She crouched down and scooped up the cups. "Lexi! What were you thinking?"

I looked up at her and started crying. "I drank blood," I wailed.

She shook her head and wrenched me to my feet.

A woman hurried in behind her and pursed her lips. "My word . . . she drank all this wine?" She yanked the cups away from Beth. "Like mother, like daughter," she whispered.

Beth shot her a look and dragged me out of the kitchen. The corridor was crowded now, and all of the adults stared down at me as we passed. My sobs grew louder as I realized the preacher's eyes were following us, his brow furrowed.

Beth didn't stop pulling me along until we were out in the parking lot. I could see in the daylight she had tears under her own eyes. "Lexi," she sighed. "Why would you do that? Why would you—"

"I was hungry." I struggled to catch my breath. "I want to go home. I want Mom and Dad."

Beth started crying even harder.

Out of the corner of my eye, I saw Donnie sprinting toward us.

Beth turned away from him as he took my hand. "I thought I told you to bring her to Sunday school."

He looked down at me, his eyes locking onto my stained lips. "I did. I—"

That was the only time I set foot in the church before the night of the fire.

CHAPTER TWENTY-ONE

The other day, out in the middle of nowhere, in the silence with Kael and Whisper . . . that's my church. Not this building filled with hollow people, staring at me as if I also died years ago.

I immediately regret coming in here.

I hadn't thought about how it would feel to see all these people again. They seemed so much larger than life back then, like these dark, towering villains. But now, they seem so small and deflated. I can't believe I ever cared what they thought.

Hypocrites, I can hear my dad say. Eventually he'd come to mutter the word under his breath after any encounter with a church member in town.

Kael lets out a long breath beside me as we negotiate through the crowd of interested but quiet young people and edge closer to the scowling elders across the room. "I feel like everyone knows."

"About last night?"

His cheeks redden behind a shy smile. It doesn't help optics that Kael insisted on going casual in solidarity with me. We're the only ones wearing T-shirts and jeans.

"They probably all do." Just from looking around, I can spot a few people who live on the other side of my family's land and need to drive directly by Kael's house to get to church. "Looks like your mom's been running damage control all morning." I nod over to her, cornered by a couple of withered old women at the entrance to the reception hall.

She's smiling, but her expression flickers when she sees us coming toward her. Her eyes zero in on Kael's simple clothes. The women she's talking to turn and follow her gaze, leering at us.

"Good morning, Mrs. Abernathy," Kael says, positioning himself in front of me like a shield and extending his hand.

Abernathy. Her husband's a deacon, or was at least. They were pushing eighty the last time I saw them, and she hasn't aged a day, no new smile lines around her signature scowl. My dad used to joke that her garden was so gorgeous because the flowers were terrified of disappointing her.

She limply shakes Kael's hand. "Why aren't you ever at service, young man?"

He sighs, but his friendly smile remains in place. "The ranch keeps me pretty busy on Sundays, ma'am." Good, solid excuse. It's the same one so many of the wives use here to hide the real reason their husbands don't want to come with them to church. "And Mrs. Brown, how are you?"

The other woman softens when Kael addresses her. "The sun is out, so I can't complain now, can I?"

Kael's mom reaches for me and clasps my hand between hers. "And of course you ladies remember Lexi."

Mrs. Brown's lower lip pokes out, and she tilts her head to the side. I suppose she's trying to look sympathetic. "We heard about sweet Beth. It's a shame she never got to come back."

Gaining distance from this place seemed to put this town in perspective for Beth. She'd never ventured far from Sola before, and the community we found in San Francisco brought her incredible comfort near the end. She forged more genuine friendships in the city than she ever did in her forty years of living here. "I'm sure she wishes she could be here."

Mrs. Abernathy purses her lips. "Hurry on up to your seats. The service is going to start any minute."

"Oh, you're right." Mrs. McPheron doesn't release me from her grasp as she ushers Kael and me toward the nearest pew.

Kael whispers in my ear, "Is it as fun as you remembered?"

I glare up at him. It's my own fault for agreeing to come here.

Reverend Butcher appears from a corridor and scans the congregation as he mounts the stairs to the pulpit, his bright-blue eyes punctuating a big, fake smile. A wolf leering hungrily at a herd of sheep. He opens his mouth to speak but pauses the second his gaze drifts to me. Everyone follows, turning in the ancient wood pews to stare at me. For a second, I feel like a teenager again, sitting beside Beth every Sunday and pretending not to hear the whispers.

"I apologize, everyone." Butcher laughs, lifting a hand toward me. "I'd like to take a second to welcome our own Lexi Rawlings back to town. It's good to see your face among the congregation."

Rawlings. Interesting choice to refer to my mom's maiden name. I don't respond, instead opting to stare down at my hands. Kael's mom reaches out and gives my arm a squeeze.

A few snickers echo through the church as the reverend continues, "It's actually wonderful timing. The Lord put on my heart, when I was preparing for today, reflections about restoration and returning home." The moment he begins speaking again, he recaptures the attention of the herd. This is how he's stayed at the head of the church. I remember now. That rich baritone voice and handsome face lend him a superficial charisma he doesn't deserve. "If you'll all join me in turning to Isaiah 61:1 . . ."

A cacophony of flipping pages bursts through the room, the air filling with the musty smell of Bibles opened only once a week.

Mrs. McPheron moves hers to the far end of her lap, so one half is draped over my thigh, presumably so both Kael and I can get a good look. I don't want to read along, but she's watching me, so I lean forward slightly.

"But we must also look to the promise of restoration in this text with special attention to from whom and through whom tangible healing, repair, and hope will come—"

Between the sound of his voice and the heat of the eyes on me, I feel that same suffocating sensation from when I was younger. His words wind around my neck like a noose. "I'm sorry," I mutter to Kael, pushing the Bible off my lap and standing from the pew. I squeeze out past Kael's knees into the aisle, my eyes locked onto the door.

"The Lord promises a return to hope and a new way of being if we accept our own past and the actions of those before us."

I push the door more forcefully than I intend to, letting it fall shut behind me with a thud. I walk toward Main Street, but I don't stop there. I'm not sure where I'm going, but I continue past the vacant storefronts. The entire street is silent, except for the engine of a lone truck rumbling behind me.

Kael lowers the driver's-side window as he approaches. "Hop in." He must've raced out to the parking lot to grab his truck as soon as I left. He probably expected this. I'm so damn predictable, aren't I?

A cool breeze brushes against my face, and I realize how red I must be. "No. You should go back. Your mom's going to be pissed."

"Forget about that. Come on, let's go."

I open the door and get into the cab beside him.

"Do you want to talk about it?"

I squeeze the side of the seat as he starts down the road. "No. I just . . . God, I hate this place. Doesn't it make you angry that Butcher is still the preacher?"

"You knew he'd be here."

I look out the window at the fields as we enter the highway. "There's just something about him that rubs me the wrong way. Not to mention he's a dick to Janna and her mom."

"You said that before, but . . . I'm not really sure what makes him so much worse than all the other people in there. He's not a bad guy."

I shake my head. "Never mind." I turn to him. "Why did you follow me out?"

"It's my fault that you were in the church in the first place. And it didn't really seem like that sermon was going in a great direction."

If we accept our own past and the actions of those before us. "Yeah, what was that about?"

"It doesn't matter," he says. "Want to drive somewhere?"

Maybe an afternoon away from Sola will do me good. "Your mom is going to hate me. I was so rude storming out like that."

He shrugs. "Eh, she'll live. She's the one who insisted we come, so it's really on her."

"Hmm."

He reaches over the center seat and takes my hand. "So? How about that drive?"

Being stuck in the city the past several years, I've missed driving around the remote north, through the redwoods that you can only see the trunks of on foggy days and the mountains meeting into the ocean. Just driving with Kael reminds me of my favorite memories from when I was younger. And there weren't many of those.

When we eventually arrive back at the ranch, Mrs. McPheron's car is missing.

Kael glances at his watch as we near the front door. "She probably already left for the evening service."

I snicker as he holds the door open for me. "What happens at the evening service?"

He shrugs and walks to the refrigerator. "More of the same minus the morning energy. Beer? Water?"

"Yes."

He glances at me over his shoulder. "Which one?"

"Surprise me."

He closes the fridge with two beers in tow. "I was thinking about it, and maybe you can find some leads at the auction."

"The livestock auction?"

"Yeah, I was planning to go tomorrow to look for a couple of calves," he says. "Maybe we can put a bug in some of these farmers' ears who are looking to expand."

I'm not sure I have it in me to spend hours in that cramped building surrounded by sweaty farmers and stinky cows. The one and only time I went to the auction was traumatizing. Beth and I had just eaten steak in the adjoining restaurant before we walked to the live auction and watched the cows from my family's farm get sold. I'm pretty sure my face went entirely white when I put two and two together. But maybe Kael's right. If anyone is looking for extra land, it'll be the livestock crowd. "So you're getting some cows now?"

He shrugs. "I'm willing to try anything. I've got a couple of stallions still out on loan with a breeder to get some money to put back into the ranch, but raising heifers is more of a sure thing."

"I guess, but you're definitely getting more money from a stud fee."

"Horses are a luxury right now," he says, running a hand over his windblown hair. We kept the windows rolled down the entirety of our drive. "Nobody around here is buying Arabians much these days. They're mostly getting sold off overseas to random millionaires for competitions."

It's probably because they're so expensive to train. An Arabian horse's default is to be stubborn and defiant. Whisper's a perfect example. My family didn't realize his strongheadedness could be dangerous, and so we mostly left him to his own devices. But growing older in Mr. and Mrs. McPheron's care has clearly done him good. "Aren't people still using Arabians in shows?" The last dressage show I went to with his mom, it was almost nothing but Arabian horses competing.

"Well, sure. But to be honest, there's more money in farrier work at those shows than selling foals and fillies to compete." He sits at the kitchen table, and I do the same. "You have an eye for cows. Maybe you can help me figure out which one is worth getting."

I take a sip from my bottle. "No. *Beth* had an eye for cows. I can tell you which one is cuter, if that helps."

He smiles. "Sure, why not? If the calf is too much of a handful, maybe I can get someone to buy it on cuteness alone."

I nod. "Okay. Let's give it a try." Anything to get out of here faster.

CHAPTER TWENTY-TWO

The scent reaches down into my stomach. Soil and dust mixed with the distant tang of manure.

I go closer to Kael, his back serving as a guard against all the people peering at me as we enter the auction room. I'm not sure which place is worse: here or the church.

An old man in the corner straightens and surveys me. Kael gives him a nod and turns to me. "Do you know the Norwoods?"

I shake my head.

He glances a few rows behind us. "I see Benny Norwood over there. Want me to introduce you? They own some land on the opposite side of the railroad tracks."

I look to where he indicated. A man with a handlebar mustache chews on his bottom lip and glares down at his phone, punching his index finger rhythmically against the screen. "Uh, sure. That's why I'm here, I guess."

Kael grins and nudges my arm. "Yes, that is why you came, grudgingly. Let's give it a shot." He leans a little over the empty seat behind us. "Hey, Benny."

The man jerks up and looks at Kael, his gaze drifting to me.

"I want to introduce you to one of our neighbors," Kael says, reaching over and shaking Benny's hand.

Benny stands up. "Oh. Neighbor?"

"Yes. She owns the farm right across from ours."

Benny's eyes darken. "The Rawlings land?"

Kael glances at me. "Yes. She's been leasing it on and off for grazing, but she's looking to sell it for good now."

Benny softens a little. "You belong to Beth, don't you?"

I shrug. I guess I know what he means.

"It's a shame. I heard she passed away a little bit ago. I was sorry to hear that."

"Thank you." I try to recall if I've ever heard Beth mention this man. He seems like one of the quiet ranchers I used to see come in and out of the feed store without a word.

He rubs the back of his neck. "We're not really looking for more land right now. With the boys gone, I've got too much to handle as it is."

"That's fine," I say. "I get it." I have no idea which "boys" he's referring to, but I assume he means his kids. "If you think of anyone, please send them my way . . . or Kael's." Kael and I turn back to the pen ahead of us where the cattle will be brought out soon. "Thanks for trying."

"We're not done yet." He fidgets with the auction number in his hands. "We're just spreading the word a little."

"What brings you here tonight?" One of the old deacons, Mr. Carmichael, walks into my view and leans back against the railing. "Can't imagine you're here to buy."

"You're right. I'm here to sell."

He raises his eyebrows.

Kael steps in. "Are you in the market for some land?"

Carmichael looks at me and chuckles. "No, I don't suppose I am. Bad luck and all that."

Kael's face reddens, but before he can open his mouth, I put a hand on his arm.

"For sure, we wouldn't want you spreading that to my farm."

Carmichael nods and then pauses.

"I think the auction's about to start," I say, pointing past him to the pen.

He scurries back to his corner.

"God, he's insufferable," I mutter to Kael.

He shakes his head. "Even worse, he's dumb as dog shit."

The small crowd behind us goes quiet as the auctioneer appears in the booth behind the pen. He taps the microphone and then adjusts his cowboy hat.

"So, we're looking for a calf, right?" I whisper.

"Yes, a heifer calf I think would be good."

We watch as the small livestock, the chickens and goats, come and go. A few men and women drift out of the room to claim their buys. Right as they bring out the first calf, someone appears two seats down from me.

"This one looks good, right?" Kael asks, nodding to the calf in the pen.

"Sure, she's adorable."

Kael laughs and raises his number as the auctioneer calls out the first bid at one hundred dollars.

"Hundred dollars. Can I get a hundred fifty?" the auctioneer calls. After a moment, he looks beside me. "We have one hundred and fifty dollars. Two hundred, anybody?"

I turn to the person in the seat near me. It's Butcher. He leans back in his seat and places his number on his lap. "What's he doing here?"

Kael shifts. "He keeps some cows in the pasture behind the rectory."

Of course he does.

Kael lifts his number again.

"Wonderful! We have two hundred dollars. Can I get two fifty?"

I glare at Butcher. Two hundred dollars is already more than what that calf is worth.

He ignores my stare and raises his number.

"Two fifty! We have two hundred and fifty dollars. Three hundred?"

Kael would be crazy to bid three hundred. I look at him, and he shrugs.

"Sold for two hundred and fifty!"

Kael slumps a little in his seat. The next calf they bring out, he looks at me. "I'm going to bid on that one."

"You don't want a steer, Kael."

"He said this is the last calf for today." He raises his number. He seems desperate to buy today. Maybe things at the ranch are even worse than he made it sound. He's the only bid for the steer.

"Sold for one hundred!"

Kael relaxes a little. "Are you going to talk to anyone else about the farm?"

I glance around the room and shake my head. "I think I'd rather get stomped on by that bull they're bringing out right now."

He grins. "Okay, I'll go ahead and pick my steer up from the back so we can head out. Meet me out front in ten?"

I nod, and he gets up from his seat. After he leaves, Butcher shoots me a look and then stands up as well, walking down the rest of the emptying aisle to the door.

I follow after him, drawing farther away from the crowd as they begin to stand. Once I reach the hallway, he's disappeared from sight.

"You can't just ignore me, Tom." His whispered but harsh voice carries.

I peer around the corner to see him facing the wall, his phone to his ear.

"I need to talk to you *immediately*. Call me back." He lowers the phone and then, after a minute, glances over his shoulder at me. "Are you looking for me?"

I continue until I can see him standing there, his back obscuring part of the parking lot from view. Other than the light of one flickering streetlamp, outside is entirely dark. "Yes," I say.

He stares at me. "Well then? What can I do for you?"

"You have some nerve."

He raises his eyebrows. "Oh? How so?"

"Who goes around flaunting offers to buy people's land out from under them?"

He smirks. "I see. This is because I outbid the McPheron boy on that calf?"

"No. It's about you throwing your money around to try to take their ranch. He's not selling. He doesn't need an offer. Especially not from you."

"I was throwing him a lifeline," he says. "That place has been losing money since his father was running it. It's not the kid's fault his old man wasn't savvy enough to do what was needed. Adele's basically already handed me the deed."

"What?" Kael's mom wants to sell?

He nods. "She doesn't need the trouble any more than he does. She wanted me to try to reason with him, but it's inevitable at this point." He glances past me toward the auction hall. "So, I suppose you two are an item now?"

"Me and Kael? No." I haven't really wanted to give it much thought. It seems pointless since it's only a matter of time before I leave here.

"Then I'm not sure he needs you acting as his guard dog."

Maybe he has a point. But it pisses me off even more. "How does a preacher acquire so much money that he can buy half the town anyway?"

He holds my gaze but says nothing.

Maybe I've struck a nerve. "You're taking advantage of people who want to believe in whatever it is you're shilling."

He scoffs. "You sound like Paul."

Good. "You don't know anything about him. Don't pretend like you do," I say.

"I ran into him a lot back then, Lexi. He was always stirring up some kind of problem around here. Looking for trouble where there wasn't any. Does my presence offend you somehow?"

Yes. "Not particularly." God, even now, I can't seem to stand up to him. I can't get into trouble with the "grown-ups" anymore for running my mouth, but something about him scares me.

"Why did you run out of the service the other day?"

I cross my arms over my chest. "I have a low tolerance for bullshit these days."

"Hmm." He narrows his eyes. "Paul had hardened his heart against anything he couldn't understand. Don't make the same mistake." I watch him turn around and walk toward his SUV parked at the front of the lot, where a man finishes latching his trailer back into place behind a baying calf.

I expected to have some sense of satisfaction about confronting him, but I feel nothing. Should I tell Kael that his mom actually would love to sell their ranch to Butcher?

The clatter of boots sounds in the distant auction room. Kael's probably already finished loading up his steer by now. It'll be easier to meet him around back. I start in the opposite direction that Butcher went, following the curve of the dark building toward the smell of hay and damp fur. There's some movement in the parking lot behind me as cowboys chatter and truck doors slam. As the solid tin wall turns into holding corrals, I realize how still it is out here right now. Most everyone must've already picked up their cattle. All the pens to my right are empty from what I can see.

I pick up the pace. Only a few moments pass before a small snap sounds, and I freeze. It's almost impossible to make out in the darkness, but a man is standing yards ahead of me. He doesn't move. I can't tell if his back is to me or if he's staring at me, but something about the way he stands causes my heart to race.

I've seen him before.

"Lex? Lex!"

I'm first aware of the hay stabbing my palms. I can't remember how long I've been sitting here, my knees to the ground as I crouch in the pen, the cold metal bars pressing against the back of my shirt.

Kael steps out of the darkness by the building, his hat visible from the light of his truck's headlights behind him. "Lexi!"

I open my mouth but hesitate; my body feels permanent here. Like this is the only safe space. I swallow. "I'm here!" I grip one of the bars and try to stand but nearly collapse as pins and needles stab my legs.

Kael turns in my direction and approaches the pen. "What are you doing in there?" He unlatches the gate and runs toward me, putting his arm around my shoulder as I bang against my legs in an attempt to revive them.

I think about the man standing in the shadows. The familiar stance. "I was coming to find you."

He furrows his brow. "In here? I've been looking for you. I was calling your name. Didn't you hear me?"

The pain dissipates from my legs, and I straighten. "I, um . . ." To be honest, I'm not entirely sure what I was doing. I can only assume I came here to hide. But he's already looking at me with concern. I can't imagine telling him I darted from a shadowy figure I potentially may have imagined will help matters. "Did you get your calf?" I start toward the gate, my hands still shaking.

CHAPTER TWENTY-THREE

I'd never even told Beth about the ghost. About the voices at night. Or about what I saw the night Grandpa died. How can I say it to Kael?

Kael's been quiet since we got in the truck. I feel like I should break the tension, but I don't really know what to say.

"That was weird earlier." I shake my head. "I just got turned around."

He doesn't believe me. And I don't blame him. "I'm sorry there weren't any good leads back there."

"No, it's okay," I say. "It was a good thought."

He takes his eyes off the road for a second to glance at me. "Are you finally going to tell me what the deal is between you and the reverend?"

"What do you mean?"

"I saw the way you looked at him. And it seemed like you wanted to punch him when you saw him at the ranch. What gives?"

I stare out the window. "He's not a good guy. And I don't like that he's trying to buy the ranch. That's all."

He doesn't say anything.

"Kael?" I turn to him. "Your mom doesn't want to get rid of the ranch, does she?"

A small crease between his eyebrows appears. "What? No. Of course not."

"Did you tell her about Reverend Butcher's offer?"

He shrugs. "What's the point? She would never want to sell the place." I can tell by the flicker in his eyes that he's not entirely convinced of the truth of this statement.

"It sounds like Butcher already made the offer to your mom, and she wants to take it."

His body stiffens.

"He's always plotting something underhanded. Doesn't that bother you?"

His grip tightens around the steering wheel as we pull into the driveway.

He only meets my eyes again once he's unloaded the calf into the barn for the night. "It's late. Will you stay here tonight?"

"So forward of you. What about your small-town values?" I tease.

A tiny glimmer of a smile cracks through his tired expression. "You're a bad influence, I guess."

"I'll head back to the motel. I need to shower off this cattle smell."

Something about that triggers a look from him. He steps toward me and pulls away a stray piece of hay from my sleeve. It must've been stuck to me from the cattle pen. I can tell he wants to press me further about the episode, but instead he just frowns. "Stay. There's a perfectly good shower here."

"Is that an invitation?"

A true grin forms on his lips now. "Do you want it to be?"

Yes. If anything can take my mind off of the unsettling events earlier tonight, this would be it. I take his hands and lead him down the hallway to the bathroom. The space is so small that I leave the door open instead of closing it behind him before I lift his cap off the top of his head. I run my fingers through his hair, and the brown locks spring back to life.

His arms wrap around my waist, and he pulls me toward him. The way he looks at me sends a jolt through my chest.

I tug at the hem of his T-shirt. He raises his arms, and I lift it off over his head before I discard my own shirt beside his on the floor.

He follows me toward the shower, stooping to kiss my neck as I reach in and turn on the faucet. He unfastens my jeans and I loosen his belt buckle. We step under the water, the heat only intensifying the temperature of our skin. He pins me against the wall, droplets gathering between our faces as our lips meet.

Whatever this feeling is—love, desire, maybe just lust—it's so good that I know I'm going to miss it when I leave. I pull away to look at him as we move together under the water, and I hold his face between my hands. He's so gorgeous. He's wasted in a place like this.

When we finally break apart, he leans his head against my shoulder. "What are you doing to me?" he breathes into my ear. His fingers trail along my waist and down my leg.

"Me? This was your idea."

He laughs and looks at me under his wet mess of hair. "Not just this. All the time. You're driving me crazy. I can't stop thinking about you, Lex."

Good. "I'm not sure I understand the problem."

He glances away from me and turns the faucet off. He steps out and hands me a towel before grabbing one for himself. He wraps it around his waist, his hair dripping onto the wood floor.

"What's wrong?" I ask, winding the towel around my body.

He stares at me and then shakes his head. "Nothing. I should just enjoy this while it lasts, right? Before you leave again."

My heart sinks. I open my mouth, but I can't speak.

He turns and walks out.

I follow him into the bedroom. "What do you want me to say?"

He grabs a T-shirt from the top of his dresser and pulls it over his bare chest. "I don't know." He opens a drawer and hands me a set of shorts and a shirt.

I take the clothes and toss them on the bed. "I can't stay here forever."

He avoids my gaze. "I know. Believe me, I *know* you can't stand this place. You never let me forget it."

I cross my arms. "There's no reason you have to stay here. Your mom wants to get rid of the ranch, so let her. Then there will be nothing keeping you here."

"I can't just leave. Most people can't move on that easily," he says, his muscles tensing as if he's defending himself from a blow. "My father dedicated his whole life to this town and this ranch. And besides, aren't you the one who practically wanted to deck Butcher when you found out he made an offer?"

As much as I hate the thought of Butcher getting his way, even more horrible is the idea of Kael toiling away on this dried-up land until he dies. "You can't hold on to things forever, Kael."

He sinks onto the edge of the bed and meets my gaze. "I'm not ready to give up yet." He looks broken even as he says it. I remember his look of desperation at the auction earlier.

"How bad is it?"

He sighs and hangs his head. "We're not just behind on income . . . there's a lot of debt. *I* have a lot of debt tied up in this place."

I sit down beside him. "I don't understand. Why you? Wouldn't your mom be able to take out a loan for the ranch?"

He glances at me. "She did. We put this place up as collateral for the biggest loan. But it wasn't enough to keep us going. I took out as much as they'd let me on my own a few years ago."

"How much?"

"Too much."

He must've just been around twenty-five at the time. It's hard to believe they'd loan out too much to someone so young without good cause, but the look on his face seems to suggest otherwise. "Why would you do that? Does your mom know?"

He shakes his head. "I don't want her to worry about it."

My stomach twists. "What did Butcher offer?"

"He wants to buy it outright. We could pay off the loans and have a little extra."

I place my hand on his. "Kael, you have to take the deal."

He pulls away.

"You shouldn't be in this position . . . it's definitely not what your dad would've wanted for either of you."

"He would've done whatever it took to save this place."

"Maybe," I say. "But he wouldn't have asked you to do the same."

He shakes his head. "You don't know what you're talking about."

"I knew your dad, Kael. And I can guarantee that he didn't want you to have piles of debt hanging over your head before you even turn thirty. He'd be heartbroken."

He stands up suddenly. "Let's stop talking about this, okay? I'm too tired to argue with you right now."

"I wasn't arguing with you. I was just—"

"Please?" His eyes plead with me.

"Okay." I stare down at the borrowed clothes in my lap. "I should go."

"No." He touches my shoulder. "I want you to stay."

I stand beside him and get dressed as he steps out and brushes his teeth across the hall.

He flashes a weak smile at me when he returns. "Do you need some water or anything?"

"No. I'm good."

He nods and slides underneath the sheets, glancing at me expectantly.

I settle onto the bed next to him. I can feel him looking at me from the corner of his eye.

"I'm sorry . . . it's not easy for me to talk about all of that."

"I know." And I do. But it's hard to accept that Kael is deeper in this trap than I knew. Once Sola has a firm grip on you, you can never get out.

A dull thud wakes me. I lay in the dark bed for a moment, turning to look at Kael beside me. He doesn't stir, his breathing deep and even.

I sit up as another bang sounds. It comes again after a few seconds, from outside.

I swing my legs over the side of the bed. I glance back at Kael for a moment before walking out of the room, toward the front door. My body feels light, like I'm not really inside of it, moving it.

I reach the living room and a light catches my attention out of the corner of my eye. A light from the barn.

I think back to Kael's story. About his father's ghost. I think about what I didn't tell him as he recounted the story. That I've seen a shadow too.

My hand doesn't feel like it's attached to my body as I turn the doorknob and walk onto the porch.

There isn't much noise coming from the barn other than a few low snorts from the horses. I stare at the path the barn light has formed along the grass outside. The stream of light is solid, no movement breaking through it.

I step onto the grass, the dirt cold and damp on the bottoms of my bare feet. My ears absorb every sound in the night air as I move forward. The screech of crickets. The soft slop of hooves into wet soil.

My heart slows as I reach the entrance. All the horses are awake in the corral, but only Whisper is visibly agitated and nodding his head.

The scene feels too familiar, and my eyes search the dark space beyond where the overhead light reaches in the barn, seeking the shadow from years ago. The one I saw earlier tonight.

My feet carry me inside, my gaze swiveling frantically between the shadows, imagining a shape in each one of them. I reach Whisper and put my back to him against the fence.

Nothing in my view moves.

The tension eases from my body, and for the first time I ask myself the question I should have before leaving the house.

What would I have done if I *had* seen the ghost?

2003

I remember when my grandfather's dog had puppies. Lady was still relatively young since Grandpa had gotten her to replace his original farm dog, Barker.

Dad was the first one to notice. "Looks like we're going to have puppies," he'd said, seemingly at random. But all of our young eyes followed his to see Lady waddling into the kitchen that morning.

We'd seen her here and there over the weeks but noticed only then how much more rotund she'd become.

I'd been thrilled at the idea of having puppies, but Mom and Dad made it clear to all of us that we couldn't possibly raise all of them. In theory that was fine, but when Lady finally had her babies, I became someone else. That was when Dad amended his earlier statement to "we can only keep one."

I was a devoted puppy nurse, sneaking out to the barn in regular intervals to check on them before their eyes had even opened. One morning, I dragged myself out of bed just after midnight. The chill of my feet hitting the wood floor shocked me awake. I tiptoed past Natalie's and Donnie's rooms to the staircase, taking them two steps at a time. I twisted the lock and slowly opened the screen door so it wouldn't make its usual violent squeak.

Once I closed it behind me, I switched on my flashlight. It didn't occur to me until my foot left the porch that the barn light was already on. I halted in my tracks.

I never left the light on. There was a heat lamp Dad had helped me to set up for the puppies that stayed on, but I only ever used my flashlight on my late-night check-ups. I peered into the darkness on either side of the barn, the wind rattling through the tall grass nearby.

Only when the wind subsided, I heard the faint but frantic whimpers. I ran into the barn; the heat lamp had been cast aside, and Lady was crying, a horrible, strained moan I'd never heard from an animal before. She looked at me from beside a bucket that was filled with water. All five puppies splashed and paddled blindly, their cries growing higher and more desperate.

I dropped my flashlight and knelt in front of the bucket, fishing them out, one in each hand, and placing them onto the hay bed we'd made for them. The last one, Rocky, had stopped paddling by the time I reached him. His body was still warm, his tiny pulse panicked against my fingers. Lady curled around her babies immediately.

My body trembled as I picked up the heat lamp and directed it toward the litter. I grabbed the nearby blankets and dried off each puppy gently, the question turning over and over again in my mind.

How?

A hand gently shook me awake. I opened my eyes to find Donnie crouched beside me, his brow furrowed as he surveyed the puppies. He and Dad were always the first up in the morning. The sun was barely peering through the opening of the barn, and Donnie's overalls were already covered in dirt. "What are you doing out here?"

I rubbed my eyes, leaning away from the hay bale jabbing me in the back. I'd been scared to leave the puppies alone after the water incident, so I'd sat vigil with them. "Someone put the puppies in the water last night."

He frowned and extended his hand to help me to my feet.

I stood, shaking the stray bits of hay off my legs and glancing at the sleeping puppies nestled against Lady. "Where's Rocky?"

Donnie pressed lightly against my back, directing me to the barn door. "Go get some sleep, Lex."

I looked over my shoulder at Donnie petting Lady's head.

I didn't think to ask about Rocky again until I came downstairs later after almost everyone had finished breakfast. Natalie and Amy were watching *Animaniacs* in the room next to us, but Mom, Dad, and Donnie all turned to look at me as I approached the kitchen table.

"Lexi, come sit down." Mom patted the table.

I'd nearly passed out once I'd returned to the house after Donnie woke me, but my eyes were still a little blurry. "What's wrong?" I sank into the chair beside Donnie.

Mom and Dad exchanged a look. "Your brother told us that you were sleeping in the barn last night," she said.

I rubbed my eyes. "I went to check on the puppies, and someone put them in water. I wanted to make sure they were okay the rest of the night."

"Did you see Grandpa go into the barn?" Mom asked, her brows knitted together.

"No," I said. "Why?"

Mom leaned across the table and clasped my hand. "Grandpa is not well, and sometimes he does things by accident. Did you see him put the puppies in the water?"

I looked at Dad. "Why would Grandpa put the puppies in the water? They could have drowned."

Mom sighed. "He doesn't want to hurt them, Sweetie. But sometimes . . . he's not thinking clearly. He's sick."

I pulled my hand away from her. Grandpa? Grandpa loved the puppies. Whenever I brought one in the house, he held it close to his chest, and sometimes he liked to give Peach a ride in his shirt pocket. "Grandpa's sick?" The backs of my eyes began to sting.

Donnie tugged lightly on the ends of my hair. "It's okay, Lex. We can just find a new place to keep the puppies."

Dad gave me a small smile. "Maybe you can keep them in your room for a little while, Lexi? Would you like that?"

I wiped at my eyes. "Yeah."

"Okay," Dad said. "Why don't you go up to your room and get some sleep? We'll feed the puppies this morning."

I pushed away from the table and walked around the corner past the kitchen.

"She's going to be so sad when she finds out," Donnie said.

Mom sniffed. "I know." Her voice trembled.

CHAPTER TWENTY-FOUR

The next morning, I leave with a muttered whisper to Kael before he can fully wake up.

After turning off the light in the barn and then returning to bed, I couldn't fall asleep. I continued listening to every sound in the night, expecting to hear that voice. To see the shadow appear again.

Mrs. McPheron is kneeling outside her flower bed at the front of the driveway as I approach. She waves at me before I can make it to my car. Great, if she had any doubts that Kael and I were sleeping together, she surely knows now.

"I wanted to talk to you the other day. About church." She tugs back the wide brim of her sun hat. "Why did you rush out of there in a hurry? Is everything okay?"

I knew this was coming. "Yes, I'm sorry about that," I say. "The sermon was a little too pointed for me."

She squints up at me briefly before returning to packing the dirt around the small bulb. "Pointed, dear?"

I shouldn't have said anything. Why can't I ever just leave well enough alone? I always just have to poke and poke and—"Yeah, it seemed like a lot of nonsense about returning home and forgiving shit others have put you through."

She stops patting the earth. "And what exactly makes you think that applies to you? What do you think others here have put you through?"

I hold her gaze. "You and Mr. McPheron were always very kind to me, but the rest of this town . . . they didn't make my family feel welcome."

"I think everyone was doing their best. Your mother hurt a lot of people, Lexi."

By leaving this town? Hardly an unforgivable offense, in my book.

"We have long memories here." She shakes her head, stabbing her trowel into the topsoil and standing. "And although it's maybe not fair, seeing you is like seeing Emma. It brings up a lot of memories of what she was caught up in."

Caught up in? "What do you mean?"

She pulls off one glove and then the other. "I'm not going to speak ill of your mother, Lexi. And it doesn't matter. Not now."

A knot begins to form in my stomach. What could she possibly be referring to? "You all but said it still matters. So what did my mom do? Is it that much of a crime that she married an outsider?"

Her eyebrows raise. "Your father has nothing to do with it. But anyway, you're right. I shouldn't have said anything. I just want you to know it isn't a reflection of how we feel about *you*."

I watch as she walks toward the house.

Isn't it odd to be planting bulbs so early in the morning? Part of me wonders if Mrs. McPheron was waiting for me to sneak out. I shake my head and orient my gaze on the road ahead. As the sky turns from black to a pale gray, I realize just how empty the road is.

Sometimes, in moments like these, I think about how easy it could be. To simply not exist. Right now, I could let go of the steering wheel or merely close my eyes and hit, well, anything. Or I could dive below the surface of the lake at the ranch and just not come up.

The idea is sad maybe, but *I* wouldn't be around to deal with it. I wouldn't be around to deal with anything ever again, like selling the farm, like missing too many people. And if I'm wrong and there is an afterlife, I would know with absolute certainty what it looks like. And if I'm right and there's nothing, I won't care because I will simply cease to be.

The thoughts creep in that easily. It's not that I want to die. But sometimes, I don't exactly *want* to live. Beyond that, it feels as though my mind is at odds with itself about whether this whole living thing is worth it. Sometimes I worry that the part of my brain that wants to self-destruct will take over one day, and I'll be dead before I can realize what's happening. It's hard to explain.

I shift in my seat and exhale. If I were dead, though, I wouldn't be around to feel the sun on my skin. I wouldn't be able to touch the soft grit of Whisper's fur. I wouldn't be able to look into Kael's eyes ever again. I guess I like my job well enough. And I'd miss out on eating so much great food.

It's a simple exercise that I've learned over the years. I think it was something a doctor told me about after my second attempt. For some reason, it helps to think about what a living Lex can do that a dead Lex wouldn't.

But a dead Lex wouldn't need to think about the ghost, about the tapes. Or that horrific, familiar scream on the phone. Or the body in the field.

My grip on the steering wheel tenses as I spot the Ringer Bros. sign up ahead.

Coming here has brought nothing but darkness. And confusion. But maybe there are answers somewhere if I go looking far enough for them.

The store always opens early for farmers and commuters to grab coffee, but there's no way to know if Janna is in. I'm banking on the idea that she never outgrew her teenage insomnia and she hasn't slept since yesterday.

Apparently I was right. She's standing behind the counter, her eyes focused intently on a book between her hands.

"Hey," I say, lightly tapping the countertop.

She looks up and blinks. "Oh. What are you doing here so early?"

Great question. And apparently, that's all I have right now—questions. "I, uh, figured I'd take you up on that candle session."

She stares at me. Maybe she thinks I'm mocking her. "Why?"

"Honestly?" I sigh. "I figured this might help me figure things out."

She raises an eyebrow. "I don't think it's a good idea."

"I can't believe you. *Now* you don't think it's a good idea? You didn't have any problems shoving the candle at me a few days ago."

She shakes her head. "You want to do it for the wrong reasons."

"The wrong reasons? What's the right reason?"

She grabs her book and moves out from behind the counter. "This is a *spiritual* practice, not psychological."

I follow her toward the back. "Why can't it mean one thing to you and another to me?"

She pauses, glancing back at me. "You really want to do this?"

I have no idea. But maybe it'll trigger something. Maybe there's a memory buried deep about the ghost. Maybe it's something I'm ready to understand now. "Yes."

She wrinkles her lips and then nods for me to follow her. She leads me to the back door and locks it behind us after we walk out. "What exactly are you trying to 'figure out'?"

"I just want to clear my thoughts," I say. I don't really feel like disclosing my entire psychiatric history to Janna. The morning light illuminates the dirt path through a thin patch of trees that opens to a small rust-colored house. "I've had a lot of memory-lapse problems and—" Dissociation. According to my doctor, it's my mind's fun little way of protecting a brain that was steeped in cortisol and adrenaline far too young. When I think back to the night of the fire, it was the first time I had that feeling. Like I was outside my body and like time had passed without really passing. It creeps in now and again, but yesterday with the shadow at the auction and then the light in the barn—"I just wonder if maybe this can help me remember anything."

"How long have you been having those lapses?" She turns to me.

"Since the fire, I guess. I have these fragments from that night. For a while I thought it was because I was so young back then, but there are pieces of a lot of years afterward that I just can't get a grasp on." The image of the body in the field and the blood on my hands flashes through my mind. What had happened right before I came to?

"Interesting." She opens the front door to the house and steps inside.

It's completely black inside. Not only because all the windows are covered but because the walls are painted black. She turns on a lamp in the tiny living room, revealing that the paint is actually dark-eggplant colored.

"We'll do it here." She taps the long wooden coffee table in the center of the room. The surface is covered in flecks of candle wax and tapers in various stages of melting. "Have a seat."

I sink onto the ornate rug. This whole thing creeps me out, but it's especially unsettling that most of the house is completely shrouded in darkness. I watch as she lights certain candles. It appears she does it in a specific order, although I can't make sense of it. "I saw your dad yesterday, by the way," I say, trying to focus on something other than the candles forming a triangle on the table.

Janna makes a face. "I'm sorry."

"What's the deal with that? How is he still the preacher here?"

She sighs. "Why are you surprised?"

"I mean, I figured that things may have changed by now." Or that someone would have noticed the bruises or burn marks. Although, every time I've seen Janna since returning, she's still been wearing long sleeves. "I thought maybe people would've realized—"

"He owns half the town now." She shrugs. "And people believe what they want to. Isn't that what you always say?"

She turns off the lamp nearby and sits across from me, leaving only the tiny flames dancing in front of us. "Let's focus now, okay?" Her eyes are pale, almost translucent from the reflection of the candlelight.

"Um, okay." My body has never felt tenser than at the idea of sitting here for God knows how long, pretending to believe in this. "Have you actually ever done this candle thing before?"

She stares at me like I slapped her in the face. "I've helped a lot of people reconnect with their loved ones this way."

I have so many follow-up questions.

But before I can ask, she nods to the candle. "Focus on the flames. Watch how the flames flicker."

I look away from her face and directly into the fire. The light hurts my eyes, but I can't look away.

"Let your breath become soft. Let it become so quiet and soft that you can't hear it."

All I can see is the bright orb of flame bending and twisting against the darkness.

"You're safe here, Lex."

I am safe here.

"Your mind is open here."

My mind is open.

"Your family is here. They want to help you remember."

My family is here.

I can see them, as if I'm standing in front of them right now. Natalie, reading a Nancy Drew novel she found on Grandpa's bookshelf, her foot dangling over the edge of the sofa. Amy standing behind Natalie, her mouth moving as if she's saying something to me, her fingers expertly weaving Natalie's strawberry blonde hair into a braid.

"What are you saying?" I ask. My voice comes out small and young. "I can't hear you."

Amy and Natalie exchange a look and then turn to me, both sets of lips moving now. Amy drops Natalie's hair and steps toward me, her expression growing more pained.

"I can't hear you!" I yell.

Natalie's mouth opens, and she lifts her head upward, pointing her finger at the ceiling. Amy follows suit, turning and pointing at the same spot in the ceiling. My head won't move, frozen forward, looking upon their terrified faces.

Suddenly, behind them, a tall shadow appears. My heart races. It's the ghost. The ghost from Grandpa's room that night.

I scream, but they don't look at me. The shadow swallows them, and they disappear. It moves across the floor until the shadow looms above me. No eyes. No face. Just a black mass.

I run, out of the living room and into the darkness beyond the porch. I sprint into the barn, bits of gravel scraping the bottoms of my feet like razors. I weave behind the pens and dive under the loft.

The shadow approaches. He bends down toward me and reaches out to me, and all goes black.

Out of the darkness appears a scene that makes my heart stop. I'm back in the living room. Amy and Natalie lay sprawled on the floor where they stood only seconds before. Amy's skull is split open, the cut running between her eyes. Natalie's neck is nearly sawed off. Their bodies are nearly unrecognizable as human, hacked up like the body in the field the other day.

"Lex?"

A voice calls to me as though it's miles away.

"Lex!"

"Thank God." Janna kneels by the sofa. "Honestly, I kind of freaked out. I couldn't snap you out of it. You were in the zone."

I squeeze my fingers into a fist.

"Did you remember anything?" she asks quietly.

No. It's not true. The shadow, the bodies . . . it's something my mind made up in the absence of true memory. "Not really."

She sighs. "I'm sorry. I really thought you might've been onto something, and that's why you were in so deep."

I turn my head to look up at her. "I . . ." My voice is raspy, as if I haven't used it in quite some time.

She bites her lip. "Maybe this was a bad idea. Here, have some water." She hands me a glass.

I pick my head up off the cushion, intense pain shooting through my temple. What did she do to me? I sip at the water, my tongue like paper.

"Do you want to try again? You're way more suggestible than I would've thought."

That's not good. I sit up. "I think that's enough for now."

She stares past me for a moment toward the hallway. "Okay. Of course." She blows out the one remaining candle and immediately switches on her lamp. I follow her out of the front door.

Outside, the sun is much higher than when we went into her house. "How long were we in there?"

She locks the door behind us. "I don't know. A couple of hours."

That long? I rub my eyes. They still feel so heavy. "Is it okay that the store's been closed this whole time?"

She shrugs, leading the way to the store. "Yeah, it's fine. I make my own hours. Everyone knows that." She glances at her phone. "Besides, Wayne is probably in by now."

"Wayne?"

"Yeah, you know him. He works part time at the motel."

So that's the creep's name. "He works at the store too?"

She nods. "Just until I find more help. He's already spread pretty thin with the motel."

"I'm sure." It must be exhausting to sit behind a desk and spend all day ignoring the only guest's complaints about a leaky sink.

She opens the door to the back of the store, and it's unlocked.

"I'm going to head straight out. I need to take care of some things at the farm."

"Oh good," she says. "I have someone who called earlier. They wanted to schedule a walk-through."

For the first time in weeks, I feel a little bit lighter. "That's great. When?"

"Is it okay if I bring him by tomorrow morning?"

"Of course." I'll need to pick up the pace on clearing out the barn, but it's doable. "Do I need to meet you there?"

"No," she says. "Potential buyers get a little weirded out when the owner is around, especially on the first viewing. I'll text you when we leave."

"Okay, sure." I'm a little skeptical of how Janna might represent the farm. I know she'll keep quiet about the details of the fire, but she might not be able to hide her distaste about the barn. Even though the graffiti is gone and the stalls are almost completely cleaned now, she probably still doesn't see it as an asset.

"See you later, Lex." She smiles and then disappears through the door.

CHAPTER TWENTY-FIVE

After leaving Janna's, I scrubbed for hours in the barn, lost in thoughts about the shadow figure and the bloody visions.

The remaining daylight has completely disappeared by the time I get out of the shower and wrap myself in a towel. I begin to comb through my wet hair as a knock raps on the door.

My entire body tenses. In a matter of days, I've had too many unwanted visitors knock on my door like that. My hair drips on the tops of my feet as I tiptoe to the door and peer through the peephole.

Janna stands in front of the door, casting shifty, urgent glances over her shoulder.

I open the door, and she startles. "What are you—"

"Bad vibes at my place." She pushes past me, the wheels of her TUMI suitcase squeaking along the floor. "I don't know what followed you back from the other side, but there's some scary-ass masculine energy."

Masculine energy? Did I talk out loud about anything when I was in that state? "How did you know which room was mine?"

"Wayne."

"How comforting." He probably would've handed her a key, too, if she'd asked.

She rolls her bag to the small desk in the corner. "I mean, this place is tiny. It's not like I wouldn't have found you eventually." She eyes the empty potato chip bags and canned coffees pouring out of the garbage can. "Do they not clean rooms here?"

"I leave the Do Not Disturb sign out." I don't want Wayne rifling through my stuff every day. Although, I'm not convinced that sign has been much of a deterrent.

She wrinkles her nose. "Well, at least the bed is pretty big."

"Come on, Janna. Whatever freaked you out is just—"

"No, Lex, you weren't there." She sinks onto the edge of the bed. "I blew through two sticks of sage, and that dark energy is still all over the place."

I sigh.

"It started in the store a couple of weeks ago. I'd hear something shift in the attic occasionally. Stuff goes missing, things aren't where I left them."

"So, it's not because of me, then?"

She shakes her head. "I don't know anymore. I'm just tired."

I've resigned myself. I guess this sleepover's really happening. I go into the bathroom and close the door. I slip my T-shirt over my head and pull on my sleep shorts before walking out. "That suitcase looks a little heavy for one night, so let me be clear—I expect you out by morning."

She rolls her eyes. "Believe me, I don't want to be here either. But the thought of staying and running through an entire cleansing ritual tonight is too exhausting." She unzips her suitcase and pulls out a brown paper bag. "Are you hungry? I brought some mozzarella sticks and steak fingers."

"From where?"

She rips open the bag down the middle and sets it on the nightstand. "I was so upset I stopped by the café on the way here."

I laugh. "I swear, some of this shit food at the café has a hold on me, even after all these years." I sit down and grab a mozzarella stick. "Have you had the patty melt recently?"

She bites into a steak finger. "Oh my God, it's amazing, isn't it? I found out it's because they use two different kinds of cheese."

That explains it.

She looks at me. "This is nice. It kind of reminds me of spending the night at Beth's place."

Beth's was by far the chosen spot to hang out at. The rectory where Janna lived was always under constant renovations, and her father was lurking in the background, ready to deliver an odd mini sermon when we did something he didn't approve of.

"How was everything at home? After I moved away?"

She pulls apart a cheese stick. "Honestly, I was angry with you. I still am, a little."

"With me?"

"Yeah, I mean, it all just happened so suddenly," she says. "I knew you hated this place, but you were really the only person I actually liked around here, and one day you were gone before I even had a chance to process it."

I shove another steak finger into my mouth before I say something I'll regret. Like spitting out all of the reasons I had to leave.

"But to answer your question, it was as miserable as it always was at home," she continues. "At least until I was able to get out on my own."

"To be honest, I was a little surprised to see you living alone. I seem to remember your father had a theory that a woman should only be allowed out from under her father's roof once she was married."

She laughs. "Yeah, that went out the window as soon as Mom died. I stopped caring about appearances and really leaned into all my weird shit. He couldn't get me out of the house fast enough, and he was willing to pay for it."

The news of Mrs. Butcher's passing had made its way to Beth after the funeral had already happened. "I'm so sorry about your mom." Mrs.

Butcher had been the perfect picture of the long-suffering wife. She put up with years of serving her husband in the shadows while he ignored her existence and wouldn't even bother speaking to her on and off for long stretches.

"Thanks." Janna glances down at her hands. "You know, he was actually nice to her near the end. When he found out how sick she was and how little time we had left with her, he treated her with a little more respect."

I clench my jaw. It seems unfair that a woman needs to die to be treated with respect, especially by her own husband.

"We still don't get along great, but he's been trying to do better."

This is how men like him get away with it. They behave like insufferable, abusive assholes for decades, and then performing the bare minimum is lauded.

"It's been a rough time out here, and he's really been pouring back into the community."

"In what way?" The question slips out in a more accusatory tone than I intend. She doesn't seem to notice.

"He's been investing in the small businesses around here. When the feed store was about to go under a few years ago, he bought it so Handley wouldn't lose it. And when some farmers were struggling, he bought that huge stretch of land right by the Trents' ranch all the way to the Norwoods' land."

When she said he'd bought half the town, she wasn't kidding. That land alone must be upward of four hundred acres. Buying Kael's family's land must be nothing for him. "Where did he get the money to do all of that?"

She shrugs. "He's been saving up all this time. Anyway, he's doing a lot of good."

I glance over at the paper bag. We've somehow managed to eat all the food already. "Maybe we should go to sleep. I'm exhausted."

As I lay next to Janna with her eye mask and noise-canceling headphones on, her portable oil diffuser polluting the air with the scent of lavender, I can't help but wonder if there's any amount of good that man can do that would make him tolerable.

True to her word, Janna was out first thing in the morning, off to go open the store before meeting the buyer at the farm.

Still sore from all the cleaning yesterday, I roll over and continue sleeping after she leaves.

By the time I wake up, my stomach is growling, and my head is throbbing. I throw my hair into a bun and grab whatever clean clothes I still have in my bag.

As I lace up my shoes, I notice my phone screen lighting up on the bed. It's Janna. "Hello?"

"Lex!" she screams over the phone. "You won't believe it! We have an offer!"

A small wave of relief flows through my body. "What? That's awesome! Who is it?"

"It's anonymous . . ."

"Wait, what? Why?"

She sighs. "Does it really matter? Let's celebrate! Not now because I'm in a rush to get into town, but later, okay?"

Anonymous? I guess it shouldn't matter. A buyer is a buyer. But still . . . "Um, yeah, of course. So what do I do now?"

"Just wait until I get some paperwork together, and we'll talk then."

CHAPTER TWENTY-SIX

I turn into the driveway, parking in front of the remnants of my family's old house. I exit my car and walk past it toward the barn, a heaviness spreading throughout my limbs with each step. The same sentimentalism that struck me when I saw this place in the daylight last week hits differently. This feeling of loss is more urgent.

I guess, even without knowing what was going on with the land in the past, I always had a sense that the farm would be here when I chose to return. The thought of someone else taking it and making it something completely new by destroying the remnants of the house and the barn knocks the air out of me.

I wander inside the barn and stare at the antique implements by the old desk. I considered removing them last night, but I thought they might add a little charm for the prospective buyer. Or maybe I did it in a faint attempt to persuade them to keep the barn up. I walk over to the tools hanging in the dark. I poke the rusted prongs of the pointiest tool on display. I never knew what any of these did. Except a couple. I turn to look at the far end of the wall at the hammer and hoe. A prickling sensation raises the hair on the back of my neck. The sickle is missing. I'm sure I saw it when I first came back here.

I peek my head into the open doorway of the barn. My stomach sinks when I spot the forest-green car parked at the far end of the property. It might blend in with the railroad crossing if not for the sun shining down on it. Is that Evan's car?

I pull my phone out of my pocket and scroll for his number. It's a little weird that he hasn't sent any more texts since his outburst at the motel. I click the number to call him. It doesn't ring and instead goes straight to voice mail.

I squint at the car again. I'm almost sure that's his. If that little shit is ditching work just to mess with me, he has another thing coming.

I take a step in the direction of the field when the sound of a door slamming nearby draws my attention away.

The door of a parked car on the other side of the house opens, and a tall man with neatly trimmed gray hair steps out. I was too locked in on Evan's car to notice this one drive up.

The man's gray eyes widen behind his large-framed glasses as he surveys the ruins. "Alexis?" He closes the door and walks around the front toward me, brushing his hand against his dark suit.

Oh God, who is it now? "Yes?"

He smiles. "I'm Jim Ridley." He extends his hand toward me. "You probably don't recognize me. The last time I saw you, you were little."

Like Larson, his hair was much darker back then. I shake his hand. "Oh, yes. Hi. I wasn't expecting you."

He surveys the barn. "Yes, well. I thought I'd make a bit of a field trip to see how you were getting on with the property."

A field trip? It's nearly a four-hour drive. "I actually have an update on that. My Realtor received an offer."

"Oh! That's great news." His gaze flits to the direction of the house. "I had my doubts, but I'm glad it resolved quickly."

I survey his outfit. For the first few years of my life, my father only wore suits like that during the week. "You and my dad knew each other for a long time, didn't you?"

He lifts a shoe and shakes off some dust that's gathered on top of the leather. "A very long time. We actually met in law school. He was in the top third of the class, and I was in the bottom." He grins. "I didn't pass the bar exam the first time, and he convinced me to give it another shot. He even tutored me. Your father was just as kind as he was smart. I hope you remember that about him."

I didn't expect such a passionate response from someone I haven't seen since the funeral twenty years ago. "Well, as someone who knew him so well, did he ever say why they wanted to get a will done back then? I never knew they had done that." It would've been out of character for them to tell their young daughter about their estate planning, but still . . .

"Paul brought your mother back to San Francisco after your grandfather died. They wanted to clear up the title to the farm after she inherited it and get everything sorted out for you kids."

For some reason, it isn't until he says this that I begin to wonder why Grandpa did leave the farm to Mom rather than Beth. Mom hadn't lived in Sola since she was seventeen. Was he hoping to tie her permanently back to the town by giving her this enormous land to take care of? Or maybe he just knew a struggling family of six would never be able to make it in the city on a civil rights lawyer's salary. "Oh, okay." Larson hadn't been willing to give away much about my parents, but maybe I can crack Jim here. "Did my dad ever mention any marriage problems?"

His lips twitch. "Um, I mean . . ."

"I know that Mom left him with my sisters and brothers before they had me."

He relaxes slightly. Now he doesn't have to feel so bad about blowing the lid off of things. "I see. I do know that they went through a bit of a rough patch, but that's not anything out of the ordinary."

I've tried to bury the memory of those kids summoning the dead the first night I checked on the farm, but their words have lingered in the back of my mind since I heard the tape. *"It was the dad."* "Did he ever tell you why?"

"No. I'm sorry."

I study his face. Just like Larson, it's hard to read him. He's probably a pretty good liar. He's a lawyer after all.

Ridley glances down at his watch. "I'm sorry. I need to make sure I get back to the city for a dinner meeting." He turns toward his car.

I follow after him, turning to look across the field. Evan's car is gone.

He pulls his key ring from his blazer pocket and looks at me. "So, how did you find this buyer?"

"I don't know actually," I say. "It's some anonymous buyer."

He narrows his eyes. "Anonymous? How much are they offering?"

I shrug. "I have no idea. I'm supposedly waiting on some paperwork."

"Hmm. Let me know when you have an update, and I'll happily make the trip back out to negotiate and go over the paperwork with you." He grins. "Congrats."

I glance at the barn. "What if I wanted to find a way to keep this place?" I almost don't believe the words are coming out of my mouth.

"I'm sorry? I'm not sure I understand." His brow is knit together.

"Well, if I decided I didn't want to sell, but I can't pay the taxes . . . is there like a loan or something?"

He sighs. "I'm afraid I don't see that as an option. You would just be constantly chasing your tail trying to keep this place afloat."

I think about Kael. He's dedicated everything to his ranch, and it's still floundering.

"If this offer pans out, your best way out of this mess is to take it."

I sigh. "I know. I was just wondering."

My mood drops even lower when I see Wayne smoking in front of the motel again, blocking my way to the staircase. I hate that he always hangs out so close to where my room is rather than on the other side by the front desk.

He nods as I approach. "I thought you were too good for religion." He doesn't move so I can reach the stairs.

"What?"

He grins. "I saw Janna here. What are you doing hanging out with the preacher's daughter?"

I debate whether I should just shove past him, but I really would rather not touch him at all. "She's an old friend. And I'm *not* religious."

He takes a draw from his cigarette. "Bunch of fuckin' hypocrites at that church, aren't they?" Bitterness drips from every word.

I eye him. There's something about his smell that's so familiar. Maybe it's the cigarette smoke. Or maybe it's just the mustiness of this place. "You said it, not me."

He pulls a pack of cigarettes out of his pocket and extends it to me. "Want one?"

For a second, I'm actually tempted. I haven't smoked since college, but if Wayne has dirt on the church, I want to hear it.

Out of the corner of my eye, I see Butcher's Lincoln pull into the driveway.

"Maybe some other time," I say.

Wayne glares toward Butcher and lets his cigarette drop to the dirt. As he walks away, I crush the lit tip with my shoe.

Butcher looks at me before he and Wayne enter the front door of the motel together.

CHAPTER TWENTY-SEVEN

I can't believe I'm doing this. Again.

"You know, we can just drink wine and watch *Top Chef*, right? We don't always have to do this to hang out." Janna smirks, handing me a cup of tea and sitting across the coffee table from me.

For some reason after my encounter with Wayne, I found myself driving here. Past the motel, past the bar, and right to Ringer Bros. Once I realized the Away sign was in the front door of the store, I walked straight to Janna's little house and knocked. "I know. Sorry." I shake my head and laugh. "This is so stupid. But last time, it felt like some memory was coming through and then . . . I just lost it."

"I don't think it was a memory. It was a message."

I roll my eyes. "Just to be clear, I don't think this is an 'other side' type situation. But it seems like this kind of *meditative* state might be helpful."

"Right. Meditative." She sips from her steaming cup. "So where is all this coming from? Why are you suddenly so into this? Did you have another blackout?"

"There's just a lot of stuff about the past that's coming up." For some reason, I hesitate. What will she make of all this? "I think someone is angry . . . about my parents or maybe me. I keep getting these phone calls."

She furrows her brow. "What kind of phone calls?"

"It's my parents," I say. "I found an old tape in the barn. And on it was a recording of me and my family . . . and my parents arguing. Someone is calling my room late at night and playing the audio over the phone."

Shit. I shouldn't have told her this. She looks terrified. But no matter what, I'm done with this whole sleepover business.

"I don't understand. Why would someone do that?"

"I have no idea." I stare at the unlit candles between us. "But someone is messing with me." I shake my head. "I mean, who would even know about those recordings? *I* didn't even know they existed."

She gnaws on her lower lip.

"What?"

She leans forward a little. "Are you sure it's a *person* doing it?"

It takes me a minute to realize what she's getting at. "Janna, come on—"

"No, I'm serious. Spirits will attempt communication in any way possible."

I sigh. "Let's agree to disagree, okay?" The events of the day have left me weak. Maybe she has a point. It's not like I know any better.

"Okay . . . shall we get started then?"

Also, it's not like I can really blame her for pushing her crazy reasoning on me. After all, I came to her to do some weird candle ceremony tonight.

She strikes a match and lights the arranged candles between us before switching off the lamp. "This time, I want you to just focus on the sounds of the flickering flame."

Oh my God. What am I doing here? I train my focus on the candle directly in front of me, watching the flame whip to the side as the air-conditioning clicks on nearby.

"Just focus on the warmth and the comfort of the fire."

It's funny she could possibly think I find any kind of fire comforting after my childhood.

"I want you to open your ears and open your heart to whatever message you need to hear right now."

I realize where I've heard this tone before. It's her father's preaching voice.

"Focus on the flame, Lexi."

I'm about to call it and stand up, but suddenly I can't look away from the wax. It's odd how a single flame can seem to have a life of its own, isn't it? It dances and grows and shrinks so erratically, as if there's something living inside of it. I follow the point of the flame as it descends closer to the wick.

"What do you think, Lex?"

I examine the pumpkin Dad holds level with his head. "A little bigger."

He turns and nods. "I think you're right. Let's keep searching."

Our mission is clear. He told me to find the biggest possible pumpkin for carving, and his head is our measurement guide. Natalie and Donnie voiced their apathy, but Amy and I have big aspirations for carving this year. It's the closest we'll be getting to a real Halloween out here. Mom warned us that trick-or-treating isn't really an option in Sola. The church doesn't approve of it, and apparently even "Monster Mash" is considered forbidden. The only seasonal indulgence allowed by the community here is the pumpkin patch and corn maze set up in the empty lot beside the church on Main Street.

Dad made a point to bring me out on the first day so we can grab the absolute best one here. Other people apparently have the same idea. There are already a lot of kids running in and out of the corn maze and snatching up the smaller pumpkins.

Dad notices me looking toward the maze as he picks up the next prospect. "Why don't you give it a try?"

"I thought you wanted to go together."

He grins, pushing his dark hair away from his forehead with the back of his hand. "You figure it out and then show me later. I'll have the perfect pumpkin waiting when you get out."

"Deal!" I weave through the mess of children standing outside of the cornfield. Most of them hold caramel apples purchased from the church ladies who set up a booth nearby. I walk into the cornstalks, and within a few steps, the sounds outside dull to a low hum. Everyone must've already completed the maze because it's empty inside.

I round the first corner, proceeding confidently at the next turn without hesitation. It won't be hard to backtrack. I run around another corner and then another until I reach a dead end. I turn on my heel and go the opposite direction. Another dead end.

My heart begins to pound as I stare up the tall stalks at the sky. A small ring of children's laughter sounds in the distance. I part the corn in front of me and run through it until I reach another pathway, panting.

A tall man is looming near me, a little girl by his side. His eyes widen at the sight of me. "Hi there. Lexi, right?"

I nod.

"Are you lost?"

"No," I say quickly, trying to calm my rapid heartbeat.

The little girl taps her foot beside him. "Dad," she hisses.

He doesn't turn to her, his gaze locked on me. "Okay. Do you want to walk through with us?"

My breath begins to return to normal. I take a few steps toward them. "You're the preacher."

He nods. "That's right. This is my daughter, Janna."

She stares at me as I approach.

The way he's looking at me is so intense, his dark eyebrows punctuating the blue eyes that watch my every move. "Go ahead, Janna."

She runs ahead of us, her long black ponytail bobbing around the corner.

I try to catch up to her, but the reverend holds out a hand.

"Just let her have her fun. I know the way out, so don't worry." The way he walks so closely to me makes me nervous. "You're Emma's daughter, right?"

"There you are!" Dad bounds toward me as soon as we emerge from the maze. "I was just about to come in after you." His eyes dart up to Butcher for the first time.

Butcher's face contorts into a hostile grin. "You really shouldn't have let her go in alone."

Dad's posture tenses. "What are you doing? It's none of your business."

I've never heard him speak that way to anyone before.

Butcher looks at me, and Dad steps directly between us.

"Mind your own damn business, okay?" Dad grabs my arm, steering me toward the parking lot.

"Dad—"

"Don't ever talk to him again, Lexi."

The shock of his demeanor silences me. When I look up at him, I don't see anger; I see fear.

I blink and I'm in the room again at the back of Janna's tiny house.

She's staring at me, her eyes wide. The candles have all been blown out.

"What happened?" I ask, flexing my fingers to restore feeling.

She shakes her head. "Um, I'm not sure. You . . . something about corn?"

My stomach sinks. "What did I say?"

"I mean, it wasn't really you."

I sigh. Of course. What did I expect other than her half-baked theories on the paranormal. I stand up. "Okay, I knew this was pointless."

"Lexi, I'm serious. You were saying some weird things."

"Like what?"

"Something about 'the preacher.'"

The words cause a chill to run down my arms.

She furrows her brow. "Were you talking about my dad?" She holds her hand to her heart as if it's in danger of flying out of her chest.

I look down at my hands. "I have no idea."

She stands up beside me. "Do you remember what happened? Did you see anything?"

"I don't know." I see the look on my dad's face again as he drags me to the parking lot. "I have to go."

"Oh . . . okay. Are you sure you don't want to sit for a little while, make sure you're okay to drive? That was really intense."

I switch on the light in the kitchen. "No. I need to leave." I reach for my keys and bag on the kitchen table. As I swing the bag onto my shoulder, it strikes the corner of a folder and knocks it onto the floor. Papers slip out from the folder.

Janna rushes up to me as I stoop to pick them up. As I gather them, the address at the top of the page catches my eye.

"Oh, are these for the farm?"

She nods and reaches to grab them, but I pull away.

I scan the first paragraph, and my stomach turns. "When exactly were you planning to tell me the anonymous buyer is your father?"

She sighs. "I mean, I figured you'd find out eventually."

I stare at her. "I can't believe you! You know what? Actually, I can. You just cover everything up for him, don't you?"

Her eyes blaze. "Wow! I got you a fantastic deal on your shithole farm, and this is how you repay me?"

"If I'd known it was him, I . . ." I'm not in the position to turn down a buyer. But maybe I would've rather just let the county have the place than for Butcher to get his hands on it.

She shakes her head. "What is it with you? If *I* can get over what he did in the past, why can't you?"

"Because he's . . ." I glance at the papers in my hand. "He acts like this holy, spiritual leader, but he's been living a lie. And he thinks he can buy whoever and whatever he wants in this town. It's not right."

"See? I knew this would just make you upset. That's why I didn't want to tell you." She gestures to the papers. "Isn't this what you wanted? You've been desperately looking for a buyer, and he was nice enough to offer."

Nice. I shake the papers at her. "This isn't nice. There's nothing *nice* about him trying to buy up even more of this pathetic town so he can own everyone. Tell him I said no to his offer."

Her eyes widen. "You have no idea, Lexi. He's offering way above market value for that place. If you have *any* sense at all, you'll just take it, okay?"

I tear the thin stack in half and throw the shreds down on the floor.

CHAPTER TWENTY-EIGHT

My clothes feel too tight suddenly, like the neckline of my shirt is going to creep up and strangle me while I drive.

I tug at my T-shirt until I can breathe again. Butcher?

Had my dad been trying to keep me away from him?

I swallow as the beam of my headlights flashes across the motel windows, and I pull into the parking lot.

The voice of that town kid with the homemade Ouija board my first night back in Sola plays through my mind.

"I heard the dad did it."

I sprint up to my room and dig the tape recorder out of where I hid it under the dirty clothes in my duffel bag. The recorder whirs as it rewinds. I stop midway and play.

"I thought we had an understanding of how things would go once we were here," my dad's voice says.

I turn up the volume. The clatter in the background sounds like breaking glass. The fear in Mom's voice as she responds is more noticeable than I remembered. *"Stop. I won't bring her again. I'm sorry."*

I hit the pause button. Was this about Butcher? All the fighting, the shards of glass on the floor the morning Beth dragged us to church.

I rest on the edge of the bed and stare down at the recorder.

A new layer emerges in my memories of those Saturday mornings in our city apartment. I can hear the yelling over the sound of the cartoon show and the sizzle of the oil as Donnie dropped the batter into it. I can see the red, irritated skin around Mom's eyes when she and Dad came out of their room finally.

Was that all about me? My recollection of the incident at the corn maze had sparked a question that I just couldn't shake. Why would Dad be so desperate to keep me away from Butcher? In the fight between my parents on the first tape, my dad specifically mentioned he didn't want Mom to bring *me* to church. Why just me?

Was Dad so upset about the reverend because he knew or suspected Butcher was my biological father?

Was my dad so tormented about this that he could've hurt his own family?

I click play again.

"Did you hear that?" Dad asks.

I dig my phone out of my pocket and pull up Tom's number as the tape continues to roll silently. Tom's the one who mentioned that Mom came here alone before I was born. Is that when it happened? Is that when she began an affair with Butcher?

Did Tom know about that?

The call rings and rings before rolling to voice mail. I hang up.

"What are you doing here?" Grandpa's voice booms through the recorder. *"I'm calling the police!"*

There's more to the recording.

The audio cuts in and out for a moment, as if the wind is beating against the microphone. Who was Grandpa yelling at? Who was recording?

My knuckles hurt as I bang on the rectory door. I continue knocking even as the light turns on in the window.

The front door opens and Butcher peers down at me. It's hard to distinguish whether he's more tired or surprised. "Lexi? I'm afraid you're a bit early for church."

"How did you know my mom?"

The blood drains from his face. "Your mom?"

"Did . . ." I can't even get the words out.

Yet somehow he understands. His eyes dart past me toward the empty church parking lot. "Let's talk inside." He opens the door and ushers me through it. "Why are you asking me about your mom?"

I want to yell or scream at him. But that would require actually asking the question I dread the most.

He clenches his jaw. "I meant to tell you. Now it seemed right. But you've been so angry." He runs a hand through his white hair. "I should've told you before Beth took you away, but—"

"What are you talking about?" Maybe if I play dumb, he'll take it back. I won't need to believe it and doubt everything I ever remembered about my parents.

"Emma came back into town for a few months in '92." His gaze is so intense I almost look away.

My body feels cold. I already know. It's like I'm looking into the pale, tormented face of Reverend Dimmesdale himself. "Why?"

He sighs. "She and Paul were having some trouble . . . I know you don't want to hear this."

"Go ahead."

"Apparently, she found out that he'd been having an affair."

The stone settling in my stomach makes it hard to ignore how painful it is to hear. "No," is all I can manage. I comb through my memories. Had Mom ever looked at Dad with suspicion? It had been hard enough to believe Mom would ever cheat on Dad, but to accept that both of them had been unfaithful . . . were they ever as happy together as I'd once thought?

"That's what she told me. She was very upset at the time. She left your siblings in San Francisco with him and came to stay on the farm for a bit to think things over."

"Who was it?"

"What?"

I dig the tip of my shoe deeper into the carpet. "Who did Dad cheat with?" I almost can't believe the words even as they come out. This combined with everything else is just a reminder that I never knew my parents.

"What does it matter, Lexi?"

He's right. It doesn't.

"While she was here," he continues, "she started getting involved in church. I think she was looking for an answer for how to move forward from any source."

Maybe that's why she brought us that one time when we moved here. The church had come to mean something to her, perhaps.

"I've thought about telling you this for so long, but I'm still not sure how to say it." He averts his eyes. I notice for the first time a line of sweat has appeared just above his lip. "We had a history together, and we started to *see* each other." His hands fidget on the table. "While she was here . . . we had an affair." He glances up at me for my reaction. I'm not sure what my face conveys, but he presses on. "She was upset about her marriage, and I was facing a crisis of my own. I wasn't sure if I'd made the right choice in marrying Madison. And we bonded over that."

I recall the tapes and the rage underpinning each of my dad's words to Mom. The warnings about church. Even if it's true and he had been unfaithful, too, my existence complicated everything. "I can't believe you." I spit the words.

He knits his brow. "Clearly you must've already known some of it. That's what you came here this morning for, isn't it? You think I could be your father."

I turn away from him, focusing on the cross at the entrance to the sanctuary. "You could have denied it. It's the very least you could've done."

"I don't want to deny it anymore. I've tried keeping it to myself. But things change as you get older. You start taking stock of your life and realize what's important. Family's the most valuable thing in this world, Lexi. And you've lost so much. Isn't it worth it to find out if you could be part of ours?"

I shake my head. Paul had loved me as his own, hadn't he? Maybe I had chosen the best memories only and he wasn't actually perfect, but he provided for us. He was always there for me. Or had he secretly hated me, even for a moment when he first had doubts?

He swallows. "I understand this must be hard to hear—"

"And to be clear, you're not getting your hands on the farm either. I know about your offer, and I'm rejecting it." I turn around and burst through the door. The sky has begun to fade from dark gray to blue.

None of what he said can be true. Not about Dad. Not about Mom.

It can't be. They were loving, to each other and to us.

But if it is true, does this change the possibilities of what happened that night? Could Dad have just lost it over this entire situation?

The idea makes me pick up the pace until I reach my car.

I sink into the driver's seat and stare toward the church. A light from the center console catches my eye. My phone screen lights up, revealing a new notification. A call from Larson. I press the button to call back.

"Lexi, sorry. I hope I didn't wake you."

"No, I was already up." I lean forward and rest my head against the steering wheel. "Is everything okay?"

I can almost hear his mustache twitching through the phone. "I have an update about the body you found . . . it was Tom Miller."

I sit up.

"Lexi?"

"Yeah." I think back to the bloody scene.

"We don't know exactly what happened yet. But it wasn't an animal attack."

I let the words sink in. "What does that mean?"

"It looks like possible foul play. We're investigating it as a homicide."

Homicide? "Who would've . . . *how* would someone do that to a person?"

He sighs. "I don't know. But, regardless of who did that, you need to be careful. Okay?"

I should tell him about the tape. And about the calls. I should ask him if any of what Butcher said is true. "Okay."

CHAPTER TWENTY-NINE

Thank God Kael is home. I spot Mrs. McPheron's car on the dirt road just outside their driveway. She stares at me through the window as I drive by.

Kael is standing on the porch with a cup of coffee in his hand. He smiles when I walk up the steps toward him. "Hey. I was just thinking about you." He opens the door, and I step inside. He's dressed in his usual after-hours sweatpants and T-shirt.

"I hope it's okay I stopped by. Your mom is out early."

"Yeah, she told me she was going to head to church early to prepare for Bible study or something. I haven't really even gone to bed yet. Got called out to an accident near Penman a couple of hours ago." He sets his mug on the table. "How are you doing with everything?"

God, he doesn't even know the half of it. "I got a call from Larson this morning. Apparently it was Tom."

He raises his eyebrows.

"The body."

His gaze darkens. "Tom? But—"

"They think he was murdered."

He places a hand on my back. "Come on, you should sit down." He gestures to the sofa. I follow and sit beside him. The TV is playing in front of us.

"I can't believe it." He leans against the cushion and glances at me. "Why Tom?"

"I don't know . . . how did nobody realize he was missing?"

He frowns. "He mostly keeps to himself, and now that I think about it—he didn't have any days on the schedule with the VFD this week."

I stare ahead at the screen. I can sense Kael wants to talk about this more. And I can't handle it. I just can't.

He follows my gaze and reaches for the remote from the coffee table.

"It's fine. Leave it," I say before he can turn it off. It's clearly a made-for-TV thriller. Maybe the acting will be bad enough to take my mind off of this mess.

Kael leans back beside me as a blonde woman on-screen turns to a pasty man in a police uniform. *"It can't be,"* she recites rigidly. *"He's my father. He would never hurt a fly."*

Fuck. Really? The word *father* makes me shrink into my seat. The thought of Butcher and his confession turns my stomach.

Kael slides his arm around my shoulder. "Are you good?"

I consider lying. "No."

He frowns. "Me neither. I can't stop picturing him in the field like that."

"I know." If only for a moment, the conversation with Butcher had managed to push the image of Tom's mangled corpse from my mind. I can feel Kael's gaze on me, but I don't want to meet his eyes.

"Did you talk to Larson about your ex?"

I turn to him. Even if Evan is loitering around to fuck with me, he would *never*. "There's no way you think Evan would do something like that. Why would he ever do something to Tom of all people?"

He looks at me, puzzled. "I don't necessarily. The timing is just odd. I—"

"Has it ever occurred to you that the real monsters, who may be capable of hacking a man into raw meat, are right here in this community?" After all, almost no one here is as wholesome as they want people to believe. Butcher is a liar, and he's been able to get away with it for so long. What else is he hiding? I stand up from the couch.

"Lex, I'm sorry if I upset you." Kael follows me to the kitchen. "I'm just worried about you. I didn't mean anything by it."

I open the door. "But you did. And that's the problem. Just like everyone else here, you think this place is perfect, if it weren't for the horrible outsiders contaminating it."

He shakes his head. "Lex—"

I slam the door behind me. I'm so sick of having this same discussion. I know Kael has longed to be free of here (or at least he did once), but he can't truly understand why I hate this town. He can't know what it is to be an outsider, to lose everything and still feel shut out. He can't or he *won't* see what these people really are.

He races out to me. "Come on, Lex, you're upset. Let me give you a ride." He takes a small step. It's subtle, but he's positioning himself between me and my car.

"Kael, back off, okay?" Instead of feeling numb or separated from all of this, I'm sunk so deep in the anger and confusion. I can't trust what else I might say to him right now.

He doesn't move. "You're not acting like yourself." His voice is so soft I immediately feel bad for raising mine.

If what Butcher said is true, then I'm not even sure what I even really know about myself. "Believe me, I know."

He raises a hand toward mine but then lets it fall by his side. "I really wish you'd stay. I don't think it's safe for you to be alone right now. Especially not if Tom was m—"

"I'm fine." I move past him and open my car. "Give me some space."

I can't think clearly the entire drive back to the motel. The bad thoughts play through my mind on a carousel. Dad. Tom. Butcher. Dad. Tom. Butcher.

I park the car and storm up the stairs to my room. As I look up, I freeze. My door is open a crack.

Everything screams in me to go back to my car and drive away. Maybe it's nothing.

I push the door and immediately step back, expecting someone or something to blast out of the room past me. A familiar smell reaches me. It's this primitive scent that fills me with adrenaline.

Nothing happens.

I squint into the room, making out the shapes of the nightstand, the TV in the corner. I dig for my phone, clutching it as I reach my hand across the threshold. I flick on the light and scream. And I don't stop screaming.

"Lexi?" Sheriff Larson avoids my eyes.

I continue to stare straight ahead at the motel. The ambulance left with Evan's body a few minutes ago. The sheriff's men are still rooting around inside my room and the parking lot.

"Maybe it's a good idea to head back home," he says. "Let me take you home."

He's right. I don't know how to move past this. But I'm sure it doesn't involve going back to San Francisco. Not now. Not after this. "I can't." I clutch my hands tighter around my stomach. "Who would do this?" I shake my head. I can't unsee Evan's body, sprawled across the bed, his head a mess of blood, nearly severed from his neck. His bloodied hand, missing his ring finger.

"You certainly can't stay here tonight. Not alone. Do you have somewhere to go?"

"I'll figure something out."

"Lexi—"

"Really. I'll be fine."

He sighs. "Did your friend have any next of kin that you know of?"

Yes. I've been thinking about them nonstop since they carted his body away. "Yeah, his mom is in Sacramento. I don't have her number, though." She's going to be destroyed. Absolutely devastated. Evan wasn't perfect, but he had been the rock of his family since their dad left when he was little. "He has a little brother, too, but I don't have his number either. His name's David if you can search Evan's phone."

Larson frowns. "We didn't find his phone."

"It wasn't in the room?"

"Can you tell me what it looked like? We're going to scan around the whole motel to see if we can spot it."

I just realize for the first time that his car isn't in the parking lot either. "What about his car? It's not here." How did he get here? And why?

He nods. "We're searching for that too."

"Okay. Um, well, his phone was a silver iPhone, but it was in a navy-blue case." I can't think of the brand of the case right now. "Did someone bring him here? If his car isn't around?"

"We don't know for now," he says.

I recall spotting the car across the field when the lawyer came to visit the farm. "But I . . . I just saw his car. At the farm."

"When?"

"A couple of days ago," I say. "He was parked by the railroad tracks."

He shifts his weight and glances down. He doesn't want to upset me. I think it's too late for that.

"What?"

"Nothing." His gaze goes to my motel room. "Are you sure you don't need a ride somewhere?"

I shake my head. "Really, I'm fine. Don't worry about me."

He watches me for a moment before reaching out and squeezing my shoulder. "I'll check up on you tomorrow." He turns around and walks toward the motel again, joining a man and woman in uniform at the base of the staircase.

I climb into my car and start driving away. I'm not really sure where I'm headed until I pull into the driveway behind his truck. Even though hours have passed, his mom must still be away at church.

Kael spots me from the window of the house as I get out. "Hey!" he calls and walks out the front door. "I'm glad you came back. Look, I'm sorry if—" He stops when he notices how rigid I am.

I don't even know what to say. I shrug.

"Come on, let's go inside."

I follow him into the house.

"Have a seat." He grabs a glass and fills it with water from the tap and sets it on the table as I sink into a chair. "What happened?"

I wrap my hands around the cold glass. "Evan is dead." I look up at him.

"What?" Genuine surprise flashes across his face. Good. Of course he's surprised. He sits across from me. "Are you sure?"

"Yes. I found him."

Surprise turns to horror. "Lex . . . I'm so sorry. So he was still in Sola?"

"Apparently," I say. "I honestly can't make sense of it right now. I went back to the motel and he was . . . on my bed." Head and gut split open. The hack marks were similar to the ones on Tom's mutilated body, but I'd recognized Evan immediately. And that was much worse. "Someone killed him." A lump forms in my throat. "Oh." I pull my phone from my pocket.

"What are you doing?"

"I have to call work. They need to know."

He touches my arm. "Just . . . let's take a minute, okay? Slow down. You've been through something."

Maybe he's right. "But Sanders has his mom's phone number. I need to give it to the sheriff. He needs to tell Evan's family." I stare at him. "What should I do?"

His lips twitch. "I don't know . . . if I were his family, I wouldn't mind believing he was still alive for a few more hours."

I don't even know if Sanders contacted Evan's family when he didn't show up to work. His family probably doesn't even know he left town. I drop the phone on the table. It's hard to think about the last interactions I had with Evan and realize that he's gone now. And he went out in the worst way imaginable. "God, this is my fault."

Kael furrows his brow. "That's not true."

"There's no other way to look at it. He came here because of me. And now he's dead." Dead. I still can't really believe it, even though the image continues to flash through my mind. "I should've never come back here."

"You can't talk like that. It's awful, but it doesn't make a lick of sense to blame yourself, Lex."

I rub my hands over my face. "It was . . . horrible. Someone . . ." Split him open. Chopped him up, like he was nothing. Like he wasn't loved by so many. Like he didn't matter. "And it's because he was here to see me."

He reaches a hand across the table and rests it on my arm. "You haven't done anything wrong. He came here on his own."

"I just don't understand it. Who would do that to Evan? Why?"

"What does the sheriff think?"

"Nothing," I say. "They have no idea. They can't find his phone or car."

He shakes his head. "About what I said earlier. I hope you don't really think I meant Evan had something to do with Tom. I feel like that's important to let you know, especially given the circumstances."

"I know. I was upset, and I was taking it out on you." There's no point in not talking to Kael. Internalizing my feelings is always the source of my problems. "I found out something this morning," I begin. "And if it's true, everything I thought I knew about my parents is a lie."

He holds my gaze but says nothing and waits for me to continue.

"I saw Butcher and he told me that—" I shake my head. "He thinks I'm his daughter."

Kael's eyes widen. "I'm sorry. What?"

Despite everything, a small laugh escapes my lips. "Yeah, that's what I thought too. He says my mom walked out on my family when Amy was two and came back here. And, according to him, during that time they rekindled their high school romance. Nine months later, I was born."

"Do you believe him?"

"No," I lie. "But, it makes sense with the recording, doesn't it? Dad said he specifically didn't want me going to church. Maybe that's why."

Kael looks down.

"I'm having a hard time accepting what he said about my dad too. According to him, my dad had an affair, and that's why my mom left him for a little while." I shake my head. "What the hell am I supposed to do with that?"

"Maybe try to take it with a grain of salt," he says. "After all, your parents aren't here to defend themselves."

I run a hand through my hair. "I don't know why I'm even still thinking about all of that. There have been two dead bodies in a week. That's more important right now."

He meets my gaze. "Is there anything I can do for you?"

"Can I stay here tonight?"

"Of course. There's no way you're going back to that place."

"Thank you," I say. "I think I'm going to lay down for a bit. I need to borrow some clothes if that's okay. I, uh, couldn't bring anything from the room . . . because it's a crime scene." God, hearing the words come out doesn't seem real.

Kael nods. "I'll go grab you something." He stands and gives my shoulder a light squeeze before walking down the hallway.

I rub my eyes, trying to wipe the flashes of Evan's body from my eyelids.

Kael reappears, carrying a pair of folded sweatpants and a T-shirt. "Is this okay?"

"Yeah, whatever is fine. Thanks." I take the clothes and walk to the bedroom. I never even touched the body, but it's still a relief to change into new clothes.

I crawl under the sheets and stare up at the ceiling fan. The early-afternoon light dances through the blades.

Kael leans against the doorway. "Do you want to be alone?"

"No."

Kael walks to the bed and slips in beside me. I turn toward Kael and put my arm around his waist, clinging to him.

It's comforting to be near him right now, but it fills me with guilt. Not long ago, I shared a bed with Evan. God, poor Evan.

He pulls me closer to his chest. He doesn't need to say anything, but I can feel the warmth spread through me from just his presence. He holds me for a long time in silence, until his grip goes limp and his breathing deepens.

I look up at him, unable to stop picturing Evan's body at the motel.

2003

Being new in town, it wasn't easy for us to make friends. Natalie and Amy had each other—they were only one grade apart and had the same lunch and gym period. But I was on my own, listening to the whispers of my classmates. It didn't bother me too much, though, because I always carried a book from Grandpa's home library with me to lunch.

While the rest of us were just managing, Donnie was the most well liked. He didn't play football, so he wasn't at the top of the popularity pyramid, but he was good looking, kind, and funny, putting him leaps above most of the kids in this town.

It wasn't anything strange for Donnie to invite kids over to study or play video games. Nat and Amy always found a way to involve themselves, but I was mostly just interested in the snacks that came with a visitor.

When Mom knew we had a friend coming over, she would break out the homemade lemon squares and the boxed brownie mix. She would pour the brownie batter into these mini cupcake holders and spread store-brand frosting on top. The best part was the sodas. Normally, my parents would keep the sodas hidden away, for special occasions, but when a guest came over? Full-size cans of Coke, Pepsi, and Sprite would be lined up in the fridge. And just as mysteriously as they appeared, they would be gone the second a visitor left.

The day Donnie brought over his weird friend, I specifically remember that Mom had picked up a bag of sour cream and onion Lay's from Ringer Bros. Those were my favorite flavor, and I shoveled a fistful of them in my mouth right as the front door swung open and Donnie came in.

"Hey, Lexi."

"Hey," I said through my full mouth before I resumed chewing.

He grinned at me and grabbed a chip from the top of the bowl. Unlike Natalie and Amy, who went out of their way to put me down in front of friends, Donnie never seemed to care what his friends may or may not think. He was always just Donnie. He gestured to the boy who slipped in behind him. He turned to the boy. "This is my sister."

His friend stared at me and gave a little wink. I recognized the long hair that looked wet around the roots. He was the boy from church. The one who gave me the bread and the blood.

Mom walked in behind me. "Oh, hi."

The boy avoided her eyes and walked past Donnie to the kitchen table. He grabbed three brownies and stacked them on top of one another, then shoved them in his mouth.

Mom looked to Donnie.

The boy grabbed the pitcher of lemonade Mom put on the table and raised the brim to his lips, gulping until nearly a third of it was gone.

"Hey!" I shouted.

Mom placed her hand on my shoulder. "Are you planning to play video games?"

Donnie's cheeks were flushed, and he nodded. "Yeah, come on. I'll get it set up in the living room."

The boy didn't respond and instead dug his fingers into the tray of lemon squares, scooping two out of the container and turning to Mom. He smiled at her as he followed Donnie out of the kitchen.

I looked up at her. "Mom—"

"Why don't you go play in your room, Lexi?" She smoothed down the top of my hair and walked over to the container of lemon squares, peering down at it.

I stood in the hallway, watching Donnie and his friend in the living room as they set up the game consoles. The boy wiped his hand on the edge of his T-shirt.

"Oh," Donnie said. "The bathroom is at the end of the hall on the right." Donnie waited for him to leave and then returned to the kitchen.

"He doesn't get to eat a lot at home," Donnie whispered to Mom. "No one really takes care of him there."

Mom nodded, her forehead still tensed in confusion. "Oh. Why don't you ask him to stay for dinner? I'll make something he can pack for home."

I heard the soft click in the distance and took off in the same direction as the weird boy. I passed by the open bathroom door. The light was still off. As I approached Grandpa's room, I heard the light shuffle of pages. When I rounded the corner, I saw him standing by the nightstand, holding Grandpa's Bible.

"What are you doing?"

He didn't look at me and instead, a smile crept over his lips as he ripped up the pages.

"Hey!" I ran to him and tugged at the book.

His gaze drifted to me, and he pulled harder.

I intensified my grip.

When he suddenly let go, I stumbled backward, falling down against the wall, the book flying from my hands. "Little bitch." He laughed.

I rubbed my head as the sound of stomping feet approached.

"Is everything—" Donnie's head poked around the door, his eyes darting to the ripped pages littering the floor beside me and then to the boy. "What's going on here?"

His friend shook his head. "I don't know, man. I was just reading and she came in here and ripped it away. She's crazy."

Donnie stepped inside the room and offered me his hand.

I took it, feeling the heat spreading through my face. "That's not it! *He* did it!"

Donnie studied me for a moment, then waved to his friend. "Come on, let's get out of here."

On the way out of the room, I looked over my shoulder and saw the boy smirking at me.

I was still scrambling to pick up the pages when slow, labored steps approached from the other end of the house.

"Lexi?" Grandpa looked down at me from the doorway. His eyes trailed from me to the cast-aside Bible on the floor.

"I didn't do it!"

He sighed. "All right."

It was such a strangely simple response and so calm. The pages stuck to my sweaty hands as I clutched them and stood up. "You believe me? Donnie thought that I—"

"I've been around," Grandpa said and grinned. "I know a good egg when I see one. Donnie is still learning."

CHAPTER THIRTY

I must have fallen asleep at one point, though, because I wake up in Kael's arms. It's almost as if we never parted.

"Good morning," he says, brushing a strand of hair from my face.

"Morning? What time is it?"

He picks his head off the pillow and looks at the clock over my shoulder. "Seven a.m."

We must've been so exhausted. I don't even remember waking up in the middle of the night. I melt deeper into his embrace. For a moment, I almost forget all the shit from yesterday.

"Did you sleep okay?"

"Apparently." It was nice to have been completely absent from the world for so many hours.

"I need to get up." He brings his lips to mine. "Do you want to sleep a little more?"

There's nothing in this world that I want more than to never leave this bed. "I can't. I need to . . ." I swallow. "I need to call my boss."

Kael runs his hand through my hair. "Are you going to be okay?"

I'm not even sure how to respond. What happened to Evan will never be okay.

"I'll make you some coffee."

I watch him stand up and walk out of the bedroom, and I already feel a sense of emptiness. I turn over and stare out the window. God, what am I going to tell Sanders? How can I even begin to explain Evan's horrible fate?

A knock sounds against the front door.

I jump up and swing my legs over the edge of the bed. I pause before stepping out of the bedroom. What if it's Kael's mom again, ready to clutch her pearls when she sees me in her son's clothes?

The door swings open. "Good morning, Sheriff," Kael says. "How can I help you?"

I resume walking, hurrying out to Kael.

"Morning." Sheriff Larson looks over Kael's shoulder as I approach, his eyes taking in the oversize T-shirt I'm wearing. His lips curve into a disapproving frown. "I'd like to speak with you. I'm sure you heard what happened yesterday."

Kael nods. "I did. And, uh, yeah. Whatever you need." He opens the door wider.

"I'd prefer it if we could speak alone." Larson looks between the two of us.

Kael looks at me. "Sure, we can talk outside."

"Wherever you're comfortable," Larson says.

I grab his arm, glowering at Larson. "What's this about?"

"I just need to ask Kael some questions."

Kael steps outside onto the porch.

"Can I speak to you for a moment, Sheriff?"

He gives a curt nod and steps inside, closing the door behind him.

"What are you doing?"

He blinks. "Lexi, we have to follow up on all possible leads. Wayne told us about the incident in the parking lot between Kael and Evan."

"Incident? They were just talking."

"I'm sure. But it's one of the only interactions Evan seemed to have here in town. Nobody else saw him after that."

That can't be true. If Evan had been around Sola since I last saw him, he must have crossed paths with other people here.

"Look, I know you two are close. But you have to admit, it doesn't look great. Your ex-boyfriend comes into town and gets into an argument with Kael and then turns up murdered?"

Oh, I had considered it, although briefly. Once the initial shock wore off, I tried to conjure an image of anyone who would want to hurt Evan in or near Sola. So of course, I remembered Kael and Evan in the parking lot. But it was an entirely verbal interaction between them. Kael had even made a joke. And I know Kael. I *know* he wouldn't do something like that.

His brow furrows. "I wasn't aware that you two were, uh, together. Did he tell you to come over last night?"

"No. *You* told me to stay somewhere else for the night, so I did. And what business is it of yours who I'm seeing?" I realize a little too late how juvenile I sound.

"You must see that it's relevant to what happened last night," he says. "Unless you have some other information you haven't shared, this is the only viable lead we have right now."

"Why aren't I a suspect? I'm the one who found Tom . . ." Sure, they'd determined his time of death was long before I found his body in the field, but still. "And now my ex-boyfriend turns up dead in my room?" My voice cracks as I say it. I can't even believe what I'm saying. Evan is dead.

His gaze softens. "It isn't possible that you could have done that to him. The force that it would've taken for someone your size to land those types of blows . . ." Mercifully he doesn't finish.

My stomach turns, and for a moment I'm not sure I can open my mouth again. "But why was Evan there in the first place? And how could Kael have known he would be? It doesn't make any sense."

Larson sighs, his mustache twitching. "I suspect Kael will have some input about that. And it turns out there have been some security issues at the motel recently. Particularly with your room door."

I stare at him. "What does that mean?"

"Apparently, that door lock has been popping open on some other guests before you came along. The only way to make sure it stays shut is with the dead bolt from the inside."

"That's bullshit. It hasn't popped open on its own once since I've been here."

"Wayne showed us the complaints from previous guests."

"Then why didn't he fix it? Or why didn't he put me in a different room?" I'm pretty sure I know the answer. The sicko probably wanted a plausible reason to be in my room if he was found scavenging through my things.

Larson readjusts his hat. "Good questions and I asked them all. But it seems to me he's clearly just a lazy moron."

"Be that as it may, Kael didn't do anything to Evan. There have to be better leads."

"We're just talking to him, all right? Nothing to get worked up about. We talked to you as well, and you're free as a bird."

I cross my arms over my chest.

"Now, can I get back to work?"

I nod.

"It won't be long," he says. "It's standard procedure, all right?" He steps out onto the porch and joins Kael before closing the door.

I should call Sanders, but all I can do is stare out the window as Kael and Larson talk. Kael's back is to me, his body obscuring Larson's face from view. He doesn't fidget, only giving an occasional nod or shrug.

With a final nod, he turns away from Larson and walks up the porch steps. Larson remains where he stands until Kael reenters the house, before lumbering to his cruiser.

"What did he ask you?" I watch Larson's car as it disappears from view.

Kael walks to the coffee maker. "He wanted to know what I was doing yesterday."

"And? What were you doing yesterday?"

He glances over his shoulder at me, coffee container in hand. "You sound a little . . . you don't think I had something to do with it, do you?"

I shake my head. "No, of course not. I'm just a little on edge, I guess."

He begins to shake grounds into a filter. "For the record, I was with you yesterday morning. Remember? You came over, and then we had an argument, and you left."

That's right. I can vouch for Kael's whereabouts yesterday morning because I was here. "Did you tell that to Larson?"

He sets the filter into the machine and clicks the button on top. "I did. I guess he didn't think it was necessary to ask you about it." He's clearly trying to hide how bothered he is by my questioning.

"I don't like the idea that you're even on the radar for this. If anything, that shifty motel guy should be the one getting questioned."

He leans against the counter. "He was. That's how they found out about the confrontation between Evan and me."

"I hate the people in this town. They creep around, watching people and twisting things. There was no *confrontation* between you two. He and I were getting pretty aggressive, and you were the peacemaker."

He shrugs. "I'm just glad they're taking it seriously. That's all that really matters right now."

I stand up from the table. "I need to call my editor. I'll be right back." My heart drops to my stomach as I retreat to the bedroom and sink onto the bed. I listen as the phone rings. Part of me selfishly hopes Sanders won't answer right away.

"Hello?" His voice sounds groggy.

I can't seem to open my mouth.

"Lex? Are you there?"

I clear my throat. "Um, hey . . . is now a bad time to talk?"

"No, it's fine," he says. "What's going on? Everything okay?"

I take a deep breath. "Evan—" I swallow a new knot that forms round my tongue. "Evan's dead."

Silence.

"He was murdered."

There's a soft exhale on the other line. "I'm sorry . . . what?"

"I found him dead yesterday." I wish I was able to convey any type of emotion in my tone, but it sounds so flat. So numb.

"I don't understand. What happened?"

"The sheriff's office is trying to figure it out right now," I say. "I was wondering if you have his mom's phone number? The sheriff wanted to inform her."

"Yeah," he says, a slight crack in his voice. "Um, I'll text it to you if that's all right."

"Yes, thanks." The pause between us is deafening. "I'll keep you updated if I hear anything."

"Sure . . . are you going to be all right, Lex? I'm so sorry."

I stare down at the floor. "I'll talk to you later."

"Okay. Be safe. Call me if you need anything."

"Okay, bye." I end the call and lie backward onto the mattress.

Kael appears in the doorway. "How did it go?"

I turn to look at him. "I feel . . . nothing. Is something wrong with me?"

He walks over and sits beside me. "You're in shock."

Maybe. Yes. That must be it. I sit up. "When Evan and I broke up, he was so angry that I couldn't react."

Kael reaches for my hand.

"I feel like I should cry." But nothing comes out.

CHAPTER THIRTY-ONE

The rest of the day goes by in a blur of unanswered calls and text messages.

> Janna: You OK? Wayne told me what happened.

> Sanders: Spoke with his mom. She's on her way out there with his brother.

> Sanders: How are you holding up?

> Jim Ridley: Any updates on the sale? Did you get the paperwork yet?

The worst part, perhaps, were the repeated missed calls from Butcher. I toss my phone behind the bale of hay I'm sitting on. There's a satisfying thwack as it hits the dirt. Unfortunately, that won't break the damn thing. I've dropped it no less than fifty times over the past couple of years without even a crack.

I turn my attention back to Whisper. He has craned his head down over the top of the fence so I can reach his snout easily.

Kael left reluctantly a few hours ago for his night at the VFD. He tried to see if someone would swap nights with him, but no takers. I reassured him over and over again that I'm fine. But I'm not so sure. I feel so empty.

Whisper stares down at me. It's been a while since I've given him a peppermint. I stand up and walk to the table on the side of the barn. The peppermint tub contains only empty wrappers crumpled on the bottom. Maybe Kael has another box somewhere. I turn around and spot the large metal cabinet near the back. I kick a feed bag out of the way to get to it and swing open the doors. Damn. No peppermints. For some reason, this feels heavier than it normally would. Like it's the last straw or something.

I slam the cabinet closed and push back the feed bags. There are a couple of hay bales stacked behind that. Of course peppermints wouldn't be there, but I shove the bales over just for good measure.

"Lexi?"

I turn around to see Mrs. McPheron standing near Whisper, her arms crossed over the front of her peach sundress.

"Can I help you find something?"

I look down at the overturned bags and the lopsided hay. My heart is still beating so fast. "I was looking for peppermints."

She purses her lips and walks up to the cabinet. The doors squeak on their hinges as she opens them and peers in. "Looks like we're out, doesn't it?" She closes the cabinet and peers at me. "Why don't you come sit down?"

I follow her back toward Whisper. She walks past the hay I was sitting on to pet Whisper and carries a long stool from near the forge and sets it down by the corral. She sinks onto the far end and pats the side closest to me. I obey and sit beside her.

Penny had walked up to join Whisper. Mrs. McPheron reaches up and strokes her head. "I'm sorry about your friend. It's horrible."

Whisper stares down at me, but my arms are too heavy to lift.

"Maybe it's time for you to go home now, Lexi."

Maybe she's right.

"I know it can't be easy for you to come back here and especially now . . . you've lost so much." Her tone is soft, but the words cut me. She has no idea truly how much I've lost by coming back here.

"Did you know?" I ask. "About Butcher?"

She frowns.

"You said my mom 'hurt a lot of people.'" I thought about it not long after I confronted Butcher. "You knew about him and my mom, didn't you?" Originally, I assumed she meant by turning her back on this community.

She stops petting Penny and places her hands in her lap. "I did. In fact, so did his wife."

So it is true. It's hard to tell if this makes me feel better or worse.

"He confessed it to her when she got sick." She shakes her head. "Can you imagine?"

That the reverend would confess something horrible to his dying wife to alleviate his own conscience? Yes, I can imagine.

"But I knew before that. I . . . stumbled upon them once." She sighs. "Of course, I'll spare you the details, but that incident seemed to kind of snap Emma back to reason."

"You talked with my mom about it?"

She glances at me. "I did. I'm not sure if you know this, but your mom and I met when I first moved out here. It was the summer before she left for college. We'd known each other for quite a while. I guess that's why she trusted me to talk after that incident. And do you know what she told me?"

Maybe I don't want to hear this.

"She told me how badly she wanted to go back home." She gives me a small smile. "She felt horrible for leaving Paul and your brother and sisters behind for so long. And she was scared that she may not have much of a home to go back to."

"Did she tell you why she left? Did my dad . . ." I can't finish the sentence.

She holds my gaze. "It doesn't matter, dear."

"It does."

Whisper nudges Penny out of the way to get closer to us. "I'm sure Kael told you about Mr. McPheron's passing."

I nod.

"It took me a good three months before I could stomach looking at his things," she says. "I started going through his closet, and behind all his work boots, do you know what I found?" She turns to me, her lips pressed into a hard line.

"I have no idea."

"Black Sabbath."

I blink. "I'm sorry?"

"The band. Black Sabbath. I suppose it was well before your time, wasn't it?"

Oh. She means the secret albums. I guess Mr. McPheron had hidden his favorites in the house that Kael never discovered. "No," I say. "I'm familiar with them."

"Well, I was furious. I had forbidden those albums when Kael was younger, and I thought I threw them all out. I must've told him a dozen times *that* music was not appropriate for a good Christian household, and he pretended that he understood. But there they were, squirreled away in secret all these years." She burst into a small laugh. "And you know what? I realized it just didn't matter." Her eyes have begun to water at the edges. "It was something that made me see him a little bit differently, but ultimately, it didn't change my memories of him or how I felt about him."

I see. I suppose it's a nice sentiment. "So, I'm just meant to move past the fact that my parents were probably trapped in a secretly miserable marriage the entire time I knew them before they died?"

Her smile fades. "No. You sit with it for a while. You feel sad, you feel angry, and then you remember the parts you knew about them."

I stand up. "I should probably get going."

"It's already so late. If I'd known you were out here earlier, I would've . . . well, did you have some dinner?"

"No, it's fine. I'm not hungry." I edge toward the entryway.

She follows me to the dark driveway. "Lexi." She catches up to me outside my car. "Think about what I said, all right? None of us are all good, but none of us are all bad either." She reaches up and moves a lock of my hair behind my shoulder.

I'd like to say a lot of things right now. I'd like to tell her that her late husband hiding classic rock albums is different from finding out both of my parents were probably unfaithful. And that it is *wildly* different from discovering my dad was likely not my biological father. Instead, I settle for saying only one thing: "Good night."

CHAPTER THIRTY-TWO

On the way to the motel, my eyes focus on the middle line of the road. The dotted line appears and then disappears rapidly as I continue driving.

The thought drifts into my mind again, the heaviness of it bearing down on my body.

Just let go.

It feels harder to resist this time as the weight works its way down into my stomach. My mind is numb. I can't think of a single thing I'd miss if I were gone. I can only picture how welcoming the darkness would be. I've been able to manage this feeling pretty well over the years with therapy. But when Beth got sick, all my time and money went to getting her better. The urgency kept most of my dark thoughts at bay. I had to find a way to survive so Beth could.

Just let go.

And I would finally know if it were just darkness behind this life.

Let go.

I wouldn't hurt anymore.

I raise my hands off the steering wheel and close my eyes. I can sense the car drifting to the left, rolling over the subtle bump of reflective tape as it crosses the center.

No.

My hands clamp down onto the wheel, and I rip open my eyelids. I release an exhale and steer back toward the right lane. "Jesus Christ . . ." I shake my head. What am I doing?

As I near the edge of the lane, my headlights flash on a tall figure standing in the road directly in front of me.

I jerk the wheel, and I swerve away from the figure. The car runs off the side of the road. A roll and a sharp thud sound before my stomach drops and the airbags explode against my torso. Up is down. I can't catch my breath as the car rattles to a stop.

My arms are braced below me against the crumpled roof of the car. I inhale, and a sharp pain crushes against my chest.

A clicking sound approaches from outside the car along with the sound of rustling grass.

I breathe in again and cough. I can't reach my seat belt. My legs begin to tingle under the pressure of the open airbags.

Out of the corner of my eye, I see movement through the passenger's-side door. Pain shoots through the back of my neck as I turn to look. My heart stops. The shadow of the figure from the road walks toward the car.

It's him. The shadow.

I want to scream, but I'm not sure I can open my mouth.

Maybe this is what I see before I die.

I remain frozen in place, a tremor beginning to spread throughout my body. His pace quickens, and the sound of clicking intensifies. I press my eyes shut.

Moments pass, and all is silent. I open my eyes. The shadow is gone.

"Hello?" A car door slams. A beam of light flashes along the grass near me until it shines in my face. "Lexi?" Sheriff Larson kneels down beside my busted door window. "Are you hurt?"

I don't answer.

"Lexi . . . I need to know if you're hurt anywhere before I can help you. Do you feel any pain?"

I try to focus on my body. Everything feels so distant and numb. I shake my head.

"Good. You're doing fine." He shoves against the airbags. "Are you able to move your arms?"

"Yes," I whisper. My voice doesn't sound like my own.

"Okay, good. Can you press your arms to the ceiling? As hard as you can."

I adjust so my forearms are rigid against the roof. They immediately weaken from the pressure and tremble.

He pulls his uniform jacket off and lays it across the shards of glass below me.

"I'm going to unfasten your seat belt, but I've got you, okay?" He stretches an arm across my waist.

I nod.

He reaches his other hand up, and the buckle clicks. My full weight presses against his arm as he eases me down on my side. The broken glass rattles underneath his jacket as I crawl through the window.

I'm only able to focus on his face once I'm out of the car. I'm terrified of looking in the shadows behind him.

He glances me over and then his eyes dart to the car. "We need to move, okay? I'm going to help you." He stands and stoops to help me up.

My fingers dig into his arms as my legs wobble. I let him lead me closer to the road as my eyes swivel and search the darkness.

He practically carries me up the ditch to where his cruiser is parked on the shoulder. He turns me toward him and examines me with the illumination provided by the headlights of his car. His gaze zeroes in on my arm. “We’re going to the hospital.” He guides me to the passenger side and opens the door.

I slump into the seat, and he rushes to the driver’s side. I stare out the window at my car down below. It doesn’t seem real when it’s flipped over like that.

I catch a glimpse of movement near my car as Larson begins to drive in the opposite direction.

Should I tell him? About the shadow? About the ghost?

CHAPTER THIRTY-THREE

"I'm fine." I say it as soon as Larson appears in the doorframe of my room.

His eyes flash to the IV I'm hooked to. "That's because of the morphine."

He's not wrong. If I wasn't already spaced out enough, the morphine has certainly finished the job. I feel warm all over.

"We'll see what the X-rays show," he says.

I sit up and lean against the pillow behind me. "Really. I'm just a little banged up."

He frowns and points to my arm.

I look down at the gauze wound around it. "It's a scratch." The doctor figured it probably came from the impact of the airbag or the window shattering.

He shakes his head. "What happened?"

What can I even say? He'll think I'm crazy. "I thought I saw something."

He takes a step toward me. "On the road? What was it? A deer?"

I shrug. "Something like that."

"The past few days have been rough . . ." He lowers his voice. "You know this will pass, right?"

This is the reaction I was worried about. Over a decade ago he and I were in these exact same positions, except back then my stomach was freshly pumped, and he didn't have quite as much gray in his hair. He knows that I've let the darkness win before. He was the one who transported me to the psychiatric facility after I was released from the emergency room. "It wasn't like that. I was tired and I just swerved too far to miss something. Really." Maybe the accident could have easily been what he thinks, but the Lex who wants to live won out. I opened my eyes. I gripped the steering wheel before falling off the other side.

He studies me. "Okay. If that's what you say happened, I believe you."

Will he believe me if I tell him about the ghost?

"But this is as good a time as any to tell you that if you ever need someone to talk to, I'm around."

"I know," I say.

"Can I get you anything? Are you hungry?"

"No, I'm good."

"All right, well, I expect we'll hear whether or not they want you to stay overnight soon." He crosses his arms over his body and leans against the wall. He clearly isn't planning to leave. And I actually don't want him to.

Sitting here in the well-lit hospital room with him nearby and the sounds of nurses and doctors stirring in the background . . . it makes what happened with the shadow feel like a dream. "How bad is my car? Can I drive it?"

He raises his eyebrows. "I don't suppose you can, Lexi. It's totaled."

Shit. I sigh. I guess it would take a miracle for an old Corolla to survive a drop and rollover like that.

The nurse pops his head in and taps lightly on the open door. "Alexis Blake?" He smiles at me and then turns to Larson. "I need to speak with the patient alone, sir."

"No," I say. "He can stay."

The nurse steps closer to me and runs a hand through his shoulder-length blond hair while he reads from the clipboard in his hand. "So, looks like you're free to go. No fractures, no internal bleeding. You're very lucky. From what I hear it was a nasty accident." He glances at Larson. "The power of seat belts, I guess."

Larson looks at me. I wonder if he's debating whether to force a hold on me. Maybe he doesn't actually believe me.

The nurse sets the clipboard at the edge of the bed and pulls two latex gloves from a dispenser and approaches me. "How are you feeling?" he asks, pinching the IV and sliding it from my hand and replacing it with a swatch of gauze.

"I'm fine." I look at Larson. He's the one who needs the most convincing.

I nod absently as the nurse goes through the spiel about signs of whiplash or concussion. "If you have any of those symptoms, follow up with your primary caregiver as soon as possible."

As I trail Larson out of the room and into the lobby, he constantly glances over his shoulder at me.

Once we reach his cruiser in the parking lot, he opens the passenger's-side door and hands me a small plastic shopping bag. "I had a deputy go gather your things."

"Thank you." I peer inside and grab my phone from the bottom of the bag. I get into his car and close the door. I scroll through my notifications. It's just a good night text from Kael shortly after the accident followed by a missed call an hour ago. "No one else was called to the wreck, right?" If Kael responded and saw my car like that, he must be beside himself.

"No. Just the tow truck since I brought you here." He sinks into the seat from the other side and starts the car. I look at the time on the dashboard. Even though it feels like I've been in the hospital for days, it's only been a few hours. It's nearly 2:00 a.m.

"I'm sorry. You must've been up all night because of me."

He shakes his head. "You don't worry about that. Do you want me to take you to the motel? They put you up in a new room, right?"

"I don't know." I stare down at my phone. I don't know how to tell Kael about this in the morning. Thank God he wasn't the one to find me. He's done enough worrying about me.

Larson pulls into the motel parking lot and turns to me. "Why don't you sit here for a minute?" He climbs out and pushes through the door of the motel lobby.

I glance out the window into the dark, empty land on the other side of the building. Did I really see what I thought I saw?

The door opens again, and Larson sits beside me. "I got you a new room." He extends a key toward me.

"Oh. Thanks." I take it between my fingers and stare down at it.

"I've got nothing better to do if you want me to bring you back home."

Home? He must mean all the way back to San Francisco. "You're trying to get rid of me?" I laugh, but his grave expression doesn't change.

"I'm not sure it's a good idea for you to stick around here."

I sigh. "Good or not, I'm not finished here." For a few reasons now. It's not just about the house. It's about the ranch. It's about Kael. My stomach sinks. It's about Evan.

He stares out the windshield at the lower level of the motel. "I know it's none of my business, but . . ." He closes his mouth.

"What?"

"Is there any particular reason you're not staying at Kael's tonight?"

I shift in my seat involuntarily, triggering a dull pain in my side. The morphine must be wearing off. "What kind of question is that?" I'm still cringing internally from Larson seeing me in Kael's T-shirt yesterday morning.

His cheeks redden. "I just mean, is there any reason you may not feel safe there after what happened to your friend?"

I shoot a glare at him. "Kael had nothing to do with that. I have no doubt in my mind about that."

He nods. "All right. But if you *did* suddenly have doubts, you would tell me, wouldn't you?"

"Yes." I answer without really considering the truth. Surely I would. It doesn't really matter, though, because Kael would never—"I'm going to go up if that's all right."

"Of course," he says. "Let me . . ." He opens the car door again and steps out. The trunk is popped open. He lifts the lid and pulls out my old duffel bag. He yanks off a yellow tag clipped around the handle. "I had them process your things as quickly as possible." He leans into the trunk again and pulls out my laptop, cradling it between his two hands.

I grip the laptop. I don't even want to know what being "processed" involves. "Thank you."

He leads the way to a door on the first floor not far from the lobby and sets down my bag. "This is your new room. Try to get some sleep."

"You do the same." I take the key he gave me and open the door. I glance over my shoulder to see him get back into his car before I tote my belongings into the room and sink onto the bed.

With all that talk about Kael, I should probably call him back. It's so late, but he might be worried. I roll over onto my side and set my phone on the pillow beside me. It can wait.

As I close my eyes, I can see the shadow outside my car running closer and closer toward me. This time he doesn't stop. He bends down and crawls in through the window. I can see his face. And it's blank, smooth and stretched skin over an anonymous skull.

My entire body is rigid when I wake up. My fists are clenched and my neck tucked tightly against the bed. I turn on my side and look at the strong light streaming through the window past the curtains. I sit up, pressing a hand to my temple as a sharp pain shoots through my head. I need to find those painkillers from the hospital.

My legs don't feel quite steady as I stand, but I manage to make it to the window. I pull the curtain farther to the side and peer out. Larson is still sitting in his car in the same spot as last night. He's leaning against the headrest, a book held up to his face.

I walk out through the door and hobble toward his car. He looks up as I approach and tap his window. "What are you still doing here?" I ask as soon as the window begins to roll down.

He sets his paperback on the dashboard and fidgets with his hat on his lap. "How are you feeling?"

I lean against the car. "I told you I'm fine. You weren't out here all night, were you?"

"I just wanted to be around in case you needed something." His eyes drift to my scuffed-up jeans from last night. "Didn't get much sleep, did you?"

I glance at the phone in my hand as it starts to buzz. It's Kael again. He's probably heard about the accident by now. "Please go home. Or work. Or something."

Larson nods to the passenger seat. "First, get in."

"Why?"

He reaches across and opens the door for me.

I sigh and walk around to the other side and sit beside him. "What's going on?"

He doesn't say anything but begins to drive.

Suddenly, a feeling of déjà vu washes over me, like it did last night. Long ago, he and I were sitting in these seats. He was silent back then because he probably didn't know what to say to a sixteen-year-old girl who had tried to end it all hours earlier.

Would it be so bad if he *is* bringing me back? After all, I'm not entirely sure what I've been seeing.

I turn to the window as we pass where my car rolled over. I spot some small debris in the flattened grass where it must have happened.

Maybe I'm *not* well. Maybe losing Beth, and now Evan, has brought something to the surface that I thought I'd buried.

"You're lucky," Larson says.

Lucky. I've heard that before. Lucky to survive the fire. Lucky to survive my first suicide attempt. And then the second. But at what point does luck run out?

Once we drive past the feed store, Larson turns down a road by the railroad that I haven't been on before. A small house emerges from behind the trees, and he starts the car down the driveway.

Is this his house?

He parks the cruiser by another car and fishes in his pocket for a moment.

"What are we doing here?"

He extracts a set of keys and hands it to me.

"What are you doing?"

"I'm letting you use my car."

I wrap my fingers around the key ring. "So, I wrecked *my* car and you're giving me yours? Does that really seem like a good idea?"

"Don't talk me out of it, wise guy. I'm *this* close to taking those keys back."

"What about you? What will you drive?"

"I can make do with the patrol car for now. This is a little newer than your Corolla, so why don't you look around and make sure you know how to work it."

I roll my eyes. "I think I can manage." I open the door and peer inside. "A back-up camera? That's pretty fancy."

"Do you feel all right to drive it back? I'll follow behind you."

I turn the keys in the ignition. "Give me a break, I'm okay. Please stay and take a rest for fuck's sake."

He frowns at me. I get the feeling he's about to reprimand me for cursing but then I realize he's holding back a grin. "Keep your phone close by. I'll be calling to check in later."

"Will do." I buckle my seat belt. "Thank you for this." I tap the steering wheel. It's so shiny and stain-free.

He shifts his weight to his other leg. "Well, I don't want you to be stranded out here . . . and please, if you're going back to the farm, make sure someone goes with you."

"Like Kael?"

He exhales.

"Come on . . . you don't really believe he would hurt anyone. You've known him forever. There isn't a violent bone in his body."

"Lexi, I've learned to never underestimate what the people in this town are capable of." He places his hand on the roof of the car and leans closer. "Drive safe."

"Um . . ." I stare down at my hands. "I don't think I really thanked you about last night, so . . . thank you."

"Of course." He taps the roof and takes a step back.

"And, one more thing." I look at him. "Have you found out anything else about Evan?"

"I'm trying," he says. "That's actually why I was working late last night. I've been running the deputies pretty ragged on that case, so I started taking up extra patrols."

"I see."

"Be safe out there, Lexi."

"I will." I close the door and look up at him through the window one more time before starting the engine.

I must've been lost in thought because it isn't until I'm within yards of the ranch that I realize where I am. Kael's nowhere to be seen in front of the house when I park. His truck is here, though, and his mom's car isn't.

I head to the barn and find him near the forge. The fire isn't lit, but he's polishing and cleaning new shoes.

"Hey," I say once I'm closer.

He turns around, cloth and horseshoe in hand. "Thank God. You're okay." He sets his things down and closes the gap between us and throws his arms around me. This was one of the reasons I put my hands back on the steering wheel last night. The warmth of Kael's body against mine. The way his breath rustles my hair when he holds me close. "You didn't answer my calls this morning. I heard about the accident."

I sigh. "How?"

He looks at the bandage around my arm. "Does that matter? Why aren't you in the hospital?"

"I'm sorry. I should've sent you a text or something. I'm fine. Thankfully, the sheriff was driving by not long after it happened."

His fingers squeeze my hand. "What can I do to help?"

Honestly, I have no idea. I can't even wrap my head around what I needed to do before the accident. What was I planning to do today? My thoughts are all replaying the worst parts of the last forty-eight hours.

"Wait, how did you get here? Pete said your car is totaled."

Ah. Pete, the town's shade-tree mechanic. Of course he's probably told half the town already. "It is. Larson is lending me his personal car."

"I'm so glad you're okay. What happened last night?"

I haven't thought through this part—of what to say to Kael about the accident. "I almost hit a deer." No reason to make up a new lie, I guess.

He meets my gaze, his eyes slightly narrowed as if he senses something is off. "Why don't I get you some coffee?" His fingers intertwine with mine as he leads me toward the house. Once we're through the door, he pulls out one of the kitchen chairs. "Take a rest."

I sink into the seat and watch as he pours coffee from the carafe and slides the mug toward me.

He sits beside me. "I need you to tell me the truth."

I take a sip from the cup. "The truth about what?"

He looks down at his hands. "You've been acting very strange, Lex. I'm worried about you."

I set the cup down on the table. "I've just had a lot to deal with recently. With Evan and everything."

He nods. "Of course. And maybe that's why you should be more careful. You're wearing yourself too thin. Maybe you should go back for a little while."

"Why is everyone trying to get rid of me?"

He straightens in his seat. "Maybe it's for the best if you go back home, recharge, and then deal with all of this after the dust settles."

I shake my head. "I can't do that."

"Why not?"

"I don't think I'll have the strength to come back here again after this," I say. "I need all of this to be finished for good."

He sighs. "Okay, then. Let's finish it."

CHAPTER THIRTY-FOUR

I'm really sick of funerals. And Tom's was no exception. Although I recognized at least half the town in the room, it seemed empty somehow. Kael continued to glance at me out of the corner of his eye as Butcher delivered the eulogy, and now as we walk down the corridor toward the fellowship room, he takes my hand.

"Do you want to leave?" he whispers as we trail behind the others.

"No, I'm fine." I wasn't sure what would happen when I saw Butcher for the first time after our discussion, but I felt nothing.

He stared at me on and off during his delivery, fumbling over his words as he did so. I can spot him at the entryway of the fellowship, greeting congregants solemnly before they make a beeline to the ambrosia salad.

"Where's his family?" The entire front row was notably empty during the service.

Kael's forehead tenses. "It's a long story."

The answer makes me feel worse somehow. I shouldn't have judged Tom so harshly during our interactions. I have no idea what he was dealing with or what his background was. As we near the entrance, I speed past Butcher before he can open his mouth.

"Good afternoon, Reverend," I hear Kael say.

I wait for him by the counter where the remaining funeral programs are displayed.

"We don't have to stay, Lex." He glances over at a crowd of elders lining up at the kitchen window.

"It's fine. Go help your mom." She's smiling as hard as she can and spooning giant helpings of au gratin potatoes onto paper plates as she hands them to people.

"Are you sure? I don't want to—"

"I'm really okay." I gently push his arm to steer him in the direction of the kitchen.

He gazes over his shoulder at me right before he gets swallowed by the throng of hungry mourners.

I turn around.

"Oh, watch it, little lady!" One of the deacons, Mr. Carmichael, almost trips in an effort to avoid me. His paper plate of deviled eggs wobbles dangerously, and he grips me with his free hand to steady himself. "Sorry about that."

I yank my arm away.

"I didn't expect to see you here," he says, shoving one of the eggs into his mouth before continuing. "Figured you'd be back in the city after what happened."

I assume he's referring to Evan. "I won't be here much longer."

He narrows his eyes. "Did you even know Tom?"

"Not much." I look over at Kael. I wonder if I can make a smooth exit out of this conversation and join him in the kitchen.

"Well, you probably knew him about as much as the rest of us then. He was always a quiet kind of guy."

Quiet? He seemed pretty talkative whenever he approached me. "Isn't he from here originally? His family must be here somewhere."

"Oh." He shakes his head. "No. Tom lost his family long ago."

Maybe that's why Tom's behavior always seemed so odd to me. Trauma can do crazy things. It can poison all your interactions, even the ones that seem relatively simple. "Oh. Was it an accident?"

"No, nothing like that. His wife and him divorced many years ago."

Awfully progressive of Sola to allow a divorced man to serve as deacon.

"She was always a little squirrely, and she finally just up and left him and his boy."

His boy? I turn to the kitchen. Butcher approaches Kael and pats him on the shoulder. Maybe I won't try to join him after all.

Carmichael grabs another egg. "Typical of Wayne to not even show up to his own father's funeral."

I look at him. "Wayne?" I try to think about whether I missed any subtle resemblance between the motel clerk and Tom. "That's his son?"

Carmichael chuckles. "You probably know just as well as the rest of us. He hasn't been back here for a good while. He was staying with his mother up north a ways from here."

I glance over my shoulder at Kael and Butcher. What could the reverend possibly be saying to him? And why is Kael even talking to him after everything I told him?

"It's up there, not much further up the road from Eden. Anyways, after that we never saw Wayne around these parts, and poor Tom never mentioned the boy. Eventually we all just assumed it was too painful a subject and stopped asking."

Kael nods and steps away from Butcher.

Finally.

"I think I probably need to head out," I say, walking away from Carmichael.

"See you around."

Kael closes the distance between us. He looks troubled, his forehead tightened in that way it does. "Ms. Vivian took over in the kitchen. Let's head back."

I follow him out the fellowship door and into the parking lot. "What did Butcher say to you?" I ask as we strap on our seat belts.

He turns to the steering wheel. "Just stuff about the ranch."

I don't believe him. "Was it about me?"

He looks at me out of the corner of his eye as we turn onto the road.

"What did he say?"

He shakes his head. "He wanted me to get you to talk to him."

Typical. "Of course he thinks if another man orders me to, I have to speak to him, right?"

"I don't know what he's thinking. Why would he ask me to do that? I mean, he's not worried that you might've already told me about the affair? Shouldn't he be concerned about a scandal or something?"

"No. Your mom's known about it for years."

"What?"

I look out the window as the gentle hills near the ranch come into view. "Yeah. And besides, even if people found out, no one would blame him." It was all my mom's fault as far as these people are concerned. At least Mrs. McPheron had been kind enough not to say that out loud, but I'm sure she thought it.

As we turn the corner and cross the railroad, the sight of patrol cars makes my stomach drop.

Kael says nothing as we enter the driveway, but his eyes focus on the men moving around outside his house.

"What's going on?" I stare at him.

"I have no idea." He parks behind the line of three cars and opens his door.

Larson has been watching us from the time we turned the corner and approaches.

I step in front of Kael. "What are you doing?"

A deputy comes out of the barn, a plastic bag in his gloved hands.

Larson looks past me and zeroes in on Kael with narrowed eyes. "Kael, let's go for a talk at the office."

Kael watches the people moving around in the background. "I don't understand. What's this about?"

Larson's body is completely rigid. "I have some questions for you about Tom."

"What?" I step toward Larson. "We already told you—"

"I said I need to speak to Kael," Larson says, his tone cold. "Alone." He gestures toward his patrol car. "Let's go."

Kael looks at me for a moment. "Um, okay, sure."

I grab his arm. "No. You don't have to go with him." I turn to Larson. "Are you arresting him?" I immediately regret asking, afraid he'll take it as a challenge to do so.

Larson says nothing, but steps past me and opens the back door of his car. He turns and glowers at Kael.

Kael gently pulls away from my grasp. "Everything's fine, okay?" As he says it a weak attempt at a smile barely registers on his face before disappearing completely. "It's just some questions."

"I'm going to follow you to the office."

He gives a little nod and then ducks into the car.

Larson immediately slams the door behind him. Before he can reach the other side, I block the door.

"What is this all about? Why are you insisting on targeting Kael?"

The anger has faded from his gaze, replaced with sadness. "There are things I can't ignore about Tom's murder."

"Tom's murder? Even if you think Kael is capable of murdering someone, you can't possibly think he'd be dumb enough to leave the body on his property."

"He probably wasn't planning to leave it there," Larson says. "But then *you* found it. Because of that, he couldn't carry on with his plans."

I shake my head. "You have this completely wrong. You—"

"Get out of the way, Lexi. I'm not having this discussion with you about an active investigation." He tugs on the door handle. "I'm sorry."

I fumble around in my bag for my phone as I watch them drive off. I can't think of anyone else to call.

"This is Ridley."

Thank God he answered.

"Oh, Alexis, I'm not a criminal attorney."

"Okay . . . well do you know one who can help me?"

He exhales. "Has he been arrested?"

"Kind of? I'm not sure. The sheriff drove him away in his patrol car, but—"

"Was he handcuffed?"

"No," I say.

He clicks his tongue. "I'm on my way."

CHAPTER THIRTY-FIVE

"As of *now*, he has been arrested." Ridley adjusts his wrinkled button-up shirt.

I sit up on the chair by the door to the parking lot. "What?" I stare past him toward the sheriff's office door.

Ridley stifles a yawn. "His arraignment is tomorrow at eight. They're going to charge him with murder."

I can't possibly be hearing him correctly. "I don't . . . how?"

He glances over his shoulder. "Let's go talk in the car." The word echoes in my mind as he leads me into the parking lot and over to his Buick parked in the first row.

Arrested. Kael has been *arrested*. Arrested. For *murder*?

Once we're inside, he tosses his briefcase onto the seat behind us. "They found a weapon they believe was used to murder Tom Miller on Kael's property."

Is that all? "So what? Tom's body was found on the ranch. It only makes sense that whoever did it might've left it somewhere on the property, right?"

He turns to look out the windshield. "They found it in Kael's forge in the barn."

I shake my head. "What do they think the murder weapon was?"

"They found what they think is a burnt axe handle. It's missing the blade, but the handle still had trace amounts of blood on it. Tom's blood."

I look down at my hands. I have to admit it's hard to imagine a reasonable explanation for that. But still, I *know* Kael. I know he couldn't. Right? "What did Kael say to them about it?"

"Thankfully nothing. I got here while they were still letting him stew in silence, hoping he would crack. They didn't tell him exactly what they found until I was sitting with him." He stares at me. "Did you know about the axe, Alexis?"

"No." I guess it makes sense, though, with the condition I found Tom in. He wasn't recognizable. But is there a universe in which Kael could have done that to someone?

"I'm just trying to understand what you may be mixed up in here."

I meet his gaze. "He didn't do it. I don't know what happened, but Kael couldn't have killed Tom, okay? What did he tell you when you talked to him?" My tone doesn't sound quite as confident as I wish it did.

He turns over the ignition. "I'll drive you to the motel, and I can give you a ride in the morning to pick up your car, all right?"

I say nothing but peer at the office one more time before he pulls out of the lot. The thought of Kael spending the night there makes me feel sick. I roll down the window.

"I'll help him during the hearing tomorrow morning and see if the judge will let him out on recognizance, but after that . . . I'm a little out of my depth here. I think you need to find him a real criminal lawyer."

"Did the sheriff say anything about a second murder?"

Ridley sighs. "A *second* murder? No. Why would you even ask that?" He sounds exhausted, his voice growing hoarser and more hysterical with every word.

Oh God, when he hears this, it'll put him over the edge. "Someone killed my ex-boyfriend recently. His body was in my room at the motel. And—"

"Why wouldn't you tell me this earlier? Why are you still in this town? It's clearly not safe!"

"It didn't seem relevant at the time," I say. But it *did* seem relevant. I knew when I saw Evan's body he had the same deep wounds that Tom had. The wounds that left their skin a raw, bloody mess. "But the sheriff thought Kael might've had something to do with that in the beginning, too, and so I'm nervous they may try to pin that on him as well."

"Let's just . . . I need a minute, okay?" Ridley rubs one of his eyes. "Maybe we should just have some quiet time for a bit." Several minutes pass before the motel sign comes into sight. Ridley parks near the lobby and leans deeper into his seat. "I'm scared to ask, but *why* would the sheriff like Kael for the murder of your ex?"

"My ex was harassing me, and Kael got him to leave."

He raises his eyebrows.

"It was a light, *verbal* altercation. Definitely nothing violent."

"Does the sheriff have some kind of personal vendetta against your friend?" He strokes the wrinkled part of his forehead, but it never smooths out.

"No. Not that I know of. But my ex-boyfriend Evan's body was in the same shape as Tom's. It's probably only a matter of time before they try to link the two."

Ridley holds up a hand. "Okay, okay. One step at a time. I'm going to get a room. I'm going to digest all of this information and sleep. And then I'll go to the arraignment in the morning. After that, I'll call a few defense lawyer friends and see if they're able to drive out this way. Sound good?"

No. Absolutely none of this sounds good. "I should call his mom."

Ridley pulls the handle on his door. "Kael had just called her when I was about to leave. Come on. You could probably use some sleep too."

I follow him to the lobby. Wayne glances up from his magazine at us. I can see a hint of resemblance now between him and Tom. It's so subtle though. I debate whether I should offer my condolences. It seems somehow inappropriate under the circumstances that I just got Tom's suspected killer a lawyer.

"Can I get a room, please?" Ridley pulls out his credit card and slides it across the desk.

Wayne side-eyes me before swiping it through the card reader. "Room two is empty." He grabs a key from under the desk and hands it to Ridley.

"Thanks." Once we're out the door, Ridley turns to me. "What is the nature of your relationship with this man?"

"With Kael?"

He nods.

It's hard to believe he hasn't guessed by now. Maybe he just wants to hear me say it. Maybe he can't believe the little girl he saw running around with his kids in the park is now romantically linked to a suspected murderer. "It's complicated."

He deflates. "Oh, Alexis."

"Look, I know him, okay? I've known him since before the fire, and this seems bad, but . . . there has to be another explanation."

He stares at me. "Let's speak in the morning. I'll meet you out here at seven thirty sharp." He flashes me one more disappointed look before turning toward the door for room 2.

CHAPTER THIRTY-SIX

By the next morning, Ridley's demeanor hasn't improved much. He peppered me with questions the entire way back to the sheriff's office, as if trying to figure out how my life has gotten so off track. And, to his point, I suppose it has.

But it doesn't matter. All that matters is that Kael is walking out with him right now. Free. Well, for now.

"You need to be at that hearing next week no matter what," Ridley says to Kael and then looks at me. "I'm going to make those calls today. I'll find someone who can attend, okay?"

"Thank you. I really appreciate it."

Kael rubs his eyes. He looks like he's been awake for weeks. "Yes, thank you, sir."

We wait until Ridley drives off before getting in my car. Kael looks out the window as I start down the road. "Thanks for the ride."

"Of course." Is it possible that I don't know this man at all? Maybe I was a fool to think that we could've gone all these years apart and not changed. But Kael becoming a murderer? It's simply beyond the realm of possibility.

He doesn't say anything else but leans back and closes his eyes.

It's probably for the best. I have no idea what else to say right now. As soon as I park in front of his house, he opens the door. He barely looks at me as we walk toward the house.

"Kael . . . what did they ask you?" I finally can ask when we reach the porch.

"It's what Larson said. He thinks I had something to do with Tom's death." His voice sounds heavy, as though it took great effort to even speak those words. He probably can't believe it. I still can't. "Apparently they found a note in Tom's pocket. It was some kind of note he had written that he wasn't going to cover for someone anymore. Larson got it in his mind it's somehow connected to the missing fire department funds from before."

That's right. Didn't Kael tell me that Tom had worked at the bank?

He shakes his head. "He thinks I'm the one who has been taking the money, and that when Tom threatened to blow the lid on the whole thing, that I . . ."

Chopped him up? I try to picture Kael coaxing Tom all the way out into the middle of the property and then hacking wildly at him. It doesn't make any sense. If Tom had come to threaten Kael, why on earth would he follow him so willingly to his death?

"I thought you said the money stopped going missing?" I want to ask him outright about the axe handle in the furnace, but I can't.

He shrugs. "I mean, that's what I thought. We haven't heard otherwise since Butcher took over." He rubs the back of his neck. "I'm sorry, but I think I just need to get some sleep right now. I can't even wrap my head around what happened."

"I get it."

The screen door of the main house screeches open, and Mrs. McPheron bursts out. "Oh my goodness!" She shoots over to us at a clip faster than I've ever seen from her before and throws her arms around Kael. "Are you—"

"I'm fine." It takes him a moment before he hugs her back. "Everything is going to be fine."

She releases him and stares at me. "He told me that you brought him a lawyer last night."

It has the cadence of an accusation. "I did."

Her lips quaver. "Thank you, Lexi. I was beside myself, calling every single one I could find in the area, but . . ." She covers her eyes with her hands and begins to shake with quiet sobs.

Kael's face falls. He places a hand on her shoulder. "Mom, it's okay. I didn't do it."

She nods and looks up at him. "I know. Of course I know that. But why would they—"

"Mom." His tone is firm. "I couldn't sleep at all last night. Let me just lay down for a bit, okay? Then, let's talk about all this." He turns to me. "Thank you. I really appreciate what you did last night."

"It was nothing."

He flashes what I assume he intends as a reassuring smile but it comes across as a grimace before he ascends the steps into the house.

Mrs. McPheron looks at me. "I don't understand any of it. Did he tell you anything else? What do they want from him?"

I can't tell her about the handle. It would only break her down even more. And I have no theory to explain it away. "I have no idea."

"Would you like some coffee or something to eat? You must be exhausted." Her eyes are sunken and bloodshot.

"No, I'm fine. Kael has the right idea. Why don't you go take a rest?"

She sniffs. "Yes, I suppose I'm no use to anyone in this condition." She reaches up and squeezes my shoulder. "Do we owe your lawyer friend anything for his trouble?" Her lips twitch as she asks.

"No. He was happy to help," I say. "He's trying to find someone to help Kael with the rest of the process. I assume whoever that is probably expects some money."

She nods. "Of course." She removes her hand.

"I'll be back later to check in."

"Yes, thank you." She turns and walks back into the main house as if in a trance.

I climb into my car and close the door. What now? What can I possibly do now? I look toward Kael's house. It doesn't make sense. Maybe the line connecting Tom to the volunteer fire department's money is reasonable. But if there were money-management issues long before Kael came back to Sola and joined the department, how could he be involved?

CHAPTER THIRTY-SEVEN

Larson's eyes widen when he sees me storm in through the front door. He looks exhausted, the dark circles under his eyes more pronounced than I've ever seen. He's leaning against the desk alone at the front, stained white mug of coffee in his hand. "Lexi—"

"I think you have this all wrong."

"I know that's what you think." He nods and sets his mug on the table. "But there are things you don't understand that I do."

"What are they?"

He sighs. "I'm not at liberty to discuss this with you."

"Okay." I step closer to the desk. "Then, let's talk about what *I* know. I know that money was going missing from the fire department long before Kael even joined. How do you explain that?"

He narrows his eyes. "And I suppose Kael told you that just now."

"No. I found that out when I first got here. Kael told me it's the reason Mr. McPheron didn't get reelected as chief a while back. Money was missing, and they were upset he couldn't figure it out. All of that happened when Kael was away at college."

He stands straight suddenly, his eyebrows drawn together. "When was this?"

"I told you. Kael was at college, so I don't know . . . 2010 maybe? Why? Does that sound familiar?"

He glances toward the open door of his office in the back of the empty building.

"What?"

He looks at me again and shakes his head. "It's uh . . . it's something your dad told me about. I just remembered it now."

"Really? What was it?"

"When you asked me if he was looking into something around here, I wasn't entirely honest with you."

It's what I suspected, but I'm taken aback by him actually saying it.

"He had a problem with the church."

Does he know why? Did Dad ever tell him the truth about what Mom had done? Or what he had done?

"He believed someone there was misappropriating funds. The preacher."

I stare at him. "Well, of course he is. Has no one seriously wondered before how he's been rebuilding the rectory and buying out everyone's lands and businesses? All on a small-town preacher's salary?"

He chews his lower lip. "Look, your dad was asking the same questions. But everyone here has a story that explains it. Butcher comes from old money up north or he's been investing it, growing businesses that help the community. Still, something always seemed off to Paul. He went back through the tax forms the church had filed. He badgered Butcher and the deacons."

"And? Did he find anything?"

He looks away. "I don't know."

Dad must've still been digging when the fire happened. "Okay, well it doesn't really matter though. When did Butcher join the department?"

"I don't remember."

To be fair, neither do I. For a long time after the fire, I avoided even walking by the volunteer fire department. Mr. McPheron was the only one who lifted his face shield that night to talk with Larson, and so I knew he was there, but the other firefighters were a blur to me. "The fact that he was looking into money issues in the church and then money issues popped up in the fire department is more than enough to point you in the direction of someone else who had an actual interest in killing Tom."

He raises his eyebrows. "Kael didn't tell you about the axe then."

"I know about the alleged axe handle," I say. "But anyone could've put that there. And I don't think Kael would be able to convince Tom to follow him out a hundred acres after threatening him. Do you?"

He doesn't respond.

"You have to look into Butcher. That's the only explanation that makes sense."

He grabs his Stetson from the desk and places it on his head. "Go on and get some rest. Let me do my job."

2003

I hovered by the door as Grandpa squinted down at a book in his hands. "Grandpa?" I leaned against the frame. "What're you reading?"

He frowned at the pages and quickly closed it. "Nothing, actually. I can't read a darn word."

I pointed at the wire-rimmed glasses on the nightstand. "That's because you need those."

He narrowed his eyes and followed my finger. "Oh . . . well, yes, that would help, wouldn't it?" He reached for the glasses.

"Let me read!" I bounced on my heels to the camel-back chair in the corner by his bed. I grabbed the book from his lap before he could protest. "I'm in the orange reading level this year."

He grinned and rested his head against his pillow. "Orange? I didn't know I had an advanced reader in the family."

It had been a while since I'd seen him this relaxed. He didn't talk that much usually anymore either. "What is this?" I flipped the book over on my lap. "*The Pelican Brief*?"

Grandpa laughed. "Your mom got it for me. It's not my style, but maybe it'll get better."

Up until that moment, I'd never seen such a new book in Grandpa's proximity. The bookshelves in his room were lined with old leather-bound classics that he'd read every Sunday morning and evening on the porch, playing classical music on an old stereo wedged behind his rocking chair. "What's it about?"

"Um . . . a law student and a car bomb so far."

He was right. That didn't seem like a fun book.

"What about *Treasure Island* instead?"

A twinkle appeared in his eyes. "You read my mind, girl. It's over on that shelf, I think."

I leaped from the chair and replaced Mom's gift with the Robert Louis Stevenson classic.

—

I woke in the dark. My face was cool against the pages of the open book at the foot of Grandpa's bed.

Grandpa must've turned off his lamp at some point because it was completely dark in the bedroom.

I remember the second I realized how still and stale the air was. Grandpa's snoring had been a joke between all of us the first few weeks after we moved in. Amy complained every morning how the sound carried upstairs to her room at night.

I closed the book and accidentally brushed my hand against Grandpa's foot. It was stiff. He didn't move at all.

I paused in the dark, my eyes adjusting to the darkness. I stood up from the chair and inched closer to Grandpa's pillow. He was so quiet.

"Grandpa?" I whispered.

He didn't stir.

I dropped the book and leaned closer to his face. A sour smell reached me. "Grandpa!"

Nothing. I shook his shoulders, but they were hard, like plastic. I leaped back toward the door. I turned the handle, but it wouldn't open. I pushed and pushed, but it wouldn't move.

Something rustled behind me, and I froze. I could sense a presence over my shoulder.

After a moment, I turned to look, and my body began to quiver when I saw it. In the corner of Grandpa's room, a tall, solid shadow stood, its outline discernible in the light of the open window.

I grabbed the doorknob again and twisted it, the cold brass digging into my palms.

Footsteps sounded behind me.

The next thing I remembered was the hoarseness of my throat from my screams and Dad swinging open the door and lifting me into his arms. He didn't see the shadow. As he carried me away from the room, through my tears I saw a door stopper on the floor. The large rubber one we used in the barn to keep the door open on hot days.

In the morning, when my parents told us what happened to Grandpa, they asked, their faces pale, who had lodged the door stopper outside Grandpa's bedroom door to lock me in. No one confessed.

CHAPTER THIRTY-EIGHT

I like Sheriff Larson. And I trust Sheriff Larson.

But I have my doubts about whether he sees the dots connecting as clearly as I do. As I wait in the parking lot across the street behind a large tree, I think about what Larson said. *"Your dad was asking the same questions."*

I had expected Larson to race out of the office to track down Butcher after our talk, but he remains inside for hours as deputies and visitors drift in and out.

The sun is low in the sky, nearly about to drop behind the curtain of redwoods in the distance.

I found the key hidden in the glove box before coming to see him. I was just trying to see if Larson had a stash of gum. I figured chewing something—anything—might calm my nerves. But there was only the key with odd jagged teeth buried under the car manual and a jump-starter kit. I knew it must be a spare.

When I first saw it, I didn't intend on using it, but after talking, I need to know more about the axe handle. No matter what I said to Larson, that's the only thing I can actually explain away.

But do I really think Butcher is capable of murder?

Finally, a deputy and Larson step out of the side exit, and they lock the door before they get into their respective cruisers. I say a prayer to no one that Larson doesn't spot this car, but he turns onto the highway without hesitation. He's probably on his way to talk to Butcher.

I wait until his car disappears into the horizon and then climb out of my seat. I cross the street behind a passing truck and pull the key out of my pocket as I approach the side door of the building.

The sky is getting dark, and there isn't much activity all the way out here. The sheriff's office and the county clerk's office, where I parked, closed to the public at six o'clock. I know there's got to be a deputy posted in there somewhere, but hopefully he or she isn't waiting just within the door.

I twist the key in the lock and swing the door open. The immediate hallway is empty, and I can spot Larson's office at the end of it. I slowly pull the door shut behind me without making a sound. As I continue down the hall, the other desks come into view. A deputy is sitting with his back to me, headphones on and sandwich in one hand as he watches something on his smartphone.

I continue until I reach Larson's office door. He left it ajar. He must be planning to come back soon. I push it open a little more so I can fit through. Without turning on the light switch, I walk over to his desk and lean close to the folders laid out there. Under the top manila folder is a notepad with scribbled words on it like *McPheron*, *VFD*, and *Tom*. I grab it and hold it up to my eyes. Larson's notes describe the wounds on Tom and then has the question *stabbed or sliced?*

My stomach turns at the thought of Tom's body. I set the notepad down and shuffle the folders. None of them are labeled, so I flip through them as I go. At the very bottom is a small stack of loose papers. My name is hastily scribbled on the first page of the pile.

I move it out of the way, and my heart stops. The second page is a photocopy with the address of the farm printed at the top. Below that heading looks like a log of sorts. One column has dates and times, and the other has a longer description.

I bend down to read it better.

October 15, 2003 01:02 – 911 incoming call by neighbor about fire sighted

October 15, 2003 01:03 – Outgoing call to Sola VFD from dispatch

October 15, 2003 01:59 – Mobilization of VFD unit

October 15, 2003 02:05 – Arrival at scene

Fifty-six minutes. Someone at the VFD waited fifty-six minutes to inform the on-call firefighters about my family's fire. Someone sat on the 911 call for nearly an hour before sending anyone out to help.

Minutes count. Kael was right. In a fire, just minutes can make a difference. In an emergency, fifty-six minutes is an eternity.

"What are you doing here?"

I hear Larson's steps approaching, but I can't pry my gaze away from the page. "Is this why you didn't want me to see the records?"

I can sense his body tense.

"You knew that the firefighters waited almost a fucking hour to leave the goddamn station that night." I look up and meet his eyes.

"Lexi—"

"You didn't bother to investigate that? That didn't raise a red flag in your 'pending investigation'?"

He takes his hat off and holds it down in his hand. "I did, Lexi. As soon as I got the 911 transcript and the report from the firefighters who responded and realized . . . they closed ranks. You know how they are here. They protect their own. And nobody wanted to own up to letting an entire family burn."

"And so you just stopped looking into it?"

He shakes his head. "Beth begged me to stop."

"She would never—"

"It was tearing her up, Lexi. On top of caring for and raising you and grieving . . . she couldn't handle what the investigation was doing to her each time I tried to get answers. There were no signs of arson, and that was good enough for her. She wanted to move on and forget that any questionable conduct had happened that night."

"Questionable conduct? That's criminal! What else are you hiding in here?" I flip to the next page and freeze. It's a photo from the aftermath of the fire. A wide shot of our blackened house.

"I was going to give you everything. I pulled it all the same day you gave us your request. But I . . ." He glances down. "I failed you."

"Who was on duty that night at the station?"

"I don't know. That part was left out of their incident report, and when I started asking questions, they all denied being assigned to the station that night. After that, McPheron began requiring clearer record keeping of every shift. That way there could be no doubt who was responsible at any given time."

I grab the stack of papers.

"Lexi, please. You have no idea how much I regret giving in to the pressure. Whoever neglected the call that night deserved to face the consequences."

"They will." I step toward him. "Get out of my way."

CHAPTER THIRTY-NINE

The church parking lot is full of the Wednesday-night crowd. I wade through the cars and push the doors to go inside.

Mr. Handley is standing at the back of the foyer before the sanctuary, organizing the collection plates. He looks up when I enter. "Hey!" he calls to me when I walk past him and barge into the sanctuary.

Butcher stops mid-sentence to stare at me from behind the pulpit. Everyone follows his gaze and turns in the pews toward me. He says nothing but watches as I approach down the aisle.

"I'm sorry to interrupt," I announce. The sweat from my palms has made the pages I'm holding stick to my skin. "But I wanted to see if I could figure it out."

Butcher furrows his brow. "Lexi—"

"It's amazing to me," I continue, "that after all this time you still have managed to fool everyone. Well, almost everyone." I can feel and hear the movement of people standing and gathering behind me. "But you didn't fool Paul Blake, did you? He saw you for exactly what you are."

Mr. Handley huffs up behind me. "Young lady, these good people do not deserve to be part of this little outburst you're having."

"Good people?" The words come out with such bitterness that I almost don't recognize my own voice. I turn around to face them—all of the townspeople huddled together. "Fifty-six minutes passed after the call to the fire department and before whoever was on duty that night alerted the other firefighters. Is that what 'good people' do?"

The crowd goes quiet. A few of them turn to look at each other.

"Almost an hour. For a house fire." I stare at Mr. Handley and hold up the papers in my hands. "If *your* family was burning alive, would you wait fifty-six minutes?"

He glances away.

Mrs. McPheron steps up beside me. "Lexi." Her voice is barely above a whisper.

I turn to Butcher. "Would *you* wait if your family was burning?"

He holds my gaze, his eyes wide and wet.

"None of you are 'good people.' Good people wouldn't sit for a goddamn hour while my brother and sisters and my parents burned."

Mrs. McPheron places a hand on my shoulder.

I pull away from her and run out the door, my heart pounding so loudly it drowns out all thoughts.

CHAPTER FORTY

I can barely see the road as I speed away from the church.

I skid to a stop in front of the farm, my headlights flashing against the charred ruins of the house. The sight hits me harder than usual tonight, knowing that it could've been different. If they had come right away, maybe all of us or at least one more could've been saved.

I step out of the car, leaving the engine running. I walk past the house to the barn. One door is open and lightly banging against the other with the breeze. I pull it open and turn on the light on my phone.

I wish I could recall more about that night. During that first session with Janna, I remembered running from the shadow in the house out into the barn and hiding. Did I somehow manage to escape the fire on my own before I ended up in front of the house?

I flash the light down the aisle between the stalls. If I was awake and able to get out, how come no one else in my family did?

As I reach the end of the barn, something dark catches my eye. I flash the light over to the small nook behind the last stall. There's another bundle there.

I stare at it for a moment. I know I removed that last time, didn't I? I grip my phone and sink to my knees, crawling into the smaller space until I reach the bundle of cloth. It looks a little different from last time—a blanket maybe instead of a shirt.

I lift it up in my free hand, but it's much heavier than I expected and it drops to the ground with a thud. Okay, so it's definitely not the same one as last time.

I unravel the cloth and the top of a faded New Balance shoebox appears. I jiggle the box, and a loud clatter sounds as multiple objects shift within.

I glance over my shoulder before lifting the top off. My stomach sinks when I look down. Within the shoebox are dozens of cassette tapes.

My hand begins to tremble as I reach in and grab one off the top. There's a peeling piece of tape with **10.12.2003** written on it in red ink. I set it down and pick up another one. **10.15.2003**. There's no other explanation, is there? These must be the tapes with the recordings of my family's last days. But who would have these? I still can't believe my father would record those. It doesn't make sense. I shuffle around the tapes inside. Underneath is a wad of brown paper. I bring it out.

The wrapped object squishes under my grasp. My stomach turns as the sound combines with the ominous smell, triggering an alarm bell in my mind. I unfurl the butcher paper. My eyes aren't prepared and scan over the withered finger several times before I realize what I'm holding. Dried blood is crusted at the base of the skin.

I jump back, dropping the paper to the ground. I watch as the finger rolls onto the dirt. I recognize the ring digging into the swollen skin right away. It's Evan's class ring.

I get down onto my knees and flash the light from my phone into the shoebox. I grip my phone in between my hands. But my mind goes blank. Who do I call?

The rational answer is Larson. I click his name, and the phone rings. And rings until it goes to voice mail. "This is Lex. I need you to come meet me at the farm. As soon as possible. It's an emergency. I think." I hang up and click Kael's name.

Shit! Voice mail again. As the beep sounds, I hear a movement just beyond the barn. I click the end call button and press my body against the back of the nook, listening.

Maybe I imagined the sound.

No.

After a moment, footsteps begin to shuffle closer.

I focus on quieting my breathing. Even though it's dark, something holds me back from leaning over to get a look at the person who's entered the barn. Some feeling that this person is listening for me just like I'm listening for them.

My heart races, trying to put together any cohesive thoughts. I swallow. Whoever the owner of this box is has killed Evan.

The footsteps recede after a moment. It's hard to tell, but it sounds like he's walking along the outside of the barn in my direction. I shove my phone in my pocket and bend onto my hands. As the sound draws closer, I slowly crawl out of the nook.

I look at the entrance of the barn. I can see the beams from my headlights in the distance. Whoever this is saw the car running and left it on. If I can run to it fast enough, I—

"Lex!"

Kael. Although his voice is far away, it echoes on the edges of the barn. The footsteps outside have stopped.

I need to warn Kael. I need to get us both out of here, but for some reason I can't move forward. My legs begin to shake.

Kael appears at the entrance. His eyes widen when he sees me. He walks toward me, his pace slower than usual, one leg dragging along the dirt.

Thank God. Maybe the footsteps I heard earlier were only Kael. Maybe we can get out of here right now and—

"Lex?" Kael removes his hand from his waist, revealing the torn fabric of his shirt and a deep gash. The rapidness of the blood running down his stomach spurs me into action.

My hands shake, and I press his hand harder against the wound. "What happened?"

He glances toward the open doors behind him. "You have to get out of here. Now!"

The smell reaches me. Gasoline. The smell is accompanied by a loud trickling sound nearby. I wrap Kael's other arm around my shoulder.

He inhales sharply, his tightening grip almost causing me to topple over. "Lex, go! I'm too slow." He tries to resist me, but I drag him forward.

"The car is just outside." We can make it. I have to believe we'll make it. But with how dark it's become, I have no idea who did this to Kael. He could be watching us, waiting to attack or strike a match as soon as we reach the exit.

I allow myself to take a breath of fresh air once we step outside the barn. The car is only yards away.

"Go, now," Kael whispers, his body growing limp with each step we take.

"Stop it." I'm not going to let him give up. He'll be fine. He has to be. I open the car and let him gently fall into the back seat. His face is so pale now and contorted, his nose and eyebrows drawn into a perpetual wince.

I close the door, and as soon as I take a step toward the driver's side, I'm knocked forward from behind. I land on my wrist first, sharp pain shooting through my entire limb. I turn onto my side, peering wildly into the darkness. My eyes barely register the man standing above me. It's him. The ghost.

A glint of steel flashes before he lunges. A scream rips from my throat. I can't move out of the way fast enough, and the axe slams down onto my leg with a sickening, wet crack. I reach my arm up and grip the earth, dragging myself away from the man. He rears back with the axe and swings down, but I bring my arm up to shield my face, a dull, loud cracking sounding before my arm goes numb.

The man sets the blade on the ground and with his free hand pushes my limp arm out of the way. I let it fall and stare up at his face. In my nightmares it was always the same—blank. But now the familiarity strikes me. Wayne? The dim light erases the wrinkles from his face, and his dark hair isn't pushed back like it usually is. Was he the boy from the church? Donnie's friend?

The crunch of tires on dirt sounds nearby. Wayne doesn't seem to notice, and he kicks at my injured leg. I hiss through my teeth and inch away from him. He follows so he's still standing directly over me and raises the axe again.

Footsteps approach, and the shadow turns. I follow his gaze toward Kael's truck and my car. Butcher closes the door on his SUV, blissfully unaware of the scene playing out yards away. I should scream to warn him, but it's a struggle just to breathe through the pain. I clutch at my leg, trying to apply some pressure to the wound, but I can't find it under the bloody mess.

Wayne steps past me and lunges toward Butcher as he approaches the barn. Before Butcher can see him, Wayne darts out and starts hacking. Butcher roars as he manages to push Wayne away from him, and they both tumble to the ground. After a moment, the sound of blade and flesh continues.

I drag myself toward the barn. That's when I notice the blaze that's begun to build within. It's spreading up the walls. I make it inside and brace against the door to reach up to the tools hanging. My fingers wrap around the handle of the rake when a shadow appears in my periphery. But he's not a shadow.

In the light from the flames, I can see he's only a man. Wayne's eyes are wild and wide as he swings. I duck right as he brings his blade down where my head was moments ago, dropping the rake in the process. I fall onto the ground, dirt stinging as it rubs into my wounds.

I roll over and grip the rake with my good hand. I swing it up into the air just as Wayne tries to leap on top of me. There's a sickening sound of metal against bone as the prongs connect deep into his chest.

He staggers backward, the rake handle flying out of my hands and following him, still stuck in him. The axe drops beside me with a thud, and he turns to gaze toward the fire before sinking to his knees.

I struggle to sit up. I grab the axe and back away through the door as the smoke begins to fill my nostrils.

The last I see before I reach fresh air is Wayne facing the flames with open arms.

Butcher is gasping near the barn, clutching at his gushing neck.

I drop the axe and sit beside him.

"I'm sorry." His voice is so quiet.

A strange feeling stirs in me. Fear, maybe. And loss. But surely not sadness. I can't say anything.

"It's my fault," he weeps, his brow contorted as he looks up at me. "I'm so sorry. I should not . . . I waited. You needed me, and I waited."

It was him. He was the one on call at the station that night. On some level, I think I already knew. "Stop talking. You need to stay calm. Help is coming." I look at the car. I'm not sure if I can even walk all the distance to check on Kael. But he needs me. I tear the edge of Butcher's bloodstained T-shirt and hold it against his neck. "Keep pressure on this. I need to help Kael." I push against the earth, keeping the knee bent on my injured leg.

Butcher's hand claws at my wrist. "Don't go." His eyes are wide, like a man staring into the face of death. His skin is so pale.

"He's hurt too. I need to see him." *He could already be gone.* A lump forms in my throat at the thought. I break free of Butcher's grasp and limp toward the car, the foot of my broken leg dragging in the dirt, searing pain surging through my body with each step. I collapse when I get to the door. I reach up and open the handle to the back seat. He's quiet, but his chest is rising and falling rapidly. I brace against the seat, and I lift myself up, gripping Kael's leg and shaking it gently. "Kael?" My voice breaks. The sound of sirens breaks through the crackling of the nearby fire.

He stirs, turning his head at an angle to look at me. "Thank God." His trembling hand reaches for mine. "Are you hurt?"

I grit my teeth against the throbbing in my leg. "Am *I* hurt? Jesus, Kael. I think you're dying." A sob breaks from my lips. I drag myself onto the floorboard of the car, resting my head against his chest.

His fingers go limp around mine. "Stop. I'm fine, Lexi. Just a little blood."

It's as if I've unscrewed the lid on everything that's been bottled up, and I can't stop crying into his shirt. I can't lose him too.

Through my tears, I can see the red and white lights flashing into the car from the back window.

CHAPTER FORTY-ONE

In light of what I learned, the only thing I truly know about the past is that I can't trust my own memories. All I have is what I've chosen to remember, and there are still so many blank spots.

But something shook loose when I saw the flames in the barn. Something from the night my family died.

I woke to Dad carrying me. The heaviness of smoke mingled strangely with the cold air outside. My limbs shook a little as Dad set me down, my feet dislodging a cloud of dust at the barn floor. "Lexi," he said, gripping my shoulders. "I need you to stay quiet." He looked to the dark empty stall. "Hide in there, and I'll be back, okay? Don't make a sound." His voice broke on the last syllable. He turned on his heel and sprinted out of the barn.

The sound of his footfalls drifted away as I fell to my knees and crawled into the stall. I had hidden in the regular stalls before when I played hide-and-seek, but not in this small one. My hand brushed against cold plastic, and I recoiled, too scared to touch it again in the dark.

I gathered my knees into my chest, listening to the crunch of hooves and moos in the distance. I waited until my body began to tremble from the cold, but Dad never came back.

Wayne Miller was still alive when the sheriff and the firefighters arrived that night. He had to be pulled out of the flames, and he was in a burn victim unit of the hospital for months before he was physically able to confess.

His box was incinerated. All those tapes and evidence definitively linking him to Evan's murder were gone, but he was happy enough to give his story to Sheriff Larson when his lips healed.

It's still hard for me to wrap my head around that Wayne had been so intertwined in my life without me even knowing. And to fully feel the weight of how many innocent people have been affected by him.

Apparently, the trouble Tom's son got up to when he lived with him after the divorce started small. He liked to sneak onto neighbors' property in the middle of the night when his dad was asleep and hide away. In the barn, in the attic, it didn't matter. The residents of Sola were loath to lock their doors, and he took advantage. Next came the fires. Wayne had always been fascinated with fire and took to setting small ones at the cemetery with friends late at night. But one night, October 15, 2003, he graduated to setting a house on fire. Through his smaller experiments, he'd learned how to start a blaze and make it look like an accident.

Eventually, Tom sent Wayne away to live with his mother, but that only led to more trouble. A year later, a horrible fire in River Gap claimed the lives of his mother and her new boyfriend as well as Mr. Vargas's wife. Apparently, he spent his adult years in and out of the prison system in Northern California. After his most recent stint, he'd returned to stay with Tom in Sola. Since Tom had done so much to help Butcher access and hide the VFD funds, the reverend owed him one. Butcher gave Wayne a job and a second chance.

But when Wayne realized I was back in town, something in him snapped again. I was the only living member of the family he'd obsessed over all those years ago. That past fixation got the better of him, and he got up to his old tricks.

When Tom found out that Wayne was skulking around Kael's barn and discovered the tapes he'd recorded of my family, he put the pieces together and confronted his son. Wayne had fled the scene by the time I stumbled upon Tom's body after the argument.

As for Evan, the autopsy confirmed what Larson had initially suspected based on the condition of the body—that Evan had been killed around the same day I last saw him. Evan had stuck around Sola, however briefly, and followed me to the farm. That's when he saw Wayne lurking near the barn. Evan went to confront him and met a horrible end.

Although Wayne refused to confess to that one, the evidence in Evan's discovered vehicle spoke for itself at trial. Wayne had been using the car as his own and storing Evan's body in the back for days before he decided to fuck with me at the motel.

In some moments, the guilt is almost too much to bear. If Evan hadn't followed me to town, he'd still be alive. Over the months, working at the magazine is only now becoming a little easier. I don't think about Evan and the last time I saw him every single time I walk past his old office.

"Lex?" Kael smiles when he sees me as he rounds the corner and spots me. I couldn't remember if he had his economics class in this building or if it was business management tonight, but I guess my first instinct was right. He adjusts the strap of his backpack over one shoulder and kisses me. "I didn't expect to see you here."

I hand him one of the coffee cups. "I figured you could use a pick-me-up before you lock yourself away in the library for the rest of the night. Want to grab some dinner?" Kael's night class schedule doesn't always make it easy to connect as often as we'd like, so I decided on today (a slow day) to take advantage.

"Of course." He follows my lead as I begin down the sidewalk. "Where to?"

"There's a place near the marina that I've been meaning to try." I slip my hand into his free one. "Is that too far? Do you have time?"

"Of course."

"We have to take Muni."

He kisses the top of my head. "I have plenty of time for you."

In the aftermath of the attack, so many things have changed, including how Kael and I have built a life together. In an alternate reality, maybe we would've been together much sooner. If I'd stayed in Sola or if he had stayed out a little longer during college, maybe we would've been holding hands together and walking down Fillmore Street for years by now.

Instead, it took an axe wound that barely missed his kidney for me to realize how much I wanted him around. Not just in Sola, but everywhere. Once Kael was out of the hospital, his mom told him about her decision to sell the place. A developer had begun to poke around shortly after Butcher's offer, and in light of recent events, she wanted to move closer to "downtown" (i.e., a lovely half-acre lot within walking distance to both the church and the café) Sola in a much smaller house.

Kael squeezes my hand. "How's your knee?"

"It's not too bad today." Even months after the surgery and rehab for the torn ligaments in my leg, walking downhill in San Francisco is still a struggle. Once we reach the corner of the street, I lead him in the direction toward the bay.

It's been an adjustment for both of us, probably more so for Kael. He doesn't like talking about the ranch, and he sees it as a failure in many ways that he was unable to save it. But when his mom gave him a large share of the sale money, he immediately knew he wanted to go back to school.

"Did you turn in that paper?" We stand under the train stop sign.

"Yes." He looks down at me. "You remembered that was today?"

"Of course. It's not every day I get to hear about the thrilling economics of farm management."

He smiles. "I'm honestly shocked you stayed tuned in long enough to hear the title of my paper." Instead of mechanical engineering, Kael decided to apply his existing credits toward a new major in economics. I remember the night he called me after I returned home and he told me about his decision. It's a noble goal to save modern farming, but I can't pretend I'm not a little resentful of the hold Sola seems to have on him. That being said, whatever has caused him to be here, I'm grateful to have him nearby.

The train rattles closer, and Kael gently draws me away from the street, as if he's scared it'll hit me. He follows me onto the train and stays standing as I take a seat. The one time he actually sat on the Muni, he immediately shot up when a woman got on at the next stop and there were no seats left. Now, he refuses to sit at all, just in case.

With my money from the sale of the farm, I was able to pay off Beth's old house and pay to put Whisper up in a stable in Pacifica.

As much as I'd like to be rid of Sola forever, I can't quite keep Janna out of my thoughts.

Lee Butcher will never be my father, but Janna is the closest I may get again to a sister. And she's alone there now that he's dead.

I haven't told her what Butcher said to me about the night of the fire or about his convictions that he was my "real" father, and I never will. For all the pain that man has left behind, I've decided dwelling on the possibility he was a blood relation would only make me a more permanent victim of his.

"We're here!" I announce as we get off the train. I point to the sign three doors down.

"Love to the Sea?" Kael smiles. "Seafood, I assume?"

"Wow, Ms. Banderas would be thrilled to know how well you remember freshman Spanish."

He opens the door for me, and we step inside.

The decor is much less kitsch than some of the more touristy places downtown. It's a lot more upscale than I expected from Mr. Vargas's descriptions of how Amor al Mar was floundering. Now, I'm not even sure we can get a table.

From the hostess stand, nearly every seat looks full. She looks up at me. "Hello, would you like inside or outside?"

"Oh, um, I had a reservation for outside. Lex Blake?"

The woman looks down at her seating chart and then smiles. "Aw, yes. Mr. Vargas's special guest." Before I can debate that term, she leads us to a seat in the flagstone courtyard. Our table overlooks the marina and the water, the bridge acting as a frame above it.

When I got back into town and saw the email from Mr. Vargas following up on his offer to try his restaurant, I figured it was the perfect place to bring Kael. And it looks like I was right.

Just like Mr. Vargas and his son got their new beginning, maybe we can get ours.

ACKNOWLEDGMENTS

First of all, thank you to the readers. I'm so grateful for the opportunity to continue writing so I could bring you this story about Lex and her journey.

Once again, thank you to my wonderful agent, Abby Saul, and my editor, Liz Pearsons, as well as the entire team at Thomas & Mercer and Amazon Publishing!

I also can't even begin to express my sincere gratitude for the authors who have supported me, like J. T. Ellison, Elle Marr, Megan Collins, Loreth Anne White, Brianna Labuskes, Allie Reynolds, Kathleen Willett, all of Team Lark, and so many others! Thank you for the art you share with us and for lifting up the entire writing community.

Special thanks to my parents and to my friends who have supported my writing.

Finally, thank you to my husband, for absolutely everything. My books wouldn't exist without him.

ABOUT THE AUTHOR

Elle Grawl is a lawyer and author of the psychological suspense novels *One of Those Faces* and *What Still Burns*. When she's not writing, Grawl enjoys traveling and spending time with her husband and their two dogs.